HOME

FIRES

PATTY SLACK

Cover design by Novak Illustration
Edited by Carolyn Rose Editing

For the invisible people

Chapter 1

New suit, new hairstyle, new career—if Cyndi was ever going to make a fresh start, this was the day to do it.

"Are you sure you don't want me to go with you?" Mike asked, handing her a woolen scarf.

His scarf, not hers.

"I'll be fine." A simple meeting with a property manager seemed as good a place as any to launch her career as a real estate investor. Not that she had any experience with real estate or business, but how hard could it be?

Cyndi looked at the offered scarf of dull, scratchy wool. "This isn't mine."

"I know, but this one," Mike said, pulling her fluffy scarf out from under her coat collar, "won't keep you warm. If you're going out in this weather, at least dress for it."

She snatched the purple strip of fabric back with a laugh. "Don't be silly. I'm not going on a trek in the woods. The light rail stops right in front of the property manager's building. Don't worry." She wound the scarf back around her neck and tossed the ends over her shoulder. She pulled on a pair of lined gloves and reached into the closet for a hat, passing over the practical stocking cap for the more stylish crocheted beret she'd made last winter. She pulled it on, adjusted her hair, and checked her reflection in the hallway mirror. It would have to do.

From the corner of her eye, she caught Mike smirking at her. "What? Is my hair out of place?"

"No. I just thought we'd be past our primping stage by now. What are you now? Fifty?"

"Forty-seven!" He was teasing, of course, but she couldn't laugh just yet.

Mike moved in for a good-bye peck and slid a hand behind her.

When she pulled away, she brushed his hand aside and, in doing so, felt that he had stuffed something into her coat pocket. She pulled out his ugly hat and scarf. "I'm not wearing them," she insisted, pushing them against his chest. "I want to look like a professional even if I don't feel like one."

He caught the unwanted items and held them out again.

"Take them. You don't have to wear them, but just in case. It's really cold out."

"Okay, okay." She stuffed them in her purse.

Mike moved in close once again. "You can do this. She would have wanted you to live."

She knew it was true, so why did living feel like a betrayal?

Mike opened the front door and held it open until Cyndi walked through.

"Good luck!" he called just before the wind blew the door shut.

God help her, she needed more than luck.

The light rail car was standing room only. Cyndi clenched a hand strap. She was wedged between a stout woman and a man screaming into his cell phone. A pair of pierced teenagers didn't seem to notice that older people could use a seat. Not that she was old, mind you.

How old were they? Fifteen? Sixteen? Did their parents give them permission to pierce eyebrows and lips? Would Madeleine have bothered to ask?

Cyndi shook the memory of her only child from her thoughts. Today, she told herself for the hundred millionth time, is a new beginning. Today I look to the future, not the past.

The rail car veered left. The standing passengers leaned in unison. Someone's bag jabbed Cyndi in the leg. The light rail was always crowded, but this was ridiculous.

Two more stops.

One.

Cyndi positioned herself to dash for the exit. When the doors opened, she jostled to get through them, but the press of people getting on overpowered her. The doors whooshed shut and the train started moving.

"You've got to be kidding," Cyndi said.

One of the teens smirked at her, twisting the stud in her eyebrow.

Cyndi looked past her to the green street signs outside. Fifth and Broadway. The sun glinted off them and then they were gone. The next stop was several blocks down the hill. Cyndi was glad she'd chosen to wear sensible shoes.

She pushed her way to the door. At the next stop, she was the first one out, squeezed onto the sidewalk like a marble shot from between pinched fingers. The cold wind bit at her cheeks and reached through her holey hat. She fished Mike's sensible hat from her purse and put it on, wrapped his itchy scarf around her face, and bundled her coat around her. Still, the wind's icy fingers reached down her collar and up her pant legs.

She turned uphill and leaned into the wind. Brisk weather called for a brisk walk. The scarf barely warmed the air as she breathed. Her lungs burned with cold; her cheeks felt the jabs of a thousand needles. She pressed on, head down.

When at last the automatic doors of the Cathmore Building swished open for her, Cyndi glanced at her watch. Any extra time she had planned for arranging her hair and makeup had been swallowed up by her unplanned hike. She darted onto an elevator before its doors could shut and pressed the button to go to Simms Property Management on the fifth floor.

Cyndi examined her reflection in the elevator's chrome wall. A distorting seam ran down the middle of her face. Mike was right about it being too late for preening. For all the time she'd spent getting ready this morning, she looked more like a bag lady than a businesswoman. She pulled the woolen hat off and immediately regretted it. Static-charged hair danced toward the ceiling, matching her frazzled spirit.

The elevator opened directly into a professionally

decorated reception area. She'd expected a property manager who sat behind an industrial desk holding a pen in his right hand and a toilet plunger in his left. A grouping of chairs, chosen more for form than function, made her wonder how much Simms charged his clients to afford such fancy offices.

"May I help you?" The glossy receptionist matched the decor.

"Um, I've got an appointment with Mr. Simms?"

"Ms. Finch? Mr. Simms is expecting you."

Cyndi followed the stilettoed receptionist down a long hallway, smoothing her hair with spit as she went. At the end of the hall, she was ushered into a spectacular corner office. Gray wintry light flooded through floor-to-ceiling windows, illuminating a gray room with black furnishings.

A pasty businessman rose to greet her across his obscenely grand ebony desk.

"Ms. Finch? Please, come in. Sit down."

She took off her overcoat, but wasn't sure where to put it. Mr. Simms didn't seem inclined to offer any help, so she folded it over her arm and sat, feeling as rumpled as her coat.

Chapter 2

"KEEP MOVING! YOU CAN'T SLEEP HERE!"

It was getting harder and harder to find a decent place to rest. The farmer's market, usually open only on Saturdays, was a full-time nuisance from now until Christmas. All those venders with their cozy tents and portable space heaters hogged the prime real estate. They should set up their tents in the open and leave the protected area under the bridge for people who needed it, people who had to scrounge for shelter from the elements.

People like Joe.

Joe sometimes stayed at the old mission, but he'd rather just tuck into a doorway or corner out of the wind. On a frigid night like this, Winter Housing Overflow would open some schools. He might be able to find a spot on the floor of a school gym, but that would mean a bus ride. He didn't want to spare the change. Besides, the shelters wouldn't exactly welcome Wolf. All he needed was a free doorway.

"Go on, now!" The irate shopkeeper swung his hand toward Joe as if shooing away a fly, then slammed his door. Three strings of jingle bells on the outside handle laughed at him.

"Come on, boy." Joe beckoned Wolf with a jerk of

his head. "We're not wanted here." Joe put his hands on the ground to steady himself, making sure his footing was solid before pressing on the front of his thighs. Slow and steady, he pushed himself to a stand. His stiff legs protested. He stuffed his army surplus sleeping bag into a shopping cart and leaned into the cart handle to get the wheels turning. The right front wheel hung like a hurt paw above the sidewalk.

"Come on. Let's go find a place to sleep."

Wolf stretched one hind leg, then the other and trotted up the street behind Joe, nose in the air. The husky mutt mix really did look like a wolf when he walked like that, ears perked, senses tuned.

Maybe he'd sniff them out a free meal.

Chapter 3

CYNDI PRESSED HER CELL PHONE to her ear and tried to catch her breath before blurting out the news. "Mike, honey, it's done. We're official!"

Mike, steady as always, didn't verbalize his enthusiasm, but she knew he felt it. He must. "How'd it go?"

"Good. Great, I think. I was kind of intimidated, but I did okay and we're set to go. We got the best property manager in town and the best strip mall west of the Cascades. I'm so ready to get started, I can't stand it."

"Settle down, hon. We won't clear escrow until after the new year."

Cyndi refused to let his infuriating practicality dampen her spirits. "Hey, Mike, I've got a couple of stops to make while I'm downtown. It's brutal out there. I'd better go before things get worse." Cyndi dropped her phone in her purse. She donned gloves, hat, and scarf, this time not even thinking about how she looked.

Outside, the wind had picked up even more. Tiny dots of dusty snow danced in all directions. She braced herself against the icy blast. She hopped over the in-ground light rail tracks and headed for Deja Lu. How long had it been since they'd celebrated Christmas? Too long. Well, this year, she was swallowing her grief and getting something nice for Mike. He deserved it.

Up ahead, the bookstore's green fabric awning bowed and flexed in the wind.

No beribboned holiday displays in the front window, just a random assortment of used and antique books. Beyond the display, the stacks reached to the ceiling, crowded out by still more books piled on the ground. She'd love to browse, but with the weather like this, she'd head straight for the locked cases of antique and rare books, make her pick, and scoot on home.

As she reached for the shop's door, she heard a low growl. She looked down.

Near the hem of her overcoat, a massive gray dog bared its teeth.

Cyndi's heart lurched. She stepped back.

The dog stood between her and the bookshop's door. It glared at her with glacial blue eyes. Under its feet, a large lump of green blankets lay like a tired mountain range.

"Whoa, boy," Cyndi said. She reached in her pocket. "Steady. You want a treat?" She kept eye contact with the massive animal, afraid to glance away. She found an energy bar in her pocket. Her fingers closed around it. She raised the bar to her mouth and tugged on the wrapper with her teeth. The foil tore the length of the packaging. A gust of wind caught the wrapper and blew it away.

Cyndi held the bar out.

The dog tracked it.

"You want it?" All she wanted was to distract the animal long enough to get inside the shop and out of the cold wind.

"Yeah, I want it," a deep voice said.

Startled, Cyndi stepped back again.

From under the lumpy old sleeping bag, a hand reached out, palm up. An old man exposed his face and sat up, with some effort. His ears were red with cold. His beard and mustache glistened with the moisture of his breath. Or was it snot?

Cyndi didn't want to think about it. "I'm . . . I'm trying to get in that shop behind you, and your dog won't let me."

"Who? Wolf? He wouldn't hurt you. He's a kitten."

Wolf still glared at her.

"Can you call him off, please?"

"Can I have the bar?"

Cyndi stepped forward. She watched the dog to make sure it wouldn't lunge at her as she set the food in the man's open palm. To her surprise, the man took it in both hands, broke it in half, and offered one piece to his dog.

Wolf snatched it and devoured it without chewing.

The man stuck his piece somewhere under his pile of blankets. "Thank you kindly," he said, and he scooted aside enough for Cyndi to pass.

Inside the warm shop, she stared at the books without seeing them, waiting for her racing heart to return to normal.

Chapter 4

JOE CRUMPLED AN OLD SHIRT to use as a pillow. The worn flannel did little to keep the frigid concrete from sucking warmth from his head, but it at least gave him a bit of cushion. Years ago, he could stand the weather, but now his old bones ached. Every time a cold front passed through, his joints warned him it was coming.

He scooted his back against the brick entranceway and tried to get comfortable, but an uneasy feeling that he was about to be chased away from the front of the bookshop kept him on edge. "Where to next?" he asked Wolf. "You got a plan? Maybe we should camp out in the lobby of that big old building over there." He looked across and down the street. "Wouldn't that be a hoot? I already got kicked out of there once. It could happen again."

Only this time, he would be anonymous, unlike last time, when they'd removed his nameplate from his office on the seventh floor. It was as if they'd removed it from him as well, turning him from a person to a problem the city would rather hide.

Before he could get too deep into his self-talk about the pitfalls of city government and the narcissism of the rich, Joe heard the door latch above him click. He turned his head away so the shopkeeper wouldn't see his face when he told him to leave.

"Excuse me, sir?"

A woman spoke, not a man.

Joe turned over. It was the lady who'd given him the energy bar. So now that she'd done a good deed, she felt like she had the right to tell him where to go and what to do? Fat chance.

"Sir?" She held out a hat and scarf to him. "I just—I noticed you don't have a hat on. I thought this might help."

Joe could tell they'd been worn, but in this weather, he'd take what he could get. The lady looked cold herself. Her own hat and scarf were for decoration, not warmth.

"I wish it was more," she said. She jiggled the scarf to get him to take it, which he did. "It's all I've got on me." She hesitated as if waiting for a response. "Well, anyway, God bless."

God bless. How many times had he heard that from people who tried to fix the world's problems with a Band-Aid? At least this lady had done something. Not near enough. It never was. But it was something.

He watched her bustle away in the dimming light. She clenched a paper sack in one hand—a book, presumably—and tugged her coat tighter around her chest with the other. She gripped her purse like she thought he was gonna mug her, even though she was the one who'd approached him.

She stopped at the light rail station. The four-car train pulled up and blocked her from view. When it continued down the line, she was gone.

"Thanks, lady," Joe muttered, his words swallowed by the wind's howl. He folded the scarf and positioned it on the sidewalk under the flannel shirt. It was plenty thick enough to shield his ear from the frozen ground while he slept.

Chapter 5

CYNDI SAT AT THE DINING ROOM table amidst stacks of important papers. The number of stacks and forms multiplied before her eyes. No wonder they called it piles of paperwork. How could she have let it get so out of hand?

She tipped her mug back, hoping for another swallow of tea before she dug in on her project again. Empty. An excellent excuse to go make more.

She turned the kettle on. Should she wait for it to boil or go back to work and be interrupted again when the whistle blew? She ambled back to the dining room, but balked at the sight of all the mess. Stacks of papers covered the table. More sat on chairs and on the sideboard. She used to be compulsive about organization, but now . . .

When it's hard to summon enough energy to get out of bed in the morning, filing doesn't seem that important. Even today, when this was the only thing she had to work on, she couldn't concentrate. Every few minutes, something urgent like getting more tea or dusting the mantel pulled her away.

The hum of the garage door told her Mike was home. She glanced at her watch. The day was gone with nothing to show for it.

"Hi, hon." Mike moved in for a kiss. He spied the state of the dining room and lifted one eyebrow. "What's all that?"

"That," said Cyndi, "is the ugly result of procrastination rearing its head. It's all the papers that have come in the past I don't know how many months. I've been putting off filing them, but with the new business starting up, I thought I should get on top of things. But there's so much . . . It's overwhelming. If I can't keep my own files, how can I expect to run a business? Maybe I'm not up to the challenge."

"You're just scared because it's a new project. If filing is a problem, we'll hire someone. It's a huge undertaking. Let's not give up before we've started. We'll sort it all out after Christmas, when the strip mall is actually ours. In the meantime, let's clear up this mess. How does takeout sound?"

Christmas. That was the real problem. Holidays were always hard. They'd only had ten Christmases with Madeleine before the accident. This would be the fourth without her. It didn't get any easier. Time erased the details of memories, stealing her child away again little by little, turning vivid moments into ghostly blurs. Half of it was mourning what she had, half what should have been. Life without Madi meant no slumber parties, no loud music, no pink-and-purple curtains, no reason to hang up stockings. It meant an eternity of silence that should have been filled with giggles and hugs.

The insurance company had finally come through with the money that could never compensate for their loss. They were using the money to buy a strip mall.

The project would be her rebirth, Cyndi's chance to take the tragedy of Madi's death and turn it into a reason to live again.

Or at least a way to keep from counting the days.

"I'll run pick up teriyaki while you get the rest of this stuff filed. Do you want the chicken?" Mike asked.

"That's fine." Cyndi picked up a stack of papers, copies of the contract they'd signed putting their house up as collateral on the real estate loan.

"Are you sure?" she'd asked her husband before they signed the papers. "What if we can't make a go of it? What if we lose the mall? Or even the house?"

"I trust you," he'd said.

For Madi and for Mike, she had to make this work. If she failed . . .

She couldn't—wouldn't—allow herself to finish the thought. If she didn't make a go of it, why else should she wake up each morning?

Chapter 6

JOE PARKED HIS CART IN front of Victoria's Tea Garden and pulled out his blankets.

"Where's that dinner roll? I know it's here somewhere." He shook the blankets, but nothing fell out. He checked in the bottom of the cart without luck.

"Where is it? Wolf, I brought you something from supper. I know how you like those rolls from the Fifth Street Mission. Now where is it?"

Wolf looked at him, head cocked to one side.

Joe scratched his beard.

He pulled off his faded Dodgers cap—*broken in* was what he called it—and patted the top of his head, as if he would have put the roll there. Patting his pockets one more time, he finally found the roll, flattened but edible. He tossed it to Wolf. "Here you go, boy."

Wolf waited until the roll was on the ground before snatching it up. He was a good dog that way, never grabbing stuff out of your hand no matter how hungry he was.

"They served up a good dinner tonight," Joe said. "Stew. I like that. It sticks to your ribs and warms you right up." He looked around at his feet for a suitable rock. When he found one, he wedged it behind the shopping cart's back wheel to prevent everything he owned from rolling away in the night. Then he settled down in the doorway and wrapped his blankets around his shoulders. As soon as he got situated, Wolf curled up against him.

"Of course, it is getting more crowded at those dinners. I can hardly find a place to sit anymore. It's getting harder and harder to find a shelter bed, too. It's hardly worth the trouble of looking. At least tonight's a nice night. We'll stay warm and dry tonight, won't we, boy?"

But Wolf didn't answer.

Of course he didn't. He was just a dog.

Chapter 7

CYNDI SAT ON THE SECOND row, near the center aisle, the same place she'd sat at every church she'd ever attended.

"Front row, center shows God and the church you're serious," her daddy used to say. While she no longer believed her proximity to the front of the sanctuary made her any closer to God, she was used to this view. Mike was at his regular post as usher, so he wouldn't sit by her until the sermon began. Every time he walked to the front, she watched him, looking all spiffed up in his Sunday suit. Twenty-seven years with the same man—more than half her life. It had taken four or five of those to knock the rough edges off him, but now she couldn't imagine life without him. She glanced over at him again. He stood in the aisle, scanning the room for empty seats, oblivious to her observation. His hair had thinned out years ago, but at least he hadn't gone the comb-over route some of his friends were trying. Now he sported a laurel wreath of gray-brown hair around a shiny scalp. His cheeks hung a little lower than they used to, but he was still the handsomest man in the room, at least to her eyes.

Watching Mike helped her ignore the empty space beside her. Not Mike's spot to her right, but Madi's space on the left. Ever since she died, church had been a lonely place.

Cyndi tried to pray, but her heart wasn't in it. Why ask for direction or wisdom or comfort if you knew none of them would come? Why ask anything of a God whose ears don't work?

She looked down at her program. *All to Jesus I Surrender, None of Self and All of Thee.*

Giving Sunday.

For the most part, Cascade Forest Community Church met their needs, but Giving Sunday was a tradition she could do without. Woven into the church's Advent traditions before she and Mike had moved here, it was a blatant fund-raising effort. She squirmed to hear the preacher tying God's gift of his son with the need for upgraded landscaping or a new roof. Of course, he didn't actually come out and say it that way. He framed it in more spiritual terms, but even the densest in the kingdom could recognize the thinly disguised underlying message.

Maybe she should have stayed home.

"Let us stand." The song leader started "I Surrender All." Cyndi joined the singing, following along with the words projected on a screen up front though she'd had them memorized since childhood. Song followed song, each asking for some form of sacrifice.

After the last rousing chorus of "I Gave My Life for Thee," the pastor bounded to the pulpit in four giant steps. He always began his sermon like that, as if he couldn't wait to get started. He set his Bible on the clear plastic podium and took his place beside it. One hand reached to his belt to turn on his cordless mic; the other picked up the remote control for PowerPoint.

"God gave the ultimate Christmas gift of all time," he began. His voice boomed, a little too loud. The speakers squawked.

Cyndi cringed.

He adjusted the volume on his microphone. "Sometimes the truth can be deafening," he joked. The congregation gave a polite chuckle at his attempt at humor. When the services went high tech, they all learned to expect a few technical difficulties.

"God gave us the ultimate Christmas gift, the Christ." He pushed a button on his remote and a slide came up, a Renaissance painting of the nativity. A plump pink baby sat on the lap of a haloed blonde beauty. He pushed the button again and pulled up a stock photo of a busy mall. Bustling shoppers carried armloads of bags. The picture, taken with slow shutter speed, blurred the shoppers to emphasize their hurry.

Mike slid in beside Cyndi. He gave her hand a squeeze.

"Have any of you been here recently?" Pastor Jake asked. Cyndi raised her hand, and a rustle behind her told her that many others had too.

Interesting that he'd chosen a picture of a mall. In the days since she'd signed papers on her own mall, Cyndi had driven past it every time she was out. It was just a coincidence. After all, who wasn't thinking about shopping at this time of year? Only a few more days until Christmas.

Pastor Jake turned to Scriptures and read the story of the widow's mite, the story of Abigail feeding David's army, the story of the rich young ruler. Another push of the button brought up a picture of the church building. The new modern structure stood proud and strong beside the old white steepled chapel. Rolling lawns filled the foreground.

It is a beautiful facility. We should be proud of it, Cyndi thought. But as the pastor talked about future development, her heart grew cold. She would never serve on the building committee or pick up a paintbrush. Her dreams pulled her elsewhere.

We're rich. Really, really rich. Not just compared to starving children in Africa or China or wherever. Of course we're rich compared to them. But we have so much compared to the people around us.

She didn't need to look around her to know how people were dressed. Designer clothes, fancy jewelry, more makeup and hair gel than she could guess. And the men . . . the men had plenty to spend, too, with their fancy cars and expensive toys. And none of the money could buy anything important. If it could, wouldn't she still have Madi?

A picture of the church grounds remained on the screen. A list of proposed projects overlaid the background image. The air in the sanctuary suffocated her. Cyndi bolted down the center aisle for the door.

She stood outside the entrance, under the eaves of the new addition, out of the rain. A few early leavers brushed past her. Cyndi forced herself to draw in deep breaths.

She knew she ought to go back in, but she couldn't. She'd wait outside until Mike was ready to go. He could put the check in without her, and then they could go back to their empty home.

Cyndi dug in her purse for her car keys and let herself in on the passenger's side. She tilted the seat back a little and stared out past the parking lot to the sidewalk.

Cars rushed by on the busy street. A bus approached and pulled to a squeaky, hissing stop at a bus shelter. Its yawning doors opened and it disgorged a passenger.

From the back, Cyndi could tell the woman was old. Her hunched back and the way she struggled to pull a luggage cart down the steps spoke of hardship. A layering of several coats rounded her shape. She turned around, revealing weathered skin and sunken cheeks.

The bus pulled away.

The old woman stood on the sidewalk for a minute, as if trying to figure out which direction to go. She finally overcame inertia and pushed, one step at a time, down the road.

Cyndi startled at the sound of the car door opening.

Mike slid into the driver's seat and put his key in the ignition. "You feeling okay?"

"Yeah, I'm fine. Did you see that?"

"See what?"

"That woman. The one who just got off the bus."

"Nah, I guess I missed it. What happened?"

"Nothing. I don't know, nothing." Cyndi knew

something important had just transpired. First the old guy with his dog, then the picture of the mall, now this woman. She tried to shake them out of her head, but she couldn't. An idea started to form. Come on, hon," she said. "Let's go home. I think I know what I'm supposed to do."

All the pieces were falling into place. Madi's money wasn't supposed to just keep her busy. It was for a much bigger cause.

She was surrounded with hungry people. She had a feeling she was supposed to feed them.

Chapter 8

THURSDAY AFTERNOON. ONLY two more days until Christmas.

The rain poured down.

Instead of a normal misty Northwest drizzle, sheets of water pounded at an angle from the sky in a windy deluge.

Cyndi navigated while Mike drove around the block scouting out a parking place. All the one-way streets confused him, but she kept him straight.

"I don't know. Maybe we should try this another day when it's not so wet. What do you think?" Mike asked.

"It's pretty nasty out," Cyndi agreed. "But we're already down here. Maybe we can find an awning or something to stand under. If you don't want to stay, you can drop me off, but I'm here to feed the homeless. They don't have the luxury of going inside just because of a little rain. I'm not going to either."

"You know I'm not going to just leave you here," Mike said. "Maybe we can set up under the bridge. I know that's where a lot of them hang out."

"There's a parking place up there on the left," Cyndi said, indicating a space that was no more than three inches longer than the car. She never would have tried for it, but Mike took a perverse pride in his ability to parallel park. Even so, it took him a few tries working the sedan backward and forward to get lined up to his satisfaction.

"That's good enough, honey. Let's go." Cyndi clamored from the car before he had a chance to pull out and try again. Once on the sidewalk, Mike pulled his hood up over his head and opened the back hatch.

"I'll take the card table. Can you get the pots of soup?" Cyndi looked at the amount of stuff they'd brought. "We'll have to take two trips."

She and Mike grabbed the table and the pots and started toward the main downtown hangout for the homeless, under the Humboldt Bridge. A popular farmer's market and craft market was open only on weekends in the summer. The rest of the time, anyone seeking shelter from the elements or a little community could be found along the river under the bridge.

The closer they got, the more people crowded the sidewalks.

"Oh, you're kidding. Is this a market day?" Cyndi stopped a stranger walking past. "Is the market open today?"

"Every day until Christmas Eve," the woman replied before hurrying on her way.

"I thought I planned this out so we wouldn't be here on a busy day. Shucks, now we'll have to rethink how to do this." Cyndi let the card table rest on her toes. "Let's at least get into the shelter of the bridge, and then we can think about where to set up. No use moping in the rain."

The market rocked in full holiday swing. Rows of canvas-topped shelters hosted shoppers who browsed through tie-dyed T-shirts, hand-turned pottery, wind chimes, and jewelry made from cast-off silverware. Enticing smells from the international food court danced through the aisles—elephant ears, spring rolls, baklava—

Mike took a deep breath. "Oh man, that smells good. We'll have to get lunch when we're all done. I haven't been to this market in years."

"That's because we never come to the city," said Cyndi, glad to see he was in a better mood. "This could be kind of fun, a little adventure. Where should we set up?"

Every inch of covered space was taken by a booth or a busker playing fiddle, bongo drums, or saxophone for extra cash.

They moved down the aisles toward the river, hoping for an opening down on the other end, but the market was packed all the way down to Riverside Drive.

Cyndi looked at her husband, already dripping wet and bedraggled. "You've got rain gear, right?" Like rain gear would do him any good at this point. They were both as wet as they were going to get.

"Let's do it." Mike splashed across the street to a grassy greenbelt along the river's edge. Cyndi chased after him, squealing each time cold water seeped into her shoes. They sploshed their way to a random spot in the middle of the grass. Mike unfolded the card table and Cyndi set pots of soup on it. Mike ran back to the car for a bag of hoagie rolls while Cyndi fished out her hand-lettered paper sign. She tried to tape it to the front of the card table, but the tape was too wet to stick. Besides, the paper already drooped in the rain. The ink blurred and ran like cheap mascara.

"Forget the signs," Mike said when he got back. "We'll just round up some people while the food's still warm, and then we'll be on our way. Do you want to stand here or go drum up business?"

"It was my idea. I can stay."

"I think you should go. I don't mind the rain. It's not like it's going to mess up my hairdo." Water poured off the bill of his Mariners cap.

"Are you sure?"

"I'm fine, hon. I'm not made of sugar," Mike said. He wiped the rain off his face with both hands and flicked the water into the grass. He was a good sport to come out with her on a day like this on such a fool's errand.

"Go on, Cyn. Stir up some business for us before I drown."

Cyndi smiled at him and set off in search of someone needy.

Chapter 9

ON RAINY DAYS LIKE TODAY, Joe liked to stay put. Early this morning, though, his favorite spot under the bridge was taken by a Chinese woman selling lucky bamboo. His other favorite place near the fountain was being used by a nutty old Santa singing Christmas songs and taking swigs of whatever Christmas spirits he had hidden in his paper sack. Joe made his way around the crowd to the river end of the bridge. Curse this constant rain.

It was Thursday. Thursdays he could usually find a hot meal from a church group that served hot soup out of a mobile kitchen—"Soup for Lost Souls" or something like that—from a food truck three blocks away. He wasn't sure he wanted to go that far in this downpour. He listened for his stomach to tell him if it was worth the trek or not.

It grumbled back at him.

Like an angel of mercy, a woman's voice reached him through the din. "Free soup! Need a hot meal? Get some hot soup!" Something about her sounded familiar. Not too tall, friendly face, a green REI rain jacket. She was a little on the round side, but not fat.

Nope. There was something familiar about her, but he couldn't place her. Living on the streets, though, he saw a lot of faces every day.

"Free soup over there," the woman yelled to whoever was in range of her voice.

Joe followed the finger's direction with his eyes. A guy in a baseball hat stood tending a rickety card table with two saucepans on it. He probably had enough to feed six or eight. The bag of rolls on the table was soaked through, the bread fit only to feed to seagulls.

Small-timers. Kinda sweet of them to try, but he knew he could find a better meal down the block.

"Come on, Wolf. Let's go find us some real lunch."

Joe and his dog stepped out into the downpour and walked past the wobbly card table and soggy rolls.

Chapter 10

DESPITE THE CHILL AND RAIN, Cyndi glowed with the warmth of her good deeds. This was a great idea, coming down to feed the homeless. She finally felt like she was making a difference. Not like the man selling handmade wooden trains at the table to her right, or the women vending stained-glass garden decorations to her left. Or even the shoppers, wandering from booth to booth with no direction.

She scanned the crowd for someone who might need a hot meal. Her eyes rested on an old woman stooped against one of the giant concrete bridge supports.

She trotted out to the card table where Mike, bless his heart, waited to serve people. "How you holding up?" she asked.

Mike grinned through purpling lips. "Great. We've only got a couple of servings left."

"Do you want to switch places for a while and dry off?"

"I'm okay. Just send a couple more customers our way so we can go home and get dry."

"I'm gonna give some to that old lady over there. Serve me up a bowl."

Mike opened the pot with his gloved hands and

served some barely hot meat, potatoes, and carrots into a plastic bowl. Cyndi went over to the old woman.

The stranger didn't look up.

Cyndi tapped her foot lightly against the woman's worn shoe. "Excuse me? Ma'am?"

The face that looked up did not belong to an old woman after all. Smooth skin framed tired, bloodshot eyes, eyes that barely hid the pain of life. She raised her hands to take the soup.

Cyndi placed the bowl in the cup of her palms. "Here's a hot meal for you," she stammered. How did someone so young end up so beaten down? What had she gone through to age her so fast? She couldn't be more than thirty.

"I hope you like it."

Before she turned her back, the moth-eaten castaway flashed her a thankful grin, revealing rotting and missing teeth and a remnant of humanness.

Cyndi shuddered.

Only one more and they were done. A whiff of wind pushed the scent of funnel cakes under her nose. She was getting hungry. After they gave away their last bowl of soup, she was going for an elephant ear. Or maybe some pad thai. Or maybe both.

She only needed to find one other person. No other bums sat in her field of vision, either against posts or along the perimeter of the market. She searched faces in the crowd, looking for anyone with sallow cheeks or hungry eyes.

A middle-aged couple, she with shopping bags and he with a cardboard tray of tamales.

Nope.

A young mother negotiating the obstacle course of an aisle with a double stroller.

Still no.

A teenaged girl decked out in cargo pants, black denim jacket, and heavy chain necklace, her purple hair showing dishwater blonde at the roots. She didn't look weathered like the last woman, but her eyes hid a hundred stories.

That's the one.

"Free soup! Homemade cookies!" Cyndi stepped in the girl's path and pointed her toward the card table, which, after almost an hour in the downpour, drooped almost as much as Cyndi.

The girl looked at the pathetic display and then at Mike. She sloshed across the grass toward him.

Cyndi followed, ignoring the rain streaming down her face. Why was this girl out here by herself? And why not get hot food from one of the concession stands?

"Whatcha got?" The edge of her voice was sharper than the spikes on her collar.

"Minestrone soup, rolls, and chocolate chip cookies." Mike started loading a plastic bowl and plate with the last of the food. "Would you like some? The rolls are kinda soggy."

"Yeah, I guess."

"Okay, well, this is the last of it. Enjoy!" Mike didn't have to lift the food far off the table before the punk rocker—did they still call them that?— snatched it and scurried back under the concrete bridge. As Cyndi packed dishes into an Igloo cooler, she took a furtive glance toward the girl.

She looked vulnerable now, damp and alone, eating her lukewarm soup.

Cyndi folded the card table.

As they passed her, the teen eyed them with disdain. She did not acknowledge Mike's nod or Cyndi's smile.

Cyndi was already past her when the girl's voice stopped her short.

"Hey!"

Cyndi turned around.

"Are you for real?" She gestured toward the space the couple had just vacated.

Cyndi followed the swing of her arm and stared at the empty plot of grass as if it would answer her question.

"Do you know how many people hang out under this bridge that need a good meal?" The girl crossed her arms, waiting for a response.

Cyndi was at a loss for words.

"How many?" Mike asked. He set down his cooler and stepped back toward her.

She lowered her voice as he approached. "There's hundreds that show up for the Wednesday night meals. You seriously only brought two little pots?"

"Yeah."

"And how many people did you feed?"

"I don't know. Maybe a dozen including you. Why?" He glanced back to see if Cyndi was still with him. She stood riveted, staring at him from less than ten feet away.

The girl raised her voice to include Cyndi in her opinion. "It just seems pretty sad. Hundreds to feed every day and you only brought enough for twelve? What is this? Some kind of Christmas gesture? Feed the hungry and feel better about the hundreds you spend on Christmas garbage for your kids? Where will you be in March when we're all still wet and cold? Or in July when we're dying of heatstroke?" Her voice dripped with sarcasm. "Lame."

She dropped the plastic bowl and spoon on the ground, pushed past them, and walked down one of the aisles between booths. If they let her, she'd vanish into the crowd and they'd never see her again.

They should just let her go, but something about her pulled at Cyndi's heart.

Cyndi raised her voice. "Hey, wait!"

The girl turned her head but kept walking away.

"What's your name?" Cyndi cried. A simple question. She had so many more—Why are you so hungry? How old are you? Do you live out here?—but she couldn't ask them.

"Clark," she called back, flashing a smile that looked more like a challenge to fight than a gesture of goodwill. "What's yours?"

"I'm Cyndi!" she called. "And this is Mike. I'll be seeing you, Clark!"

She didn't know how, but she was going to find that girl again.

"Wow, that was horrible," Cyndi said as she peeled off her rain jacket. After shaking off the excess water, she hung the jacket on a rod above the clothes dryer. She grabbed a towel from a basket of clean clothes and rubbed at her hair. A glance at Mike showed her he was pretty done in. She tossed the towel over to him.

"Yeah." He caught it with one hand and dried his scalp and the back of his neck. "What miserable weather. I'm so sorry about you having to stand under shelter while I got soaked in the rain. I feel bad about that."

"Sure you do." She would have been miffed if the roles were reversed, but he was a good sport. "You would have made a great carnival barker."

Mike peeked out from under the towel with a smirk on his face. "Are you saying I have a big mouth?"

"Not in so many words." Cyndi tried not to smile, but the corners of her mouth twitched and pulled until she gave in to the impish grin. "Big mouth," she whispered and dove for the door. She tugged it open and scrambled into the kitchen, slammed the door, and sat against it.

Bump! Bump! "Let me in!" Mike sweetened his words to make them singsongy, then whiney, then gruff, then playful again. When he exhausted all the ways to talk her into letting him in, he pushed on the door. That's when the fun began. She dug her heels into the kitchen floor, but she couldn't find purchase. Mike pushed slowly against her and she lost ground. Just when it felt like she couldn't hold the door shut for another second, she jumped up and ran for the stove. Mike burst through the door but not before she grabbed the teapot. Cyndi fiddled with the knobs on the stove and tried to act casual.

He stood behind her and wrapped his arms around her waist. He bent his head to her neck. "Mmm, you smell so good. Like fresh rain and wind." His breath on her ear drew her backward. "I've missed you, hon."

She relaxed back into him for a moment, finding the curve in his chest that she liked to imagine had been worn there by almost thirty years of leaning on each other. "Want some tea?"

"No, thanks. I've still got some coffee. I'll sit with you, though."

He went to the living room to wait for her while Cyndi went through the ritual of pouring a cup of tea. She walked with china cup in hand to her favorite chair, set down the cup, and picked up her coziest blanket to wrap around herself, the soft crocheted one Mike's mom had made for Madi's big-girl bed. She settled herself in her chair, pulled her feet up, and tucked the blanket in around her. Then she reached for her teacup and took a sip.

Tea helped her put the world in perspective. Teatime was comfort time. She used to say the first sip of tea was like the first breath of a prayer, a pause to quiet the spirit before launching into something important. She didn't say that anymore, not since God stopped hearing her prayers.

She closed her eyes and savored the tea. When she opened them again, Mike was looking at her from his recliner. He had that look of bemusement that often crossed his face when he thought she wasn't looking.

"I love watching that, you know," he said.

"What?" she asked. She held the teacup in both hands, letting its warmth soak into her cold fingers.

"The serenity of your tea ritual," he said. "It's nothing like watching someone desperately gulping the first coffee of the morning. It's more like you're smelling a lovely flower. I'm sorry about this afternoon, though. We really should have waited for better weather. Or had a better plan."

Cyndi set her cup on the lamp stand next to her. She looked Mike in the eye.

"Honey," she said, "when I said it was horrible, I wasn't talking about us. I was talking about the people down there. They're out in the rain all the time. They have to sit out there whether it's sunny, windy, cold, sleet, snow, ice. I can't complain about getting a little wet. I have a home and a husband and a teapot and friends and a loving church family to come back to. What do they have? Did you see that girl?"

"The one who was yelling at us? Uh, yeah, I saw her."

"She's a baby, Mike. She can't be more than a year or two older than Madi. How can she be living on the streets? How is she getting by? Why isn't she with her family?"

"Were you looking at the same girl I was? The girl I saw looked tough—pierced nose and lip, tattoo on her neck. She was no baby. She's been around the block."

"A block she never should have seen. Can you imagine if she was our little girl? I'm serious, Mike; we should do something to help."

"I thought that's what we were doing today."

Cyndi sighed. "I don't mean one meal. I'm talking about doing something big, something that really makes a difference."

"You've already signed up for a project. Remember the mall? I thought that was your dream."

"I know. It is. It's just—I can feel my heart coming alive for these people."

"You can't change the world, Cyndi. You've got to just take care of your little corner of it."

He was probably right.

Still, that night, Cyndi dreamed of Clark and Madi finger painting a mural on the wall of the strip mall.

Chapter 11

CHRISTMAS, DESPITE CYNDI'S hopes, turned out no less painful than the previous years. She gave Mike his book. He gave her a briefcase. She pretended to be grateful, but as soon as she could, she snuck away to Madi's room to cry.

She knew Mike knew she was in here, but he didn't come comfort her. She lay on the bed and clutched Madi's pillow, the one with the horses on it, letting her tears soak into its soft fabric.

"Why did you have to go?" she asked, but what she really meant was, *Why did he take you away?* It was so hard to keep her promise not to live a life of what-ifs.

Tomorrow she'd feel better. Tomorrow she'd fill her new briefcase with papers and files and brand-new business cards, but today belonged to Madi.

With the holiday behind her, Cyndi's mood improved. Three weeks later, Cyndi stood by her car in the parking lot, looking at the mall—*her* mall.

How surreal.

"Who actually owns a mall, anyway?" she'd asked Mike last night over dinner. She'd sat at the table with the deed in her hand, her own name and signature splashed across the bottom of the page. Even with the proof in front of her, it was inconceivable.

"It's not like you own the whole town, hon. It's just a strip mall."

Just a strip mall. But right now, it was the most beautiful strip mall she'd ever seen. She scanned the length of it, as she had countless times in the weeks since putting down the earnest money. Right to left, she counted off the storefronts.

On one end, anchoring the mall, a craft store. Next to that was a do-it-yourself ceramics studio, then some kind of packaging distributor. In the middle was a restaurant. It used to be a pizza place. When Madi was small, she would order cheese pizza, no sauce, and eat it as fast as she could so she could pretend to play on the race car video games before Cyndi and Mike finished eating.

Honestly, if the pizza place were still open, Cyndi wouldn't have bought the mall, but a few years ago it was bought out by a sushi bar. Recently, new management had torn out the conveyor belt and converted the restaurant space to a sandwich shop, now boldly labeled as Hometown Hero in green, red, and white.

Next door to the restaurant was an accounting firm, Spencer Ridley, CPA. That place was new.

And on the far left, the other anchor space stood vacant. The tape around the brown paper in the windows had lost its sticky in places. The paper hung as if a breath of wind would blow it to the ground. Cyndi made a mental note to tear it all down today and start cleaning the space for a new client.

She'd have to put a For Rent sign in the window.

Beyond that, she had no idea of how to find a tenant. Where should she advertise? What kind of business should she target? Her already dog-eared book on landlording would be getting more use for sure.

She'd start at the craft place and work her way down to the vacant space. If she timed it right, she could hit the sandwich place for lunch. Cyndi looked in the side pocket of her purse to make sure her new business cards were there.

She'd printed them off last night.

Cynthia Finch, Proprietor

She'd never had a business card before. It made her feel so official. One more look in the car's side mirror to make sure hair and makeup were in place and she was ready. She wanted to make a great first impression.

She just hoped she wouldn't puke.

Things started off easy, since the craft store owner wasn't in. She left her card, promising to return later in the week. The ceramics studio proprietor, a friendly bohemian woman who was happy to meet her and know how to get in touch in case she needed anything, talked longer than Cyndi cared to listen about all kinds of things that had gone wrong in other ceramics shops. Cyndi made a mental note to make sure there was enough insurance to cover damages if the kiln malfunctioned.

She paused in front of the financial advisor's door, memorizing his name before she walked inside.

Spencer Ridley.

It was late morning, and the sun had actually dared come out for a glimpse at January. It wouldn't like what it saw and would hide its face again for the next few months. But the few minutes of bright daylight gave Cyndi a flicker of hope.

She pulled the door open and walked in.

The small reception area only had four seats. The woman at the desk looked up at her. "Good afternoon. May I help you?"

"I'm Cyndi Finch. I'm your new landlord, um, proprietor, I mean. I mean, I own this building." She held out a business card, stiff armed. Everything about her screamed *novice*. "Could I speak with Spencer Ridley?"

The receptionist took the card. "I'm Mr. Ridley's wife, Allie. I'm sorry, but he is with a client right now. If you want to make an appointment, I can fit you in as soon as possible. I'm sure you understand." Allie set the card by her phone.

Something in the woman's attitude threw her off balance, like she was mad at her even though they'd never met before.

"No, I mean, yes, of course," Cyndi stammered. "I'm just trying to meet everyone. I didn't realize . . . I'll call ahead next time." She hated that this woman had such a withering effect on her. Just by being poised, she'd had the power to wilt Cyndi's confidence.

Cyndi skipped the shipping business and went straight to the Hometown Hero Sandwich Shop. Maybe she was just anxious because of low blood sugar. She'd feel better after she got some food in her. Maybe some tea, too. She wouldn't tell the server who she was until the end of the meal. She didn't want to get yelled at again for being the new owner.

A greeter welcomed her at the door and invited her to pick her seat. She bypassed the booths for a spot along the bar that had a view of the room.

It took more effort than she expected to heft herself onto a high stool. While she waited for her salad, she watched the other customers, curious what kind of people stopped at her mall.

Next to her, an elderly gentleman in a business suit read a book, propped up on the salt and pepper shakers and held open by a giant black clip. A couple of soccer moms chatted away at a booth. A steady stream of professionals came for takeout.

About the same time as her salad arrived, so did that woman from next door along with a man who must be her husband.

Allie something.

Cyndi squirmed in her seat. If it hadn't meant walking past her on the way out, she'd have left right now. Something about them made her feel small and frumpy. Why did they have to be so tall and thin? And the way they carried themselves—it was as if they knew they were better than everyone else in the room.

Cyndi hunted for croutons and cheese bits in her Caesar salad to avoid looking at Allie and her husband. She wasn't half finished when a man's voice drew the attention of everyone in the room.

"I said no mayo!" It was the accountant.

"I'm so sorry about that, sir. I'll have the kitchen make you a new one." The server looked like she wanted to disappear.

Cyndi knew the feeling.

"I've already sent it back once, but you didn't make a new sandwich, just changed the bread. What's the white stuff on my tomato?"

The server, just a high school student working for tips, scrutinized the sandwich. "It looks like mayonnaise. I'm sorry. Let me get that replaced for you."

"Again? What, so you can rinse the tomatoes this time and throw them back on the same sandwich? I don't think so." He didn't shout, but the rest of the diners had fallen into an awkward silence.

Cyndi—and everyone else in the room—heard every word, every inflection, clearly. She cringed.

Only Allie seemed unfazed by the scene. She was probably used to him getting his way.

"I want to talk to your manager," he demanded.

"Yes, sir." The server went to find her superior.

Allie and her husband didn't seem to notice everyone in the room was staring at them.

Cyndi had seen enough. She left a dollar on the counter and slid down off the stool. She beelined for the door, carefully avoiding eye contact with Allie. Wouldn't you know, as she passed Allie's table, her foot caught on something. It dragged behind her and she stumbled.

"Watch it!" Allie cried out. She grabbed her purse and snatched it against her chest.

"S-sorry," Cyndi stammered. Her cheeks warmed. She rushed for the door.

Her scalp tingled with anger. "Ooh, they made me

so mad," Cyndi muttered to Mike for the fortieth time that night. "Who do they think they are?"

"Don't let them get to you," he said, like he had several times already. "Why are you letting some secretary ruin your day?"

"I don't know. She just—they were so snotty. It was like they thought they were better than everyone else, better than me. They don't even know me."

"Give them time. They'll love you once they get to know you. They won't be able to help themselves."

"Sure they will." Most relationships weren't that simple. Cyndi retreated to her favorite chair. She flicked on the TV, but none of the prime time drivel captured her attention. She scanned through the channels three times, then pushed the off button with a disgusted sigh. She picked up her Bible, not because she thought she could concentrate on reading but because it was close at hand and she hadn't settled down enough to sit still. She bent the flexible cover back and leafed through the crinkly India pages until the book fell open at a comfortable spot.

Proverbs.

She scanned the page, not really reading, until she came to some underlined words. She'd read them a hundred times.

She read them again.

"If your enemy is hungry, give him food to eat; if he is thirsty, give him water to drink. In doing this, you will heap burning coals on his head, and the Lord will reward you."

She slammed her Bible closed.

Well, that wasn't helpful. No way was Cyndi going to go out of her way to be nice to this woman who wasn't even hungry. Or needy. Or nice.

Cyndi exchanged her Bible for the remote again and flipped to the public television station. Talking heads droned on about economics or politics or something. Their gray suits and gray hair blended with a drab background. Cyndi poised her thumb to switch the channel to something more colorful, something that might lift her up. But before she did, they cut to a photograph of an old man dressed in ragged clothes. His face was lined with years of hard living. He reminded Cyndi of the homeless man in front of the bookstore. She turned up the volume.

"—crisis of homelessness is not just in major cities anymore. This growing problem is spilling over into the suburbs. The last five years have seen a 64 percent increase in suburbs of people living below the poverty level. There are more poor people in the suburbs than in cities."

Cyndi's heart skipped a beat. She muted the program. Could that be true? It reminded her of the old woman she'd seen getting off the bus right in front of the church building right here in their neighborhood.

When she'd felt the need to feed the hungry, she'd automatically thought she had to go into the city to find them. But Riverton must have its share of hunger, poverty, and homelessness. Why had she never noticed it before?

Cyndi thought about what a fiasco trying to feed people downtown had been. But there were hungry people in Riverton, too. Maybe she could do something for the people closer to home.

An idea began to form in her head. What if, instead of renting out that extra space in the mall, she turned it into some kind of soup kitchen?

It was a crazy idea, but maybe . . .

Where to start? She'd need to check out the numbers with Simms to make sure she could afford to lose the rent on that space. And she'd need to do some asking around. And there might be some hurdles with permitting and the health department. It was an intriguing question, though.

Cyndi popped out of her chair, eager to get started but not knowing where to begin.

"Mike? Honey?" she called. She couldn't wait to find him before blurting out her plan. "I've got a great idea! I think I finally figured out what to do in Madi's memory!"

Chapter 12

"A SOUP KITCHEN? ARE you nuts?"

The idea was new to Mike. It would take him time to come around.

"It feels right," she said. "It's a perfect blend of running the mall and helping people."

"I'll tell you what it's a perfect blend of—lunacy and trouble." He set his reading book on the bedside stand. "What do you know about running a soup kitchen?"

"About as much as I know about running a mall. I'm a fast learner." She didn't want to sound desperate, but she wanted this so, so bad.

"You don't have any experience at all."

"I did work at a B&B for a while."

"Not the same and you know it."

It didn't matter. "I could visit the missions down in the city and see how they do it. I know it'll be a challenge, but I really, really want to do this." She stopped short of falling on her knees, hands clasped together in a plea.

Mike tapped his hand against his thigh. "Why don't you take some time to learn your role as proprietor before you take on something new?"

"I hate being proprietor. I just want the property manager to handle all the tenants." Wasn't that what she'd hired him for anyway?

"You've only been at it for a day. Give it time."

Cyndi felt the explanations piling up in her, racing to tumble out. "It's for Madi. I bought that mall with her money. I don't want it to be just a business or, worse, just a way to keep myself busy. I want her to be proud of me."

Mike shook his head. He patted the bed beside him. "Hon, Madi's not coming back, and nothing you do can change that. No mall, no soup kitchen, no project is ever going to replace her."

She didn't sit down. "I know she's not coming back. Don't you think I know that?" The pitch of her voice rose. Tears would follow soon. She bit them back. "I have to make her life count. She didn't have time to do all the great things I know she would have wanted to."

"I'm not saying not to do it. I'm just saying to wait awhile."

"I don't want to wait. I'm tired of waiting." She took a deep breath.

He reached out a hand and pulled her down beside him.

"If it's that important to you," he said, "then I guess you should do it. But this is your life, not Madi's."

Cyndi's heart beat a little stronger with a dose of hope. "I know."

"We'll always remember her. Just don't lose yourself."

"I won't." She rested her face in the palm of his hand. "I promise."

Already her mind swirled with new ideas. She needed a notebook. She had a menu to make.

"Where do these big pots go?"

Cyndi could hear her friend Nance's voice but couldn't see her face behind the huge pile of saucepans. "Over here on the counter for now. Thanks, Nance."

Nance shook out her arms. "That's the four big pots. I think there are still eight of the medium ones left in the van. I'll go get them."

"Don't try to bring them all at once!" Cyndi yelled after her.

Mike placed a hand on her arm. "Will you help me with the tables?"

Once she'd convinced him she wanted to do the hot meal program, he had thrown himself in as if it was his own idea.

She picked up one end of the first rectangular folding table from a stack leaning against the wall and, with Mike lifting the other end, carried it to the middle of the room. The walls and floors were still bare, and it didn't look much like the dining room she imagined yet. Cyndi pictured it full of people, working and eating together.

The city had issued all the permits. The health department had done their initial inspection. The fire inspector would be by later in the week. Most of the nasty paperwork behind her, Cyndi looked forward to the reward for all the legwork, the chance to finally do something worth doing.

Mike pulled the table legs into their extended position and helped her set the table upright. They went back for another one.

"I was thinking," Cyndi said, surveying the arrangement, "what if we put all the tables down on this end near the kitchen and leave a space up front for a seating area? Sort of an area for those who want to hang out and visit. Like gathering around the fireplace, only without the fireplace. What do you think?"

Nance came over to join them. "I think a seating area's a great idea," she said. "Maybe we could get people from church to donate old recliners and a couple of coffee tables. We've talked about feeding souls, not just stomachs. Why not give them a place they can be comfortable and get to know each other?"

Maybe we can buy one of those electric fireplaces," said Mike. "And put a TV over it for when the big game is on." He winked at Cyndi. He turned to Nance. "How's the kitchen coming? Do they need any help in there?"

"Looks like it's all under control. It's amazing how many people you know have been in the restaurant business. They have all the info about health department regulations down pat. They're arranging things and posting regs, and I was just in the way. Then again, it's amazing how many volunteers have come in from all over."

"I know," said Cyndi. "I never expected this many people to get behind this project. Pretty incredible."

What else can I do?" Nance asked.

"You want to stave off the rabid wolves?" Mike said, looking out the window.

Cyndi smacked him in the shoulder, then looked to see who he was referring to. An older couple stood at the front window, shading their eyes to peer in through the tinted glass. Cyndi recognized them as the owners of the craft store on the other end.

Oh boy. She'd been waiting for the first head to head with the tenants. She'd expected it to be the Ridleys, the accounting couple she'd had such an unpleasant start with. She tried to remember their names. It was a nautical term. Mast, maybe? Starboard?

Stern.

Chip and Amanda Stern.

From her other encounters with them, the last name fit them, though how such a bitter-looking man ended up with a name like Chip was hard to guess. It was as if the man doubled up on his sourness to compensate for his first name.

"Uh, nope," Nance said. "This one's for you. I think they might need my help in the kitchen." She shot a grin over her shoulder and hurried out of sight.

Cyndi greeted the Sterns with as firm and friendly a handshake as she could muster. "Chip! Amanda! Great to see you!" She knew this wasn't a pleasant social call, but she tried to act like it was.

Mike shook their hands and greeted them too.

Cyndi was grateful for the backup on this first face-to-face encounter with a business owner. She mustered enough confidence to say, "Please, have a seat. You're just in time. We just got the first table set up."

"And the first pot of coffee made!" came Nance's voice from the kitchen.

Bless Nance.

Mike got some folding chairs. By the time he had four set up, Nance and one of the kitchen workers had placed four cups of coffee and a paper bowl of sweetener packets on the table.

Cyndi went to look for spoons. She couldn't find a matched set but scrounged two, one white and one beige, and a handful of mismatched napkins.

"Leftovers from my kitchen at home," she said with a crooked smile. "Our supplies haven't been purchased. I know it doesn't look like much yet." She waved her arm to take in the room. "But it's coming together. We'll be ready to open in a couple of weeks."

Amanda poured a packet of sweetener into her coffee cup but didn't stir it. She kept the yellow paper in her hands and twisted it into a skinny tube, then untwisted it, then twisted it again. She avoided looking Cyndi or Mike in the eye.

Chip, though, was not shy to speak his mind. He sat in his folding chair, arms crossed against his chest. "I don't like what you're doing here," he said. "Going off and making a big decision like this without considering the impact to our businesses. You've got no right—"

"Not to be disrespectful, sir," Mike said, "but I think you're ill informed. We've gone through the proper channels, and we're filling a need that really must be addressed. A lot of people from the community are pitching in, sharing their talents. Cooks, carpenters, plumbers, electricians. I had no idea we had so much untapped talent. There's a whole group of people who are really behind this project."

"Not to be disrespectful," Chip countered, "but I think you're forgetting about us. Your clients. Remember? For you it's a project—for us it's our livelihood. And not just us, but all of us business owners."

"I hear what you're saying, but I think if you give it some time, you'll see that we're doing our best to help some people who really need a leg up. We'd love to see you get involved, too. I know you've got some talents we could use. Did you see our sign out front?"

"I didn't notice."

"I did," said Amanda.

"Pretty terrible, huh? I tried making it myself, but it's a mess. I bet you could do a much better job."

Chip ignored the broad hint. "There are a lot of other ways to fight social injustice without inviting a bunch of bums into the neighborhood," he said. "You're asking for problems."

"What kind of problems are you anticipating?"

"Parking, for one. Increased fire hazard, not to mention increased crime. And a huge drop in business. Who's going to want to come in our stores if there are vagrants hanging around the entrances? Who's going to trust their car in a parking lot full of street people? You start inviting drunks and druggies and mental cases, you know what you'll get. Trouble. That's what."

While Mike and Chip were going at it, Cyndi turned toward Amanda a little. She didn't expect to find an ally in the older woman, who, after all, was in the same situation as her husband. But at least she could try to erase her frosty glare.

"That's a beautiful vest you're wearing. Is it quilted?"

"Yes."

"Where did you buy it?"

"I made it."

Cyndi whistled. "You made it? It's gorgeous. I've always wanted to learn how to sew."

"I teach classes. You should come. A vest like this is too hard for a first project, though."

"What do you suggest?"

"Something with lots of straight lines is best."

Cyndi looked around the room. "What about curtains? I'd love to learn to make curtains."

"You could do that. Curtains are easy. What color is the room you're thinking of?"

Cyndi thought for a second. "Maybe yellow? I'm talking about for in here."

Mrs. Stern looked at the huge front windows. "You'd need to order a special kind of tension rod to fit those window frames. I have a source—" She glanced over at her husband. When she looked back, her expression had sobered. "I'm sorry. I really can't help you."

Cyndi didn't know how to respond. She ignored Mrs. Stern's concerns and plowed on with her ideas. "We need some color to cheer the room up a bit. Yellow is such a friendly color. I think we need to make this room a friendly place. Do you sell fabric at your store? Maybe I'll come by and see what you have. How much fabric will I need? Oh, and I'll need material for tablecloths, too."

Amanda stammered and looked puzzled, like she'd been hit from the side. She looked at the windows, tall tinted glass that ran the whole front and one side of the room, fourteen sections in all.

". . . minding our own business," Chip was saying. Amanda tapped his arm.

"Dear?" she said. Chip stopped talking. "Dear, did you bring your measuring tape? I need to measure some windows."

Chapter 13

April 17
Dear Mrs. Finch,

The Riverton Heights community prides itself on its safety and cleanliness. You can't just invite a bunch of bums into our neighborhood.

I know poverty is a problem, but it's not my problem. I donate plenty to the poor, but that doesn't mean I want them moving in with me.

My family chose to live in Riverton Heights in order to take advantage of good schools and good amenities.

Let's keep city problems in the city.

If you go through with your idea for a hot meal program, you can expect to hear from me again. There are plenty who feel the way I do, and we're willing to fight for our neighborhood. We're willing to do pretty much anything to keep you from moving forward.

Asking you to reconsider (politely, for now),

Buddy Kreft

Cyndi's hands shook as she read the letter. "Is this letter for real?" she asked.

"Oh, it's for real," Mike said. He left his laptop to come read the letter over her shoulder.

"Well, maybe it's just a few people. Maybe it's not as many as he says."

"Honey," Mike said, tucking her stray hairs behind her ear for her, "it's probably more than he says. Nobody's going to like us pulling the underbelly of the city into their view. But that doesn't mean we should stop."

"But is it right? I mean, what if my motives are all wrong? What if it's too much work? What if I can't pull it off?"

"Then we go back to life as normal. But for now, I think you need to be faithful to this wacky idea God planted in you."

Cyndi fought the heaviness in her heart. She'd been so excited, so eager to run with an idea that seemed to grow legs of its own. She wanted to do something important, but she wasn't looking to rile up a whole community. "If people are so against it, why haven't we heard from them?"

"Well, I guess we have. Some of them, anyway. This isn't the first letter."

"It's the first one I've seen."

"I didn't want to worry you. You know how frazzled you get when people are unhappy. And believe me, you don't do your best work when you're frazzled." Mike scratched behind his ear before admitting, "I've pocketed a few letters."

"How many is a few?"

He shrugged. "Maybe a dozen or so."

"A dozen? A dozen people are mad at me?" She felt a little sick. He was probably right to hide the letters.

"Chin up, babe," Mike said. He sat next to her, squeezing a hand for comfort. "If this is a God thing, he'll work it all out despite angry neighbors. Don't give up before you even give it a shot."

"But what if they're right? What if I ruin the neighborhood by feeding hungry people? What if I drive away our tenants? What if I fail and we lose our house? What if it's just a Cyndi thing, not a God thing? Maybe—"

Mike cut off her rising panic. "We won't lose the house. It'll be fine, but you've got to hold yourself together."

"What if we attract criminals? Drug addicts? Vandals?"

"You mean those who have lost their way? The needy? I thought that's who we're *trying* to attract. Every group, rich or poor, has its troublemakers. We'll just have to manage whoever God sends us."

Cyndi rested her forehead in the heels of her hands. "Who am I to think I can make a difference? What was I thinking?"

"If it makes you feel any better, you're not the first one to go through this. I've been doing some research." Mike got up, grabbed his laptop, and set it where they could both see the screen. He pulled up a search engine and typed a few words.

Portland soup kitchen parking.

He scanned the top results but didn't find what he was looking for. He typed in different search terms.

Portland homeless lawsuit.

Again he scanned the first page of results and came up empty.

"What are you looking for?" Cyndi asked.

"Hold on a second. I'll find it." Mike typed in a third set of words.

Portland meals limit.

This time he whispered an *aha* and clicked on the top choice. A newspaper article popped up on the screen.

"Is that what you were looking for?" Cyndi leaned in for a closer look.

"Yeah, this is it. A few years ago there was a case where a church was hosting meals for the homeless. The neighbors protested and the city shut them down."

"Why?"

"Too many people meeting in the building at once, I think. Here it is. It looks like there were some drunks hanging out around the doors, and it bothered the neighbors. So the city set limits on how many people could meet together at once. The national media jumped all over it. I can't believe you don't remember this story."

"When was that? 2000? I've slept since then. So what happened?"

"There was a big debate, mostly played out on the news, and the city eventually backed down, I think.

Actually, I'm not sure. The story just kind of disappeared after a while. Maybe it got lost in election year coverage or something."

"Doesn't it always work that way? Things like that seem all-important when they're in the public eye. And then when the media stops feeding us their line, we just forget about it. I'd like to know what happened. Even if the news coverage stopped, you know the problems of the homeless didn't. I bet a lot of the same people are still hanging out down there."

Mike typed something else in the search engine and came up with another story. "Here's one about a minister in California who was fined a thousand dollars a day for not chasing the homeless off the sidewalk in front of his church."

Cyndi whistled. "A thousand a day? We don't have that kind of fighting power. What happened there?"

"Looks like it's still in appeals."

"Shoot, honey," Cyndi said, scratching the back of her neck. "We don't have that kind of money. We can always back out now before it goes any further."

"Is that what you want to do?"

It would be so much easier to just forget it. But pictures of the old man lying on the sidewalk with his dog flashed through her head, then images of the girl, Clark, and the old lady down the street. Cyndi's dreams each night were filled with the faces of these people and others, people she'd met at the soup kitchens and shelters she'd visited while formulating her plans for her own.

She sighed. "I wish I didn't care so much about it. I

wish I could just say it was a good idea but I'm over it. Only . . . I'm not over it."

"What about the money?"

"We've still got some left from Madi's life insurance."

"And the house?"

"We'll quit before it gets that far. I'm not as worried about the money as the fight. Whatever anyone says, it's the right thing to do. This isn't about the neighborhood. It's about helping people who can't help themselves."

Mike closed his laptop. "Then we don't have a choice. We have to do it."

Chapter 14

CYNDI LAY IN BED, THE heavy down comforter pressing her into the mattress. Usually the combination of warmth and snugness pushed her right into sleep. But not tonight.

Beside her, Mike whistled slightly through his nose every time he exhaled.

Cyndi turned her back to him. She pulled a pillow over her head to drown him out. After a few minutes, she turned over the other way, then a minute later flopped onto her back with a groan.

They'd been working like crazy to get the new kitchen ready. For the last several weeks, she had spent every waking moment working on the place. It had a new coat of paint, freshly polished floors, and friendly yellow curtains, courtesy of Amanda Stern down at the craft shop.

Everything was going so well. Everything but the unexpected onslaught of opinions on Facebook.

Most people's comments were so supportive. But then there were the others, the cutting remarks, the veiled threats, the heated debates. It all made her sick to her stomach. She threw the blankets off and swung her feet to the floor.

She shuffled to the bedroom door. She stubbed her

toe on a desk chair. "Ow!" she whispered.

Mike stirred. "Hmph, what's wrong?" She could hear him patting her side of the bed. "Where are you going?"

"I can't sleep."

The blankets rustled. He'd be back asleep within seconds.

In the kitchen, Cyndi turned off the teakettle when she could hear the water crackling inside. Not that it would wake him anyway. He'd done more physical work in the last three weeks than in the past five years.

She didn't need a whole pot of tea, but part of the calming effect of tea was in the ritual. Cyndi reached for her favorite china teapot, the one with roses on it that her mother had brought back from London years ago. She poured loose chamomile leaves in and chased them with water. The pot went on a serving tray, along with blackberry honey, a spoon, a napkin, cup, and saucer.

She took her tray into the living room and set it on the stand next to her favorite chair. She curled her legs up under her and wrapped herself in Madi's blanket. Each step helped pull the world into focus.

The floorboards down the hall creaked. Mike came into the living room, squinting his eyes in the light of the lamp. "Why are you up?" he asked. "I can't sleep without you."

"I'm sorry, hon. I didn't want to wake you."

"Nah, it's okay. The bed just feels empty. What's up?" Mike cinched the belt on his ragged terry cloth robe and sat in his recliner.

"Those comments on Facebook. I feel like I need

to answer them or defend what we're doing. Do you want some tea? It's chamomile to help you sleep."

"No thanks. I was sleeping fine." Mike screwed up his face. "It's not nothing. Criticism is hard to take."

"Yeah," Cyndi said. "When we're down there working, I'm so excited. But when I look at my phone . . . All the negative stuff is killing me. I just want to run a soup kitchen."

"Hot meal service program." He smiled.

They'd settled on the terminology at the beginning, under the premise that *soup kitchen* conjured up pictures of the Depression, bums, hoboes, and the like. As if by calling someone a homeless person instead of a bum, they could raise his social status. Or by calling it a hot meal service, they could act like they were running a family restaurant.

"The problems are real," Cyndi said. "I don't have the energy to fight on every front. At this point, vocabulary doesn't even make the list of things I'm worried about."

"I know," Mike said. "The criticism is hard."

She looked at her phone. She could spend her whole life scrolling through unsolicited comments people were posting. "I don't know if I can do this. If we can't succeed, I don't even want to start. I have no intention of offering something to people who need it and yanking it away when things get tough. If we're doing this, we're all in."

He covered her phone with his hands. "Maybe you shouldn't be looking at that." He gently took it from her. "If you're going to run this kitchen, you need to get off Facebook. It'll only bring you down. May I?"

She used to love staying connected with people on social media, but not anymore. The court of public opinion was a hard place to be tried. "Yeah, okay."

He pushed a few buttons. "It's gone."

No more Facebook. No more unsolicited comments. Maybe now she could get some sleep.

Cyndi reached for her tea. She wrapped both hands around it.

"Seriously, Cyndi. It's going to be fine."

She stifled a yawn. "I'm just worried, that's all. It's what I do. I don't want anyone to get hurt." Especially not her or Mike.

"You're tired," Mike said, reaching out his hand to help her up. "No more Facebook. Let's get you to bed."

Cyndi left her phone by the chair. He was right. There were enough reasons to worry without letting other people's criticism keep her awake nights.

Chapter 15

"LOOK THERE, WOLF," JOE told his dog. "Swimming suits in all the store windows. That's a sure sign of spring." The air held the promise of warmer, dryer days ahead, but the damp of winter still hung about Joe's bones and made him feel older than his sixty-some years. Each year on the streets aged him five.

"What should we do today?" The winter's gray clouds hadn't heard that spring had arrived. They sat stubbornly on the city and refused to move. "Shopping? No? How about a game of chess? Or the library. Yeah? Sounds good to me, too. We can check the computer again."

He wasn't much for Internet, but he did keep his profile updated on Facebook and LinkedIn in case one of his daughters decided to look for him. "Don't you know if we skipped a week, that's the week she'd try to find me." He stashed his shopping cart in the bushes a block or so from the library. A look in the reflective glass of the office building next door told him he still looked homeless, but not frighteningly so. And with only two or three days since his last shower, he wasn't at his ripest. Not that that ever stopped him from going into public buildings.

"Morning, Joe," Janice, one of the librarians,

greeted him. "You're a little late today. Been busy?"

Joe grunted. He didn't aim to be predictable but found he fell into weekly routines without even realizing. "Here for the computer."

"I'll need to have your keys or license to secure one for you."

She knew what day and time he came in every week but didn't remember he didn't have a car?

"Will my library card do?" Joe asked.

It did, like always.

He missed the old microfiche machine with their copied newspaper pages, Polk directories, and old photographs. The Internet was a minefield of information, reliable and not. He didn't have much use for it and didn't like to waste time on it except for a few minutes every week. All that jumping around gave him a headache, and all the little words were getting harder to read.

He googled both his daughters' names, then his own, but turned up nothing new. He checked his profile pages for messages and looked at a people finder site to see if his daughters had tried tracking him down. Nothing.

Not surprising. They'd said they never wanted to see him again. It seemed they were serious. Once he'd found a wedding announcement for Deb, his younger girl. A couple of years later, he ran across a birth announcement. The little boy's face had long worn off the folded paper he kept in his breast pocket.

No news on either of his girls today, and no sign they were looking for him. He logged off and got his card back from Janice.

He took the escalator to the third floor and picked a carrel in a quiet corner. Then, as he did every Wednesday, rain or shine, he pulled every new law review off the shelf and started to read.

Chapter 16

WHEN THE BURLY MAN HAD loaded the oven into the back of the pickup, he'd made it look so easy.

No way could Cyndi move it herself. She'd have to wait for Mike to have time to help her.

She'd been so excited to find a working industrial stove on Craigslist for a fraction of what she'd expected to pay. A split second decision and a drive across town and she had the last piece of necessary equipment, and under budget, too.

If only she could get it off the back of the truck and in the front door.

She thought if she climbed into the truck bed and pushed the oven from behind, she could find its balancing point and tip it out slowly, then walk it to the kitchen. It was a foolish plan, but she was so eager to move it in, she couldn't wait for Mike to get here. She tried climbing into the back of the truck by swinging one leg up onto the tailgate and hefting herself up. She couldn't even get her foot as high as the tailgate. She turned her back to the truck, placed both palms on the edge of the metal, and hopped, trying to land her behind on the tailgate.

She didn't even get close.

She hopped a little higher, trying to land her larger-than-before backside on the topside of the tailgate.

No luck.

Not to be deterred, she climbed on top of one of the tires and positioned herself to scramble over the side of the bed. She hoped none of the shop owners was watching the awkward display. If they were, she'd given them plenty to talk about.

"Need some help?" She heard the man's voice from behind.

"No thanks. I've got it." She repositioned her hands a little and started to heft herself up.

He bounded into the back of the truck, letting a skateboard clatter to the ground beside it. Not a man, a boy, with spiky hair and baggy clothes. "No, really, I can help. Where are you taking it?" He readied himself to push.

"Into the kitchen." She let her leg drop back to the safety of the ground and backed up to catch the upper edge of the oven when it reached her. The boy slid the behemoth as far as he could, then started tipping it toward the ground. Cyndi grabbed the lip and adjusted the oven's angle so it could be let down with minimum effort. As soon as its weight rested on the ground, the boy bounded out and grabbed the stove top corners. Cyndi straightened and helped him ease the other two corners to solid earth.

"I'm Cyndi," she said, putting out a hand in greeting.

"Zach." He wiped his palms on his T-shirt before shaking her hand.

"I've seen you here a lot. You're the skater, right?

You're pretty good."

"Yeah, I skate."

"Isn't there a skate park around here? Isn't it more fun to hang out with other kids?"

"Nah, those guys are all posers."

"Posers?"

"You know, guys who try to act like they're *all that* but can't skate worth anything. Or worse, little kids who come with their mommies and tattle on anyone who bends the rules a little. At least here I can make my own rules, you know?" He tossed his skateboard into a patch of grass near the sidewalk. "How we gonna get this inside?"

"I think I have a dolly. Hold on a second." Cyndi unlocked the door to the kitchen. She found the dolly in the storage closet.

"If I hold the stove at an angle, it should balance its weight. Can you push and steer?" she asked.

Zach grunted.

She guessed that meant yes.

They maneuvered the monster to the edge of the sidewalk and lined it up with the door. Cyndi found a rock and propped the door open as wide as it would go.

She helped Zach tip the dolly back and push it forward, lining up with the door as he went.

She backed through the opening and tried to help him guide the oven.

It hit the edge of the doorjamb.

Zach backed it up and re-angled it to try again.

Again, it hit the jamb.

"It's kinda big," Zach said. He backed up enough

that he could set it down.

"Yeah, it is." Cyndi stared at it, as if she could make it shrink just a little by sheer will.

"Didn't you measure it?"

"Actually, no. I saw it online and I got so excited, I just went to pick it up, and I didn't plan through how to do this on my own. Hold on."

Cyndi ran back inside for a tape measure and checked the width of the door and the oven. "It looks like it will fit if we remove the top hingey thing on the door. Then it's just a matter of putting it in place. I'll need to find a professional to come hook it to the gas line."

Zach grabbed a chair and a couple of screwdrivers and set to work on the door. Cyndi stood under him feeling silly and helpless that a kid had more initiative than she did.

"Thanks for your help," she offered, by way of making conversation.

"Hey, no problem. I could tell you weren't going to get anywhere on your own."

"You're right. I don't know what I was thinking."

"My dad does stuff like that all the time—thinks he can do everything by himself. Thing is, most times he can." Zach jumped off the chair and tucked the screwdriver in his back pocket. "Anyway, what are you doing here? Why do you need such a huge stove?"

"We're starting a hot meal service program."

"What's that mean? Like a cafeteria?"

"Well, sort of. It's more like a . . ." Cyndi hesitated for a second. "Like a soup kitchen."

"That's cool. You mean, like, you're going to feed poor people?"

"Exactly. Poor people, homeless people, lonely people. Whoever comes our way."

"No way. Right here in the strip mall? That's sick!"

She chose to think he meant it in the best possible way.

"Can I help?"

Cyndi looked him over. Hooded sweatshirt, spiked hair, skater shoes, gauge earlobes.

He looked like a hoodlum.

He'd fit right in.

Zach had turned the parking lot into his personal skate park. He showed up every day after school dressed in a grungy T-shirt and saggy pants with a chain that dropped from his drooping belt line past his knees.

Cyndi grew used to the sound of skateboard wheels crackling against the asphalt. Every afternoon, rain or shine, he was out in the parking lot. She loved watching him practice his latest move. Lately, he'd been jumping the curb, catching the edge of the board in midair, and sliding off the board onto the concrete. She hated to think what damage he was doing his ankles, but he had determination, that was for sure.

She wondered if his parents knew where he spent every afternoon, or if they even cared.

Another thing he'd started doing every day was dropping in at Home Fires after he'd been skating for a while. He always asked if he could help with anything, and he'd been great at getting furniture assembled, painting the walls, and helping Mike install the TV. He'd also taken over the coffee station as his own territory and used the syrups and flavorings to concoct new coffees all the time.

This afternoon, he passed a cup across the table to Cyndi. "Try it. It's a hazelnut raspberry caramel mocha. You'll like it."

She screwed up her face. Since when did coffee get so complicated? Give her a cup of tea with cream and sugar any day. "No thanks," she said. "I'm okay. I've already had my caffeine for the day." She looked out the window through the rain. "Who's that?"

Zach looked out too. "Dunno." He shrugged and took a swig of his coffee.

Cyndi grabbed her jacket on the way out the door. A half-dozen people stood in the grass between the parking lot and the main road. She walked toward them to see what they were up to.

One of them turned his body enough that she could see he held a sign down low.

"Keep Riverton Safe!"

A good message, but why here? Why now?

A few steps closer, she saw his face. The ringleader was that Ridley guy, Spencer Ridley, the accountant who had been so rude to everyone at the sandwich shop. She'd heard he was stirring things up on Facebook. Of course he was going to protest. Of course he was going to get in her face.

Oooh, she could just scream.

She walked even closer, though she didn't have a

plan for what to do once she got to the group. Chew them out? Infiltrate their ranks? Yeah, no clue.

She turned to go back inside.

His voice reached her across the parking lot, instructions he was shouting to be heard above the roar of traffic. "Nonviolent doesn't mean passive! Yell all you want. Get in their faces, just don't touch anyone. Got it?"

Oh, that man. She should march over there and—

No. That would be exactly what he wanted. She would not deal with terrorists. She stomped back inside and flung her jacket at the coatrack.

"What? What happened?" Zach paused from flavoring up his coffee even more to ask her.

She clenched her fists. "It's those—Have you ever had someone who made you furious no matter what they did?"

"Yeah?"

"That's how that Spencer Ridley is for me. He hates me, sure. He's working against us, leading protests, writing letters to the editor . . . whatever. But there's something about him that makes me want to hit him even when he's not doing any of that stuff. Know what I mean?"

"Mmm." Zach walked over to the window and looked out. He seemed a little twitchy. Too much coffee, maybe.

"He's out there training protesters, probably setting up a schedule so they try to keep us from opening. Well, it won't work. We're opening, all right. On time. On schedule. And no matter who says what. You know why?"

Zach turned back to her. "Why?"

"Because the Ridleys do not get to decide what's best for everyone, that's why. The Ridleys only look out for themselves."

Zach muttered something on his way to throw out his cup. Cyndi didn't catch what he said, but it sounded a lot like "Not all of them."

Chapter 17

OPENING NIGHT. IT'D been a long time coming. At least, it felt like a long time, though the people in charge of permitting and codes at the city offices said they'd never seen something pushed through so fast.

Cyndi took a deep breath and let it go. She hoped this would work.

Mike used his booming teacher voice to call everyone together. "Okay, everybody! Let's gather over here by the service line for a word of prayer before everyone comes in."

The volunteers gathered in a circle.

Cyndi knew everyone here, friends and acquaintances from church and service clubs and every possible corner of her life. A few had brought other friends along, strangers who had already grown into friends in the weeks they'd worked together to prepare everything for tonight.

"It's the night we've been working for," Mike said. "Good job. You've all pitched in and helped get ready. I appreciate your standing behind my wife's vision. I can tell you're making it your own. Tonight is just the first of many, many to follow. We want to start off strong, so let's start with a prayer."

Cyndi held hands but didn't close her eyes. She didn't pray much anymore. Hardly any since God stopped hearing her.

"Our Lord and heavenly Father," Mike prayed, "bless us tonight. Please bring to us the people you want to feed. Thank you for giving us the food we need to share with them. Give us love and words to do the same. We ask you to soften the hearts of those who don't want this project to go forward. In Jesus' name"

Most everyone murmured, "Amen," but not Cyndi.

One of the older ladies was brushing tears from her cheeks. Nance was already headed for the kitchen.

Cyndi shouted to get everyone's attention. "You all know your places. Kitchen staff, don't forget to rinse the dishes in bleach water. Oh, and wear gloves. And don't serve seconds into a dirty plate. They have to get a new plate if they want more food."

Mike placed a hand on her arm. "It's all right, honey. They know what they're doing."

He was right. They had done a complete run-through last night and ironed out most of the kinks. Of course, she had to expect some bumps tonight, but they were as prepared as possible. Everyone was assigned a task—servers, busboys, drink people, dishwashers, even a greeter at the door. Cyndi's job was to be available to talk to people, to mingle with the guests.

Guests. She liked that. Instead of calling them clients or poor people or beggars, they were guests in a home. The volunteers were their family.

At six o'clock sharp, Mike threw the deadbolt on the door and a group of about twenty people surged in. Cyndi looked them over. Most of them looked like they had definitely been to other hot meal programs—a lot—maybe even today. One woman who weighed well over three hundred pounds lumbered to a chair and sat down. She shouted orders to a couple of children to push two tables together, then sent them to stand in line with the others.

There was a woman with a plaid flannel shirt and jeans. Her face was drawn and gaunt—a smoker's face. She had long, stringy red hair, except at the top, where two inches of black roots showed. Next to her was a stooped old man with a tangled gray beard. Beside him stood a young man. He wore a red T-shirt and no jacket, even though it was still in the forties. His shoulders were round, his arms skinny, and he carried an extra sixty pounds around his waist. The way his jeans were belted above his paunch gave him the appearance of a Macy's Thanksgiving Day balloon.

The line didn't seem to be moving. Cyndi moved closer to see and hear what was going on.

"Do you want green salad or coleslaw?"

The lady with the bad hair pointed to the green salad. The server, Marlina, scooped some lettuce onto the tray.

"And would you like ranch, Italian, or honey mustard dressing?"

Too many choices.

Cyndi realized it would be better to serve a simpler meal and get everyone through the line faster. She had overreacted to the fiasco under the bridge when she had gone with only two pots of soup. Now they had enough to feed an army, and variety to boot. They'd learn. Give it a few times and she bet it'd run like clockwork.

Cyndi looked around the room. There were enough seats for about a hundred. A group of twelve or so sat at the shoved-together tables. Most of the other guests sat alone, one person to one table. They would have to set up fewer tables if they wanted people to mingle. Either that or get the word out to more folks that free food was being offered. She grabbed a cup of coffee and scanned the room, trying to decide who to sit with.

She settled on an older man with a yellow handlebar mustache.

"Mind if I sit here?" she asked, pulling out a chair.

"Go right ahead," the man said. He glanced at Cyndi with a quick, nervous smile, then looked back at his food. He hunched over his plate as if afraid to drop a single crumb.

"Is it good?" How do you start a conversation with someone you don't have anything in common with? Cyndi was uncomfortably conscious of her clean jeans and department store blazer. She was way overdressed to blend in with the crowd. The man across from her wore layers—a T-shirt under a flannel shirt under a denim jacket. His hair was slicked back, not with hair gel, but with weeks of sweat and oil.

"Mm-hmm," the man replied, not bothering to look up. He took enormous bites, one after the other.

No manners, Cyndi thought. And then, *What do you expect? He's eating like a hungry man.* She looked for another way to start a conversation. "Do you eat at places like this much?"

The old man looked down at his now-empty plate, then up to the service window where food was being served, then back at his plate, then at Cyndi.

"It's okay. Go ahead and get more. There's plenty." The man pushed back from the table and raced toward the food counter with an agility that belied his age. Cyndi sat back in her chair and nursed her coffee. It would come. She couldn't expect everything to be perfect on the first night. She couldn't expect everyone to fall in love with her on the first night. They were bound to be gun shy.

They'd been hurt.

Then again, so had she. It wasn't their problem she needed to win them over to heal herself.

She looked for Mike.

He was at a table across the room, at home amongst strangers. She made her way to his side and touched his elbow to get his attention. He interrupted his conversation with an older couple—were they volunteers or guests? She wasn't sure.

"Hey, Cyndi. I think there's something you need to see."

"What is it?"

Mike turned to the couple and excused himself. He took Cyndi's hand and led her to the side windows. They had to weave between the folding chairs.

"It's going well, don't you think?" She had to raise her voice to be heard.

"Yeah. A few hitches in the kitchen, but we've got

plenty of volunteers, plenty of food. There's just one problem."

"What is it?"

"Look." Mike pulled back a wisp of yellow muslin so she could get to the shades.

Cyndi poked her fingers between two blind slats and pried them apart so she could see out. It was dark outside. She leaned closer to the window to see past the reflection. "The protesters?" she said. "I saw them earlier."

"Look again."

"There's a van."

"What kind of van?"

"It's white . . . it's a news van!" Cyndi stood up and let the blinds clap together. "It's that Whitt lady."

"You knew about the news crew?"

"She called me this afternoon. I had no idea she'd be doing a live TV report. Cool!"

"If it's so cool, why is she out there talking to them? Why not film inside?"

"She will. But look! We're on the news!"

"It's on! It's on!" Cyndi called Mike into the living room. She was exhausted, but she couldn't go to sleep without seeing the story. They'd been teasing it for the last hour. "Hurry!"

TV reporter Rebecca stood in the dark outside Home Fires.

"That's it! That's our place!" Cyndi jumped out of her chair.

The reporter started talking. "Thank you, Dan. I'm standing here in front of Riverton Plaza Mall, where there's a bit of excitement going on. Tonight, the owners of the mall opened their doors to the homeless. They are starting a hot meal service aimed at helping out the poor and hungry." She cut to the doors of Home Fires. It must have been at opening time. People were going in the front door.

"There's that lady!" Cyndi was beside herself. "And you!"

Sure enough, you could see Mike's face through the window.

They played Cyndi's voice talking about how they wanted to bless the poor in their own neighborhood.

"Do I really sound like that?" she asked.

"Shhh," Mike hushed her.

It cut back to the reporter.

"But the neighbors and tenants in the strip mall have other ideas. And they're speaking out. Here's what some of them have to say."

Rebecca lowered her oversize microphone while the news desk rolled footage of interview clips she had shot earlier.

The first one was with that awful man, Spencer Ridley. "We have community regulations on things like this. This soup kitchen is going to bring in more crime, more litter, and more danger to our kids."

They cut to his wife. "If they want to eat, they should find jobs. That's what the rest of us do."

Then to the guy who had written her the letter. "We moved to the suburbs to get away from drugs and crime. Now they're bringing it to us."

They all had the right to say what they wanted, but she wished they wouldn't.

Rebecca put her microphone to her mouth again, ready to finish the report as soon as the video clips cut off.

"I am standing here with Spencer Ridley, who is heading up this protest effort. I notice you've got about twenty protesters out here. How long do you plan to keep this up?"

She thrust the microphone toward Spencer but kept her eyes on the camera.

Cyndi wanted to spit at the TV. The story about how Home Fires was going to bless the community had been hijacked by the protesters.

Spencer spoke up. "We'll picket as long as it takes. We rented space in this building expecting the owners to do everything possible to bring customers to us. Now they've made a decision that will drive business away. That's not fair."

Whitt asked, "Why not just take them to court? Why fight them on the streets?"

"We are hoping that by putting our viewpoint out, the public can help the Finches see their error without having to take them to court. We don't want to make trouble; we just want to have our say."

"Thank you." Rebecca turned toward the camera. "We spoke with the proprietor of Home Fires today. She said she's excited to see what changes this new service will bring in the community. It looks like she's getting a bigger reaction than she bargained for. Live from Riverton, this is Rebecca Whitt, News Channel 7."

"That's it?" Cyndi screamed at the TV. "How dare they?"

Mike stood back, arms crossed. "They kinda stole your thunder, didn't they?"

Cyndi fumed. "Did they just threaten to take us to court?"

"Sounded like."

It was a veiled threat, but clear enough for her to hear it. If they thought she was going to close up Home Fires because of one little protest, they didn't know who they were dealing with.

Chapter 18

THE CORDLESS PHONE IN Cyndi' s new office in the back of Home Fires rang with its artificial old-fashioned tone. She'd been getting a lot of calls this week, ever since Home Fires had opened its door. She tried to field most of the calls and keep the pressure off Mike and the volunteer workers. She hated the PR part of this job, and it was getting worse.

"Hello? Cyndi Finch." Out of habit, she pulled the receiver away from her ear in expectation of an outraged onslaught. The man on the other end of the line had already worked himself up. "Donald Eldridge."

She searched her memory banks. Donald . . . he was on the finance committee at church. She couldn't imagine what he could be angry about. "Don, good to hear from you. What can I help you with?"

"It's about the food pantry. I understand you've been taking supplies from the church to supplement your program."

"Yes, we have. It's been a great help."

"Do you know how much that food costs?"

Aha.

She switched the phone to her other ear so she could doodle on a sticky note with her right hand. "No, I don't have that figure. Not off the top of my head."

"It's come to attention that you've siphoned off about $600 in supplies over the past few weeks."

Cyndi prickled at the use of the word *siphoned*. This was not a friendly call. "It's been a tremendous help. The elders agreed that it was better for us to be distributing the food rather than hoarding it in a closet. Maybe you'd like to speak with one of them about their decision?"

"We've worked hard to build up that supply in case we ever need it. If your bums keep up this rate, we won't have anything left in a month or two."

"Mr. Eldridge. First of all, they're not *my* bums. Their problems affect all of us. And secondly, if we didn't want people to eat the food, why did we collect it?"

Donald spluttered for a second. "For a rainy day."

Cyndi looked out the window at the water streaming down from the sky. It seemed that every day was a rainy day. "I'm sorry you feel that way," she said. "Maybe if you come down to help serve a meal or two, you'll get a feel for what a difference we can make."

"I'll be talking to the pastor about this," he said.

"You do that." Cyndi punched the end button on the phone and dropped it back into its cradle. Before it even had time to settle, the phone rang again. Cyndi breathed a quick prayer for patience.

"Oh, Mrs. Winston, how nice to hear from you."

The purple-haired old bat.

"Yes, we've opened the hot meal service. We've served two meals . . . No, not every night. Just on Tuesdays and Thursdays. Yes, poor people."

Cyndi listened to her neighbor's concerns that a homeless man was going to jump out of the bushes and attack her if she came to volunteer.

"Mrs. Winston," Cyndi explained, "we have no reason to believe that any of our guests are hanging around except at mealtime. Most of them actually live in the city and are taking the light rail over here for meals. The ones who are in the neighborhood already have their favorite places to stay."

Mrs. Winston repeated her concerns in a higher-pitched voice. Cyndi tried to calm her fears, with no luck.

"I'll tell you what, Mrs. Winston," Cyndi said, pinching the bridge of her nose and trying to rub away the headache that was forming there. "I'll keep my eyes and ears open for any problems that come up, and if I feel like there's any danger, I'll be right on it. In the meantime, if you don't feel comfortable helping out, then don't. It's not mandatory. Okay, bye now."

She should keep track of all the complaints that were coming in. Many of them centered on the fear that someone was going to get hurt. Some dealt with concerns that property would be damaged—litter in the grass, cigarette butts on the sidewalk, car radios stolen. They were silly concerns in Cyndi's opinion, trivial matters in the scheme of things, but very real to the people calling.

Her favorite, one she could laugh at, was an older volunteer who worked in the supply closet who was worried about toilet paper. How much would it take? How much would it cost? How could they keep people from stealing the excess? Should they ration it?

"What exactly would a toilet paper rationing look like?" Cyndi had asked. "Never mind. I don't think I want to know."

Cyndi opened her top desk drawer for some Advil. She lined up the little arrows on the cap and bottle and popped the top. Four pills skittered into her hand. She started to scoop two back into the jar, then reevaluated the severity of her headache and popped all four pills into her mouth. A swig of coffee washed them down. Cyndi leaned forward and rested her head on the desk.

She closed her eyes. The vessels in her temples pulsed, pounded.

The phone rang again.

Chapter 19

Zach faced Cyndi in the light rail car. He thrummed his fingers on the plastic seat next to him.

Bored or nervous? *Nervous*, Cyndi thought.

"So, what are we doing downtown?" he asked. A month ago, she never could have imagined inviting a skateboarding teen to the city with her. But he'd proved to be her most faithful volunteer. He worked most nights and came in Saturdays to help restock the pantry and clean.

"Looking for someone," Cyndi replied. A compulsion to find the old man who had planted the seeds of an idea to help hungry people drove her on what she knew would be a fool's errand.

"Someone you know?"

"Kind of."

"Do you have his address?"

"No, I'm just hoping I run into him." Cyndi changed the subject. "How's school?"

"It stinks." What did she expect him to say? "It's just like, you know, like the teachers are all out of touch with reality. I mean, who cares what the War of 1812 was about? Or the specific gravity of anything? What's it all got to do with life?"

"Good point. I never quite figured that out. It

seems like busywork sometimes, but you really *are* learning." It was the type of answer a mom would give. She changed the subject. "What do you think of Home Fires?"

Zach's whole demeanor changed as he answered her. "I love it. I mean, people can come in and get food and warm up. It's cool how everyone seems to work together. It's like we're making a difference."

"That's what I was thinking too. I wish everyone felt that way. But we're just getting started. It's just going to get better." Cyndi looked out the window. "Oops. This is our stop."

She jumped up and raced for the sliding door, Zach just behind her. They stepped down to the cobbled walk under the Humboldt Bridge. All that was left as evidence of the morning market was some litter and the lingering smell of Ethiopian chicken stew. A man in gray shirt and pants and an orange reflecting vest pushed a broom down the sidewalk. Two Rastafarians sitting against a retaining wall hummed softly in Jamaican harmony.

Cyndi looked around but didn't see him. "Let's look up top."

Zach followed her up a staircase that took them on top of the bridge. The yellowing afternoon light cheered the bleak street scene. A dozen or so people sat or leaned against the ledge of a mission shelter across the street. Cyndi wished she had something to offer them, but she was empty handed.

Zach walked close behind her, hands buried deep in his front pockets.

Cyndi looked each person in the face as she walked by, but she didn't stop.

"Hey, kid. Got a cigarette?" The man who asked couldn't have been older than forty, but the gaps in his mouth where teeth should be made him look much older.

Zach moved closer to Cyndi. He might try to look tough, but he definitely had more swagger in the suburbs than in the city.

She kept walking, ignoring the catcalls and stares of the men sitting on the sidewalk. Mingled scents of smoke and sweat, booze and body odor assaulted her. It took her a minute to realize Zach was no longer with her. She turned around to see him, eyes wild with panic, as a group of men gathered round, fingering his belt chain and his designer jacket. He pulled back, looking for a place he could step and get free.

Cyndi strode back toward him.

"Settle down, kid. I'm not gonna hurt you. Go ahead, run to Mommy," a short man growled.

Zach broke free and moved close behind Cyndi.

"Creepy," he said, looking back to see the man and his buddies staring after him.

"You're okay," Cyndi said. "Come on."

She strode with purpose, like she really did know where she was headed, though she didn't. She just wanted to get out of this part of the neighborhood. She crossed the street at a crosswalk, walked around the corner, and climbed the hill toward the Cathmore Building. Under the awning of the used bookstore, she looked for any evidence of the old man and his dog.

"He's not here," she said. She didn't know where else to look.

"Does he hang out here?" Zach asked.

"I don't know. I mean, I've only seen him here once."

"Recently?"

"Early December."

"Four months ago? He's had plenty of time to move since then. Why are you looking for this guy?"

"He's the one. The one that got me thinking about starting Home Fires. I wanted to tell him that he and his dog are welcome. I think they'd like it there."

"Hey, Cyndi!" The voice came from behind them, across the street. Cyndi turned to see a girl, about Zach's age. Tough, streetwise, with her biker jacket and punked-out hair. It took a second for the name to register; then Cyndi lit up with the delight of recognition.

"Clark!" She waved her arm in the air, returning the call of the teenage girl she'd only met once, that disastrous day in the rain. *I can't believe she recognizes me.*

Clark returned the wave, with an eagerness that surprised Cyndi. It didn't last long. She lowered her arms and stuck her hands in her pockets.

If Cyndi had learned anything in the short time she'd been working with the homeless, it was that they guarded themselves. Don't get involved, don't get attached—those were key rules of the streets.

Don't get involved.

That was a rule Cyndi couldn't keep. She stood at the curb and looked for a break in traffic. Clark stood directly across from her, separated only by a line of cars. And a million miles.

The crosswalk's red hand turned to a white man walking. Clark bounded off the curb and across the street before Cyndi had a chance to step off the sidewalk. It looked like Clark was going to run straight into her arms, but she stopped herself a few feet short of a hug and checked her face and body for excess emotion. She forced her hands deeper in her pockets when Cyndi offered a hand in greeting. Feet planted, she took on a tough-guy stance.

"So, you're back," Clark said. "I didn't think I'd see you again. What's it been? Three months?"

"Four," Cyndi returned. "I've been busy."

"Sure." Clark looked down at her toes and scuffed her foot along the sidewalk.

"No, really. Last time I saw you, you really got me thinking. Those two pots of soup were pretty pathetic. You thought I was only down here to do my good deed for Christmas. And maybe I was. But now I'm doing more."

"Oh yeah? Like what? Easter brunch?"

"Actually, no." Cyndi laughed. She could see how she deserved that one. "We've started a hot meal service. Tuesday and Thursday nights you can come for a free meal and a safe place to hang out."

Zach nosed into the conversation. "I thought Clark was a boy's name. I'm Zach, by the way."

Clark stared at him, then looked back down at her feet. "Where's the meal at?"

"Riverton Plaza. It's a mall on the main drag

through Riverton, not far from the light rail stop. We'd love to have you."

"Riverton? I'd have to ride the train half an hour to get there. Plus it costs two bucks each way. Four bucks for a free meal doesn't sound like much of a deal."

She had a point.

"We're doing it for our community, but I'd love if you could join us. Just once?" Cyndi pulled out her wallet and found a five. "That's enough to get you there and back. Come give us a try. Maybe we could work something out where you can exchange help with cleanup for train fare. If you want."

Clark took the crisp bill between her fingers. Cyndi could almost see the hunger behind her eyes, hunger for something more than a hot meal. The choice was Clark's. She could take the money and use it for whatever she wanted. Or she could invest it in a train ride and a possible way out.

Cyndi promised herself not to demand anything of the girl. She'd let her come on her own terms or not at all. Same deal as she had with Zach.

Clark crammed the bill into her pocket. She said, "I'll have to think about it."

"Six o'clock on Tuesdays and Thursdays. Or earlier if you want to help set up. Or take a shower. Anyway, I'm always there by three or so. I'll be watching for you."

"Me, too." Zach spoke up. Cyndi looked from him to Clark. He was dressed in all the latest names. His sneakers must have cost a couple hundred bucks. But he looked more lost than the girl.

"I'm Clark." She offered him the hand that she had refused Cyndi.

"Zach."

"All righty, Zach. See ya." She turned with a bounce and jogged across the street just as the flashing red hand turned solid.

That Thursday, Mike, Cyndi, and Nance stood side by side on the kitchen side of the serving line. Mike placed a roll and pat of butter on each plate, then passed it to Cyndi, who dished up the main course and salad. Nance then took the plate and added dessert—brownies tonight. The thirty or so they used to serve had spread the word, and after only a month, they were now serving almost a hundred meals every Tuesday and Thursday.

Nance handed a plate to the last person in line. Cyndi leaned through the opening to see if anyone else was coming.

"Looks like we're done," she said, peeling off her one-size-fits-no-one latex gloves and dropping them in the trash can. She went to the hand-washing sink to rinse the powder residue from her otherwise clean hands. Mike and Nance followed her.

"Things are going so great," Nance said. "Way better and smoother than I thought they'd be."

Cyndi agreed, but not completely. "You know what's getting me about all this? I thought we'd be digging into people's lives by now, but we're not connecting."

"Don't be too hard on yourself," Mike said. "You're doing a great thing. Change takes time. We're not going to break into these people's lives the first time we meet them. We have to give them time to know they can trust us."

"I think Cyndi's right," Nance said. "We've served some of them twice a week for a month, and we haven't really gotten to know anyone. They sit at their tables; we sit at ours. Are we meeting their needs? Are they really being served?"

"Well, I'm sure not."

Cyndi turned to see who had said that. Clark, the girl from the streets, stood at the window, dripping wet.

"What happened? How are you? I mean, welcome!" Why was she so flustered talking to this girl? Maybe because she seemed more human than many of the others.

"Nance, this is Clark, the one I've told you about. Mike, you remember Clark?"

Nance waved a hello to Clark. "It's good to finally meet you."

Mike was more outspoken. "I saw you that day under the bridge. You're the one who laughed at us, aren't you?"

Clark seemed to shrink a little at his words.

But he continued. "Thank you so much! Without you and your reality check, we never would have thought to start something this big."

Clark nodded. Her arms were folded across her chest. With her hair plastered against her forehead like that, she looked younger, more vulnerable. For the first time, Cyndi realized that she was probably too young to be on her own. What was her story? What made her so tough? Why wasn't she at home watching *American Idol* or hanging out at the mall right now?

Cyndi couldn't ask her any of those questions. Not yet. She needed to meet the physical needs first and be careful not to push too hard. If the girl was comfortable, she'd come back. It would take time.

"Hungry?" Cyndi asked.

"Starved," said Clark. "What's for dinner?"

"Lasagna, garlic bread, salad, and homemade brownies. Want some?"

"Yeah, a little of everything." She took her full plate and looked for a place to sit. As soon as her back was turned, Cyndi spotted Zach across the room, bussing tables. She waved her arms around to get his attention. When the boy looked up, she pointed to Clark. A smile stole onto Zach's face, and he made his way over to offer Clark a drink and a chair.

Cyndi turned back to Mike and Nance and gave them a nod and a grin.

"Now that's more like it."

Chapter 20

OVER A MONTH IN AND the protesters were still at it. Cyndi usually tried to get to Home Fires well ahead of opening time to avoid the picket line. Tonight, though, she'd had a meeting that made her late.

A handful of protesters were already marching with their signs.

"Safe Streets! Clean Streets!"

Cyndi scoffed. No rise in crime, no rise in garbage on the streets that she had noticed.

"Go Away!" read another. That was subtle.

A few more would show up before the guests arrived, but the number of protesters had shrunk while the number of diners had increased.

There was another protester now. Spencer Ridley walked right out of his office—in her own building—carrying a sign that said, "Not in My Backyard!"

Oooh, she wished there was a clause in their contract that would let her kick Mr. Ridley out of her building. He was the only one of the tenants who was publicly fighting her and he was the one who stood out of the opposition crowd. He'd written some pretty nasty letters to the editor (which Mike talked her out of replying to). He'd been active on Facebook, too, she'd heard, but Mike refused to show her the ugly fight still being waged against the kitchen in cyberspace.

They were in the Northwest, for crying out loud. Go downtown any day and you'd meet a bunch of people protesting something—furs, taxes, social injustice. Just, most of those people weren't protesting *her*. It was a new experience, and one she didn't like. At all.

She walked past the line. The protesters didn't stop her, but she heard one of them, probably Spencer, mutter, "She's the problem."

Oh, that man! She turned around to scream at him but stopped herself. Directly behind him, camera trained on Cyndi, was the news crew. She hadn't seen them. How had she missed them before? She turned back around and hurried inside.

"I am so sick of those stupid protesters." She stomped into the dining room and went straight for the window. Peering out through the blinds, she got a good view of the protesters. The news van was parked on the main street, not in the parking lot. That's how she'd missed it. "Why can't they just give up and go away? Can't they see that we're not going to give up feeding people just because they're marching around out there? Looks like they're going to be on the news again tonight."

"How many are there this time?" Mike stood beside her and peeked through a higher slat.

"Just the diehards. I'm surprised they keep coming." Cyndi let her blind slats flap together.

Mike took one last peek at the protesters. "Hello, what's this?"

"What?" Cyndi turned back to the window. She peeked through the blinds again. "Oh, that. Yeah, the news is back."

A couple of others headed to the window.

"Look," he said and pulled the blinds open so everyone could get a view.

"Sweet," said Zach. "We're gonna be on TV?"

"Not us," Cyndi said. "Them. I can just hear it. They'll tell all about the poor families that live in their perfect McMansions in their perfect little neighborhood. They'll slant it to sound like we're totally dragging down property values, trashing business revenues, like we love crime and want all the bad guys to camp out in our parking lot."

"Don't you?" Zach asked.

"Don't we what? Love crime?"

"No, criminals. And you do let bad guys hang out in your parking lot. You let me."

Cyndi resisted the urge to ruffle Zach's hair. He got it. Of all people, this punk kid skater actually got it.

Someone said, "Turn on the TV. Let's see what they're saying."

Chip turned on the set above the electric fireplace.

There was that reporter, Rebecca Whitt, with the accountant. "I'm speaking with Spencer Ridley of Riverton. Mr. Ridley has been protesting in front of Riverton Plaza twice a week since the Home Fires soup kitchen opened in February. Mr. Ridley, why is this cause so important to you?"

"Rebecca," he said. "I have worked my whole life to be able to afford a nice home in a safe neighborhood.

I've built a business and a lifestyle. I moved my family here to give my son better school opportunities. I should have the right to enjoy it." He smiled at the camera.

He was a charmer. Cyndi hated charmers.

"What about this soup kitchen threatens you?"

"On a personal note, our business is right next door to the soup kitchen. Just as business was starting to get off the ground, the, shall I say, undesirables started hanging out. But this isn't just about us. On a broader scale, Riverton is an affluent community. We simply don't have to deal with many of the crimes that happen in the city. Why invite them in?"

"Such as?"

"Such as drug trafficking on the streets, random acts of violence, auto theft, to name a few."

"And in the time since Home Fires has been open, have you seen an increase in these crimes?"

The picketers continued to chant in the background, but Spencer focused on the reporter and her camera. "I don't have the statistics on that, but there are other crimes, too—litter, loitering—"

"And those? Have they worsened? Have you actually seen a decrease in revenue at your business, or is it just a perceived drop?"

Cyndi cheered the reporter. *Those* were the kinds of questions to ask.

Someone tapped on the front door. She started to tell whoever just came in to wait a few more minutes. Guests were supposed to wait outside along the sidewalk that ran down the end of the building so they wouldn't be in front of any of the other doors in the mall.

But it wasn't a guest—it was Clark. Last time she'd come with a smile and an eager attitude, but tonight she wore a scowl. Cyndi didn't miss the fact Zach practically skipped over to say hi.

"What's wrong?" Zach stopped short of the hug he was probably hoping for.

Even though Cyndi could see Clark was upset, she hung back. She would let Zach try to handle whatever the problem was. Too many people in Clark's face would shut her down.

"Nothin'."

"Come on. It's not nothing. What's going on?"

Clark shuffled her feet. "That group out there is pretty pushy. They were trying to keep me from getting to the door."

"Yeah, we're watching them on TV. Did you tell Mike?"

"It's no big deal. I'm hungry. Can I eat?"

Zach shook his head. "Just talk to him for a sec, and then we'll get our food." He reached for Clark's hand, but she jerked it away. "He's watching the news," Zach said.

Clark stepped out in front of him and started toward Mike. After a couple of steps, she turned around and talked to Zach. "You coming?"

He bounded after her like a puppy just learning to stay.

Cyndi followed them.

The lady on the news was showing some chart

about crime rates in Riverton.

"Hey, Mike," Zach said. "Those jerks outside gave Clark a bad time tonight."

Mike looked at her. "Did they hurt you?"

If they did, so help her—

"I'm okay," Clark said. "It's no big deal."

"You're bleeding," Zach said.

Cyndi hadn't noticed before, but Clark's jeans were torn. Blood seeped in at the edges of the tear. Cyndi's mothering skills, long dormant, kicked in. "Zach, go get the first aid kit. Clark, sit down here. Mike, you call the police."

"No!" Clark practically screamed it. "Please don't. Please. Just let it go. It's no big deal."

"They hurt you. It's a big deal. They crossed the line."

"Just don't call the cops. Please?"

Cyndi hadn't seen this side of Clark. Her tough exterior was torn away, leaving her small and afraid. Maybe she was wanted for something. Cyndi didn't want to believe it, but the girl lived on the streets, for goodness' sake.

"Please?" Clark's eyes shone with unmasked fear.

She looked from Clark to Mike and back to Clark. The girl was desperate. Much as she wanted to call for help, Cyndi didn't have the heart to do the one thing Clark was begging her not to do. "All right. No police. But I can't just let this go. I've got to stop them before anyone else gets hurt. Mike, are you coming with me, or are you staying to patch up that cut?"

"I'll stay."

Cyndi turned to Clark. "I'm gonna go talk to them. Did they get you on camera?"

Clark shook her head. "No."

Cyndi stormed across the room and pushed through the door. "Well, they'll get an eyeful of me."

Chapter 21

CYNDI RAN FULL SPEED OUT the door and toward the TV camera. She pulled to a stop between the reporter and Spencer Ridley. She knew she looked like a madwoman, but she didn't care. "What do you think you're doing?" she practically screamed at Spencer.

The reporter opened and closed her mouth a couple of times like a gaping fish, but no sound came out.

"You have no right! How dare you!"

"We have every right to be here," Spencer returned, careful to keep his voice steady. Calm for the cameras, but pushing down kids the rest of the time? "It's a free country, and I'm exercising my right to freedom of speech and expression."

"I don't care what you think and what you say!" Cyndi knew her face was red, her temples bulging. "You have no right to push innocent people around! I've got a young lady in there who's bleeding. If you're all just exercising your right to free speech, how did she get hurt?"

Rebecca had regained her composure. She thrust her microphone toward Spencer.

"How *did* she get hurt?" Her voice had lost any softness. She spoke with the edge of a hardened newsman.

"I don't know. I didn't touch her, and I'm sure none of my group did either. We're about stopping crime, not encouraging it."

Cyndi shrieked, "Well, you've done a fine job of it! Stay away from my guests!"

Rebecca said, "This is Cyndi Finch, who owns this strip mall and is in charge of the soup kitchen."

Cyndi clammed up. She drew away from Spencer and lowered her voice.

Someone laid a calming hand on her shoulder.

She took a deep breath. "I'm asking you to let us help these people," Cyndi said. She enunciated each syllable, holding the things she really wanted to say just behind her bared teeth. "I'm asking you to let us do some good. One of our homeless teens was hurt by one of your protesters."

"Says you," Spencer shot back. "I'm a business owner and a citizen of this town. I have rights and you are stepping on them." Spencer leveled his gaze at her.

"What part of 'She's hurt' are you not understanding?"

"What part of 'We didn't do it' do you not understand?"

"You need to back down!" She could hear the shrillness of her request, but she couldn't stop herself.

Spencer started directly at her. "We don't *need* to do anything except stand up for ourselves. I didn't want it to get this far, but you leave me no choice. We will see you in court."

Cyndi didn't know what to say. She glared back at

Spencer, trying to think of a brilliant comeback, but she was blank.

Spencer's words hung in the air. He'd thrown down the gauntlet.

Well, fine. If they wanted a real fight, they were going to get one.

The reporter drew the microphone close to her own mouth. "And *that*, folks, is the news on the street. Live from Riverton, this is Rebecca Whitt. News Channel 7."

Mike escorted Cyndi back to Home Fires while the news crew was still packing up their gear. He didn't say anything, but she could hear his thoughts—*What have you done? What did you think you could accomplish? How is getting us dragged into court going to help anyone?*

When Cyndi finally talked, she asked, "How's Clark?"

"Shaken, but fine."

"The reporter is going to want to talk to her, take her picture. Maybe we should let them. It would show our side."

He pulled open the front door. "Maybe that should be her choice."

"Maybe."

If she thought Clark overreacted to their suggestion they call the police, it was nothing compared to the suggestion she might want to talk to a reporter.

Nope. No way. No how. Not going to happen.

So, that was that.

"Wow," Zach said once everything had settled down. "I didn't know you could run that fast."

"Me neither . . . but that man. He and his wife are doing everything they can to run us out. I can't let that happen."

"Right on," Zach said, but with less than his normal enthusiasm.

That night, the late edition of the local news showed the story again, edited this time to show Cyndi running at the camera over and over.

"What were you thinking?" Mike asked.

Cyndi shook her head. "For once, I wasn't. I was just acting on what I thought. They hurt Clark; I hurt them."

Cyndi watched herself on TV, larger than life, screaming in the face of that horrible man. Only on TV, it looked like he was sane and she was wacko.

As soon as the story ended, Mike clicked the TV off. "You can't do that again."

Cyndi took a deep breath. "I know. I'm sorry."

He pressed his mouth closed. "I don't think sorry is enough. I think he was serious about taking us to court."

Cyndi stared at the black screen. If they did sue, she'd fight as hard as she had to to keep Home Fires open.

She was on pins and needles the next day, waiting for someone to drop by with a subpoena. Was that even the right word to say when you were being sued? Or was that just for when you were being called to testify in court?

"Do you think they'll really do it?" she asked Mike.

"I don't know, babe. Do you want to go talk to them and see if we can preempt a lawsuit?"

She'd watched the recording of the news over and over. She'd played the scene in her head a hundred times. There was nothing she could do to stop those people from doing whatever they very well chose. "If we go talk to them, all that will happen is I'll start screaming my head off again. I can't stop myself. They make me crazy."

"Me, too, hon." He kissed the top of her head and went back to rolling silverware in napkins.

"What do you think?" she asked Amanda Stern.

The older lady said, "I bet they're all bluff. Protesting is one thing, but to hire a lawyer? They'd have to have proof their business has decreased. We've looked at our books, and at least for our store, there hasn't been any change in revenue. You've done a good job of making sure everything stays clean and the parking lot is still for customer use."

At least she had the Sterns on her side.

She wandered over to Zach, who was hanging out on the couch, thumbing through stuff on his phone. "Hey, buddy."

He tipped his head toward her.

She plopped down next to him. "Do you think they'll sue?"

He sat upright. "Huh?"

"Those people, the Ridleys. They said they're going

to sue. Do you think they really will?"

Zach looked down at his phone screen. It was off. "I don't—I've—um—What time is it?"

"Maybe about five. Why?"

"I-I gotta go." Before she could react, he was gone. That was weird.

She paced some more and worried some more and bugged everyone for their opinions. She didn't have to wait or speculate too long, though. By the end of the night, she had the papers in hand.

She had been served—*served* was the word she was looking for.

"It's in our court now," Mike said while they were lying in bed together. "Do we settle or do we go to court?"

Cyndi snuggled in next to him. "Oh, we're not settling. If they want a fight, I'm giving them a fight."

Chapter 22

JOE PUSHED HIS SHOPPING cart full of ragged coats across the red cobbled bricks of the public park. Much as he hated the cold winters on the streets, he hated the summer even more. After all, in the winter, he could keep bundling on more coats and clothes or snuggle up with his personal heating pad, Wolf. But during the rare Northwest heat wave, like today, there was only so much you could take off.

Wolf trotted behind him, his tongue drooping out the side of his mouth. It wasn't even nine in the morning, and the poor dog was already roasting. Joe leaned into the shopping cart and forced it to turn uphill. He had planned to spend the day at the city library. Its air conditioning beckoned him. But if he was inside all day, Wolf would have to be tied up in the sun, so he headed for the courthouse instead. The fountain there would give Wolf plenty of water.

The gray stones of the government building's facade glowed white in the hot morning sun. A set of stairs as wide as the face of the formidable building poured out to the sidewalk. Twenty-seven steps, three flights of nine. Joe had climbed them a million times. But that was a lifetime ago. He found a spot near the bottom where the railing cast a shadow. It was close enough to the fountain that Wolf could get up and take a drink whenever he needed to. In lean times, Joe had waded in this very fountain, and many others, to collect coins off the bottom. The twinge of guilt he felt when scooping up wish pennies melted away with the ice in the bottom of the slushie cup he purchased with discarded coins. He didn't understand how people could have so little regard for money that they'd throw it away on a wish, but he was thankful they helped fund his special projects.

Hard to believe he had done the same thing before. A very, very long time ago.

Tidy people in crisp white business shirts and dry-cleaned suits made their way up the courthouse steps. Joe watched the men climb two stairs at a time and the women in heels clip past him like eager horses. You could tell the ones who worked here. Self-important, deluded egotists. Lawyers and judges, clerks and stenographers all fooled into thinking they could change the world. Or get rich trying.

Others walked with less confidence. They were the defendants, the witnesses, the litigants. Joe could spot one a mile away. They were the ones who actually looked up at the building before climbing the steps. Sometimes, he could see one of them draw a deep breath. Also in suits and dresses, these strangers to the world of law looked uncomfortable, as if their clothing wore them.

One woman climbed the first set of steps and stopped on the landing. She didn't belong with the others. She oozed confidence, but she didn't have the steely glare of a young lawyer. There was something striking about her. Beautiful, even. She was made up to perfection. Her blonde hair didn't give away any secrets, though her tweezed black eyebrows suggested the blonde was purchased. But it wasn't just her beauty. There was something about her . . .

She looked up at the courthouse, then down at the street. She paced across to the other end of the landing, looked around, and walked back toward Joe without seeing him.

Joe squirmed inside. One of the most uncomfortable things about being homeless was how people looked at him . . . or didn't look at him. Most people averted their eyes and pretended not to see him. He didn't blame them. If you're trying to live in Utopia, the sight of a street bum is a shocking reminder that the whole world has not *arrived*.

The woman definitely saw him now. Instead of turning away from him, she walked straight toward him. She fished in her green leather clutch for something, maybe some coins to toss his way? But she was getting too close, closer than pretty women ever dare to get. Joe's eyes were at her knee level as she approached. She looked down at him.

"Excuse me, sir?" Sir? When was the last time anyone had called him sir? He squinted from shadow into sun, tried to make out her face.

She stepped down to his level and into the shadow.

"Yes?" His voice came out like a frog's, like he was nervous. Which, truth be told, he was. After all, when was the last time a young thing like this had approached him? Decades. A lifetime. He cleared his throat and tried again. "Can I help you?" That was a little better.

She held out her hand. Between her index and middle fingers was a card, a business card. He looked at it up close, then held it at arm's length. Darn these old eyes. He patted his chest where a shirt pocket should be and muttered, "I seem to have misplaced my glasses." He finished the sentence in his head. *About fifteen years ago.* She took the card back and read it to him.

"Rebecca Whitt, reporter, News Channel 7. I'd like to ask you a few questions, if you don't mind."

"What about?" What could a news reporter want with him?

"There's a hearing today about whether a mall owner has the right to run a soup kitchen out of one of her store spaces. Have you heard of it?"

"No. Can't say that I have."

The reporter, Rebecca, pulled a newspaper out of a satchel and pointed to a picture and article on the front page. He couldn't read the article—the print was too small—but the headline read loud and clear.

HOME FIRES SNUFFED OUT?

"Hmph," Joe said. "What's that supposed to mean?"

Rebecca pointed to a picture. There was a suburban mall in the background and a woman in the foreground. "This is the place," she said. "Cyndi Finch started up a soup kitchen there in the winter, and the neighborhood is upset about it. They say the homeless are dragging down property values, killing businesses, and raising the crime rate. What do you have to say about that?"

There was something vaguely familiar about the woman in the photo. Joe squinted to try to bring it into focus, but his old eyes just didn't have that much focus left in them. "What do I have to say? Well, I reckon it depends on the neighborhood. And it depends on the homeless people. We're not all cut from the same cloth, you know. Every one of us has a story of how we got the way we are."

"And what's your story?" Rebecca asked.

He should have seen that one coming.

"My story's my story, and I choose to keep it that way."

"Right, then," she said. "I'll stay away from personal questions, and you'll let me interview you?" She flashed him a smile and waved to a man who was headed their direction at street level. The cameraman.

"Wait . . . I didn't—"

Rebecca didn't let Joe finish his thought.

"This will be perfect. If you'll just a turn a little, we can frame you with the statue of Justice behind you. Can we get him miked up? Super."

The cameraman moved in and started messing with Joe's shirt.

Joe could smell his aftershave, feel his breath. He hadn't been this close to anyone in a long time. It felt scary but familiar, like lacing up roller skates for the first time in twenty years. Joe sat motionless, as if a wrong movement or twitch would send the man running for cover.

Do I smell bad? My breath has got to reek. Are they disgusted by me?

The cameraman backed away and picked up his equipment.

"Ready?" Rebecca asked.

Realizing she was talking to him, Joe nodded his head. "I think so."

"Okay," she said. "Don't be nervous. We won't use everything you say. We'll edit the good bits together later. So just relax and be yourself and don't worry about making a mistake. All right?"

"Um, do you have a comb I could use?" He felt silly asking. It wasn't like a few seconds of grooming would do anything to cover up years of neglect.

Was that horror on her face? Of course she wouldn't want to share a comb with him. She'd have to burn it afterward. No telling what kinds of critters might be dwelling in his hair and beard. He suspected that the persistent itching was not just from dandruff.

"Actually, sir, you look fine just the way you are." Ah. She chose him because he looked scruffy. That's the look she was going for.

"And . . . action."

Rebecca stood on the landing above him, the camera pointed at her. Joe watched her in the monitor in front of him but heard her voice from behind.

"Good morning. I'm Rebecca Whitt. This morning I'm standing on the steps of the county courthouse where, today, an important hearing will take place. It is the case of Ridley v. Riverton Plaza. In this groundbreaking lawsuit, the sitting justice, Judge Edith Ferndale, will be asked to decide whether a property owner has the right to feed the homeless if it affects the incomes of surrounding businesses."

Judge Ferndale. Interesting. It would be intriguing to see how she handled this case. She had the reputation of being pro individual rights. As an attorney, before she took the bench, she was known for prosecuting anyone who stepped on free enterprise.

"This case may indeed test the limits of faith-based initiatives. But, on a more personal level, it directly affects the people who depend on soup kitchens to survive. Today, I'm talking to—" Rebecca lowered her microphone and leaned toward Joe. "I'm sorry, sir," she said. "I didn't get your name."

"Joe," he said.

"Joe . . . ?" She waited for his last name.

"Just Joe."

She stood up straight again, smiled into the camera, and picked up where she left off. "Today, I'm talking with Joe." She took three steps down toward the camera and Joe and sat down beside him. He wasn't sure where to look. At her or the camera? He caught a glimpse of himself in the monitor and decided looking at her was a better idea.

"Joe," Rebecca started, "where do you eat most of your meals?"

"Here and there."

"Do you eat at soup kitchens?"

"From time to time."

"How does this case affect you?"

"Don't know that it does."

"Cut." Rebecca flicked her hair back and looked at Joe.

"Joe," she said, placing her hand on his shoulder. An electric shock swept through him.

"Joe," she repeated, leaning slightly toward him as if she cared. "I need you to give me more information when I ask you a question. If you could even repeat my question within your answer, I'd appreciate it. You seem like a bright guy. Give me something I can use. Give yourself a voice."

Joe felt pulled. First-year law school taught you to make sure your witness didn't divulge more information than the question asked for. He had drilled so many people in keeping their secrets. And he had lived with his own secrets for so many years. Yet he did have so much to say on the subject. And could probably articulate it better than any of the other guys out here. He smoothed his beard with his left hand and gave Rebecca a nod.

"All right. I'll try."

She removed her hand from his shoulder and said, "Let's roll."

"Joe," she said, still sitting beside him and leaning toward him as if they were old friends, as if she wanted to hear what he had to say. "What is it like being homeless?"

Joe grunted. "Now there's a word that's lost its meaning. To people sitting in their fancy houses, it means being poor and down on your luck. They see pictures of people like me and feel whatever they feel— pity, disgust, helplessness. But to those of us who are out here, being homeless means we don't have homes. No place to relax. No place to call our own. And especially, no one to welcome us in. Most of us have lost wives or husbands, children, parents, brothers and sisters. Most of our families don't want us anymore. That's the hardest part of being homeless. It's remembering the home that used to be."

"Where do soup kitchens fit into your life?" Rebecca asked.

"Soup kitchens, hot meal services, NGOs that offer free food and clothing are our mainstay. Dumpster diving, I'm afraid, is not what it used to be. Panhandling is seasonal. Civic groups and church groups come and go out here. Between Thanksgiving and Christmas it's pretty easy to find meals on the street, but when Christmas is over and the long winter comes, it gets hard to find those home-cooked meals."

"What about the social aspect of soup kitchens? Do you make any friends?"

"If you hit the same place on a regular basis, sure, you get to know some folks. Some people get tighter than others, form kind of new family groups. But for the most part, folks are pretty careful about who they trust."

"What about you?"

"Me? I'm a loner. I've lost one family, don't plan to ever lose another. It's just me and Wolf here." He scratched the dog's back. "We take care of ourselves."

"How do you feel about the hearing that's going on today?"

"I never heard of it until today. From what you've said, it rings of a faith-based initiative taken personal. It's an interesting idea. I can't say how it's going to pan out. I like the idea of putting social programs in the hands of the people who care about them. But it will take some time and several court cases for lines to be drawn and precedents to be set."

Rebecca gave the "cut" signal to the cameraman again. "Joe," she said. "I've got to say, you don't sound anything like what I expected. You're too educated. I'm not sure I can use what you've given me. I'm not sure the public will accept that voice coming out of your face."

"You're the one who wanted me to talk. If you really want to hear what I have to say, turn the camera back on. If you're just looking for a sound bite, check the guys in front of the mission down the street. There are plenty there who will sound like your stereotypical bum."

"Okay," she said. "I'll take more footage, but I'm not promising I'll use it, especially not with tonight's story. Your ideas are bigger than a sound bite. I think you might just be a story in and of yourself."

Chapter 23

THAT NIGHT, CYNDI REMOVED her makeup in front of the bathroom mirror. She squeezed toothpaste onto her toothbrush.

"He's an idiot, a complete imbecile." Mike's voice reached her from the bedroom.

She padded to the doorway in her ratty slippers, toothbrush hanging out of her mouth. "U ee-ee o ar."

Mike sat on the edge of the bed and yanked his socks off. "I mean, I don't think we could have come off sounding stupider if we'd hired a third grader to defend us."

Cyndi ducked back into the bathroom to spit, then went to sit on her side of the bed.

"I think you're being too hard on him," she said, pulling the covers up under her chin. She rolled over with her back to Mike, but he didn't take the hint. He kept on talking.

"Today's hearing was supposed to end in a settlement. 'It'll be fine,' he said. 'We'll walk away off the hook,' he said. 'I promise you we won't go to trial,' he said." Mike didn't even try to hide the sarcasm in his voice. "Promise! He promised. Now we've got all our lives sunk in this soup kitchen, half the people we know ready to walk out the door, most of our proceeds from the rent already committed just in food costs, and now we have to take it to trial?"

"We could concede," Cyndi mumbled under her covers. "We could quit and go back to the way life was."

"Concede? No way! We are not giving in. We won't quit fighting until we win. We have to stand for right, even when it hurts." Once Mike took something on as a personal project, he'd never quit. He clenched onto his beliefs like a pit bull. But when did he stop supporting Home Fires because Cyndi wanted him to, and start believing in it himself?

Cyndi sat up. "That's just what those picketers are saying. You're fighting on their territory. Maybe it's time to throw in the towel on this one. We can always do something else that won't be so controversial."

"Like what? A car wash? I don't think so. This soup kitchen is helping people, and I'm not giving up on it. We just need a better lawyer. That guy is an idiot."

"You mentioned that before. You get what you pay for, though. Maybe if we offered him his going rate, he'd put a little more spirit into the fight."

"You know we can't pay that much. We were lucky to find someone to take the case pro bono." Mike climbed into bed beside his wife.

"It's not lucky if he can't get us what we want."

"Remind me again why we're not using the guy Simms recommended? He seemed like a pretty competent lawyer."

"He's a real estate attorney, not a trial lawyer. He doesn't *do* court." Her voice of reason sounded flat and annoying, even to herself. "The light's still on."

Mike stomped across the room and hit the light switch. "Well, it's too late now. Even if we had time to find another lawyer, we could never afford one. I'll have Simms look at our budget again, but I think we're spending all the mall revenues plus a little more to keep the kitchen afloat. If we hired someone else, it would be out of our own pocket."

He stomped back to bed and climbed in beside her. Cyndi lay in the dark next to her husband, feeling very much alone and very much like everything was her own fault.

She'd thought feeding the hungry would make her feel better. That she'd be so busy she'd forget Madi. And the actual feeding was great, but this hassle with the Ridleys . . . It just might not be worth it.

Chapter 24

"SO COME ON DOWN FOR our Halloween blowout sale, where you'll scream over the lowest prices of the season at your local Ford dealer. Deals so low, they're scary!"

The common room television blared while Joe and all the other men in the shelter ate their breakfast. Cold cereal again. He shouldn't be surprised. After all, that's what most of the men preferred. At least the crunch of the sugary puffs drowned out the noise of the TV.

Joe stood up and stretched his back. He was getting too old to sleep on the ground. Technically, last night he wasn't on the ground. He'd had his own foam mat on the floor of a dorm-style room. It was better than sleeping on the street, especially now that the weather had turned cold again. Still, the kinks in his back were taking longer and longer to work out each day. Maybe it was time to look for a different life.

Loud, raucous laughter interrupted Joe's stretch.

"Hey, look! Joe's on TV!"

"Hey, Joe, it's you!"

All eyes in the room went to the television screen, where a pretty lady sat behind a news desk. Sure enough, that was Joe's picture in the little frame above her right shoulder. Dang, he thought that story would have come and gone by now.

Several of the men closest to the television set shushed the others. The common room attendant turned up the volume. The news lady's voice rose above the din.

"—an inside look at the problem of homelessness in our city from an intriguing man who articulates the problem in his unique way. Join us tonight at seven thirty for an exclusive special report, 'Street Talkers.'"

"Hey, hey!" A couple of guys thumped Joe on the back on the way past. "You're famous!"

Joe didn't even pretend to be excited about being on TV. The interview was a couple of months ago. Spokesman for the down and out wasn't exactly the kind of new life he was dreaming of. News was supposed to be instant. Why the delay? He looked back at the TV, where the news droned on. Another face appeared on-screen, a lady.

"Hey, give me your glasses a minute," Joe said to the guy next to him. He balanced the spectacles on the end of his nose and took a closer look. Sure enough, it was that lady, the one who'd given him her scarf last winter outside the bookshop.

"Be quiet up there," Joe yelled, moving closer to the television so he could hear better. The anchor was saying something about a lawsuit between a strip mall soup kitchen and the other businesses in the mall. Some video footage flashed on the screen—protesters—and then it cut back to the woman.

"Well, I'll be . . ." he said, surprised by a flutter of emotion just above his stomach. "She actually did something. Good for her."

The news anchor wrapped up the story by saying, "Whether a person has the right to serve the poor on her own property will have to be determined by the courts. And that's just what's going to happen, starting today."

The story ended and a commercial came on. Joe went back to his cereal, now soggy. He carried his bowl to the kitchen window and went to collect his belongings. It seemed he had an informal appointment at the courthouse.

Chapter 25

CYNDI SAT BACK IN THE COURT-appointed defendant's chair. Her toes ached from her grinding them into the floor.

Mike sat on one side of her, every bit as nervous as she was. Their attorney sat on the other side, looking professional and studious with his copious notes on the table. But from Cyndi's angle, she could see that the notes were a mishmash of random ideas. Surely this bozo would pull things together and bring some order to his arguments. Was that a page of football picks? Surely not.

If she leaned out, Cyndi could see Allie and Spencer Ridley, the plaintiffs. She wouldn't give them the satisfaction of acknowledging them. Cyndi turned away to snub them, but they had already done the same to her.

A door in the paneling to the left of the judge's seat opened about a foot. What was the seat called? The pulpit? No, the bench. A stenographer wiggled herself into a comfortable position. The bailiff called out, "This is the case of Ridley v. Riverton Plaza, Judge Edith Ferndale presiding. All rise."

The judge entered her courtroom.

Judge Ferndale's face was a road map to a hard life.

Cyndi wiped her sweaty palms on her slacks.

Judge Ferndale sat without any of the fanfare of swishing of robes Cyndi had come to expect from watching too many old courtroom dramas on TV and called the court to session.

"I've read your depositions," she said. "This is not a jury trial. All testimony and evidence will presented directly to me, so I expect both sides to refrain from using theatrics to sway the case. We'll hear from the plaintiff first."

One of the attorneys on the other side stood up. This guy was decked out in a tailored suit and power tie.

"Good afternoon, Judge Ferndale," he said, approaching the bench. "I'm Anthony Brine from Brine and Taylor for the plaintiffs. Spencer and Allison Ridley are residents of the Riverton Heights neighborhood and business owners in Riverton Plaza, owned by the defendants. May I have permission to present a document?"

The judge nodded.

Brine bent over his table, picked up a stack of papers, and handed it to the bailiff. Once the papers were in front of the judge, Brine explained what they were.

"This document shows month-by-month profits and losses for the businesses in Riverton Plaza before the defendant allowed the homeless to frequent a space in the mall. I've also included some property values for houses in the vicinity both before and after the hot meal service opened its doors. You will notice a sharp drop both in profits and in property values, which we assert is a direct result of the lower-class people the defendant has encouraged to frequent the area."

Cyndi thought they should object, but her lawyer sat still. They had profit and loss sheets from the other businesses, the ones what hadn't lost revenue, along with signed statements from several stating that they were happy to see a small downturn in exchange for the good they were doing.

The judge put on her glasses and looked at the documents. After a minute she set them aside.

"Am I to understand this is a simple question of breach of contract, or are you planning to bring in anything about zoning?" She directed her question at Brine.

"Both, Your Honor," he replied. "We intend to prove that the proprietor of the mall has overstepped the bounds of what is allowable on her property. Her actions have had a direct adverse effect on both businesses and personal properties."

The judge shook her head. "Start with the zoning question."

Cyndi couldn't follow the arguments presented by the Ridleys' lawyer. So many details about zoning and regulations and city planning. Why couldn't they all just speak English? She wished she could take her turn to say people were hungry. She wanted to feed them. Period.

But court didn't work that way. Apparently Mr. Brine had taken the "no theatrics" directives to heart. By midmorning, Cyndi could barely keep her eyes open. During the morning recess, she ran downstairs for a cup of vending machine coffee and supplemented it with a chocolate bar. The caffeine didn't help make the lawyer's speeches interesting, but it did give her something else to think about—how to keep her legs from jittering.

Her own lawyer seemed even less interested in the trial than she was. If she elbowed Mike, would he elbow the attorney and wake him up?

At the end of the eternal day, the Ridleys' lawyers were still presenting their case.

The evening air held a hint of winter. Tonight could bring the first frost.

"Can we drop by Home Fires on the way?" Cyndi asked Mike. "I want to make sure the thermostat is set and check the pantry."

"I'm pretty tired, hon," Mike said. "Can I drop you?"

She let herself in the front door of the soup kitchen. It whispered shut behind her.

A light was on in the back.

Cyndi wrestled out of her blazer and tossed it at the coatrack. "Is someone there?" she called.

Nance came out of the kitchen. "Bad day in court?"

"The worst," Cyndi said. She slumped down in a chair at one of the dining tables.

Nance turned another chair around backward and took a seat. "Sorry I couldn't be there. I had to work."

"It was horrible." Cyndi held her head in her hands. "We should be winning this one. Isn't our lawyer supposed to stand up for us? Or object? Or something?

Why did we hire this guy again?"

"Do the words *pro bono* ring a bell?"

"A classic case of getting what you pay for. How do we find someone better, and fast?"

"How fast? How cheap?"

"Free would be good. And before Monday."

"We could . . ." Nance seemed hesitant to offer her suggestion.

"What? If you have an idea, blurt it out. I'm desperate here!"

"Well, I was just thinking . . . maybe we should pray?"

Pray? When was the last time she'd really prayed? Not a let-the-light-turn-green kind of prayer, but an honest I-need-God's-help prayer? At Madi's bedside? Or was it her graveside? No amount of praying had healed her, and nothing could bring her back. God didn't answer the prayers that meant the most, so Cyndi quit expecting he'd answer any others.

Her friend's head was already bowed.

"Holy Father God," she prayed, "you are maker of the universe, designer of all. Entire galaxies flowed from your fingertips as you spoke the word. You set the planets in motion, you hung the sun in the sky—"

Cyndi's thoughts fixed on immediate needs as Nance wandered through the introduction. This was uncomfortable.

"—you not only know the number of hairs on our heads, you made them all. You designed all the flowers, showed the bees where to collect nectar, taught the birds to fly. You made the mountains push up out of the ground and filled the low places with water—"

Cyndi's foot tapped. She put a hand on her own knee to still it.

"—you made all these things. And then, instead of leaving us on our own, you came near to us. You loved us. You cared. Just like you care for the homeless people we're trying to serve, like you care for your church, like you care for the people in this neighborhood. And since you care more than we ever could, we place all of this in your hands and ask that you work it all out to your perfect glory. Do whatever you need to do to draw the most people to you. In Jesus' name, amen."

Why hadn't Nance told God what to do?

Your will be done? God's will couldn't be trusted. If he had a plan, it was a vague cosmic one that didn't take people's feelings into account. If he wouldn't save Madi, how could he be expected to save the kitchen? Or the house they'd put up as collateral? Or her dream?

If Cyndi had prayed, she would have given him an earful. He was lucky to hear from Nance.

Nance pushed her chair back from the table. "I need to pick up some supplies," she said. "You can lock up?"

"Sure."

Nance grabbed her purse and coat and breezed out the door, leaving Cyndi alone in the dining hall.

Cyndi put her head in her hands. Despite Nance's apparent belief that her prayer had been heard and answered, Cyndi felt like they'd left things in midsentence. She pressed her palms into her eyes and groaned.

Praying might make Nance feel better, but Cyndi needed to *do* something. She picked up her cell phone and called Mike's number.

Chapter 26

JOE STOOD ON THE SIDEWALK outside the mission. It was the third shelter he'd visited today. The third one that was completely full.

"Sorry, Joe. You know how it is when the cold hits. You've got to be here early to get a bed." The attendant at the front window said he was sorry, but he wasn't sorry enough to push the magic button that would open the door and let Joe in off the street.

"Yeah, sure," Joe said. "What about a meal?"

"You know the rules. We only have enough for the people staying here. Have you tried the overflow?"

That was his last resort. He hated that place, especially the way everyone jostled and pushed to make sure everything was fair.

What day was it? Friday? Joe stopped at a newspaper box. He had to scrape a thin layer of frost off the window to see the front page. The headline blared, "Wintry Blast!" but he couldn't read the date. He knew it was early November. Must be Friday. Yesterday was hot sandwiches down by the river, and they usually came on Thursdays. Tonight he should be able to get a meal under the bridge.

Joe shuffled through his dilapidated cart for a pair of gloves. He found one black one and one woolen one.

He tossed the black one back and overturned a few more things before he found the matching gray wool glove. They were the kind that had the fingertips missing—his favorite pair. Growing up, Joe had seen pictures of hoboes with bandanas tied to sticks slung across their shoulders and—always—fingerless gloves on their hands. Joe liked the idea of wearing a cliché. He had some nice Gore-Tex gloves that a local clothing manufacturer had given out to everyone on the street last year, but that meant everybody had a pair. He was the only one with fingerless gloves.

Joe pointed his cart downhill.

Wolf loped off ahead of him, following a predictable route to the waterfront. Rain fell and instantly froze when it hit the sidewalk. Branches sparkled like early Christmas trees when headlights shone through the ice building in their branches.

Joe gripped the shopping basket handle and measured each step. "If you slip and fall on this hill, Wolfie," he said, "you'll slide all the way down into the river." As if to prove his point, he lost his footing and went down hard on his butt. It took him three tries to stand up again with the help of his cart. By the time they reached the bottom of the hill, Joe's hip was aching from the fall. He slowly pushed his cart up the river walk to the Humboldt Bridge.

A group of street people had already gathered. It could be a scene from a movie—low-life bums sitting under a bridge. Only, instead of standing around barrels of burning garbage, they stood in circles around portable space heaters provided by whatever group was feeding the masses tonight. The heaters were a nice touch.

Joe walked over to the row of chafing dishes set up along a concrete wall. Hungry men and women stood in line to get some food. Servers on the other side of the rectangular metal dishes were bundled in coats and scarves, gloves, and hats. But so were the homeless people. The only difference between them was which side of the food line they stood on.

Joe accepted a paper bowl of spaghetti and a warm roll, butter glistening on its golden top. He took a seat on a curb. The icy chill cut through his old bones. Every year the cold was a surprise. He pushed himself to his feet, found a thick blanket in his cart, and sat down on it. Not much better, but a little.

"Old Arthur getting you down?" asked his nearest neighbor, chuckling at the worn-out arthritis joke. "You're looking a little stiff."

"Yeah," Joe said. He didn't really want to talk to this guy. Just a glance told him all he needed to know. A youngster. Let himself go. Bad teeth—probably meth.

"Yeah, winter's always hard," the man said. "It's gonna be a long one."

Joe eyed the intruder and turned slightly away from him.

The guy, unschooled in the finer points of body language, kept talking.

"Good food, huh? I love spaghetti. Always have. Sticks to your ribs. I like that."

Joe turned away a little more. This guy talked about food too much. It was none of Joe's business. He was just here to fill his belly before hunting for a bed for the night.

The guy still kept talking. "This is nothing on that place out the line—Home Fires? Oh, man, is that good food."

Joe's ears perked despite himself. He could picture this guy rubbing his stomach and rolling his eyes in pleasure, though he wasn't looking at him. Home Fires? That was the name of that place the trial was about.

"Yeah, it's out the light rail line, all the way in Riverton," Meth Man said, "but it's totally worth the trip. Good food and a nice comfortable place to hang out. I'm there every time they open, every Tuesday, Thursday, and Saturday. They just added Saturdays."

Tomorrow was Saturday. A light rail ticket cost money, but there were ways around that. He was curious. He'd go check it out.

Chapter 27

SATURDAY, CLARK CAME EARLY. In fact, she was sitting on the sidewalk by Home Fires' front door when Cyndi arrived just after noon.

The girl's face had filled out. Her color-of-the-week hair was growing out.

"Hey," Clark said.

"Hey, yourself. What are doing here so early?"

"I thought you might need some help or something."

It was a little early to start food prep. "You know, I could use some help, but not here. Back at my house. Are you free?" Cyndi held her breath, afraid she'd overstepped the line of what their relationship allowed.

Clark cocked her head. "I guess." She stood up and brushed off the back of her grimy jeans. "Walking or driving?"

"Driving." Cyndi knew she had to come up with a legitimate task for Clark before they got to the house. She drove the long way around.

"Nice neighborhood," Clark said as they drove past rows of identical houses.

"Thanks. It's not fancy, but it'll do." Cyndi regretted her observation as soon as she'd said it. Of course any neighborhood was better than where Clark had been staying lately, wherever that was. She tried correcting her gaffe. "We're happy here. That's our house up on the right." She was thankful for the time it took to get out of the car and unlock the house door.

She let Clark in ahead of her.

The girl walked into the living room and went straight to the fireplace and looked at the pictures on the mantel. "Who's that?" she asked, pointing to a picture of Madi playing in the sand.

"That's my daughter when she was about four."

"I didn't know you had a daughter. How old is she now?"

This was the part about meeting new people Cyndi always hated. The explaining. "She would be fifteen. But she died about five years ago."

Five years. Two months and six days. But who's counting?

Clark looked back at the picture. "She's cute."

"Yes, she was." Cyndi was done with this conversation.

Clark turned around. "So what's the job?"

"Actually . . ." Clark spoke slowly at first, then dove into her suggestion. "You need to take a shower, and then I want to buy you a couple of outfits." She bit her lip. She hoped Clark wouldn't be offended.

"That's the job?"

"Yeah." Cyndi avoided eye contact by gathering towel, washcloth, and soap. "Is that all right?"

Clark shrugged. "Yeah. I guess."

Cyndi showed her how to work the shower and the bathroom fan as if she were a refugee from a third-world country, not an American teen. Even as she explained, she knew she was prattling on too much, but she couldn't stop herself. "Okay, I guess you'll be fine. If you need anything, give a yell. Oh, and—"

"Go." Clark used the bathroom door to shove Cyndi out into the hall.

Cyndi paced in front of the bathroom door until she heard the shower turn on. "Stop hovering," she muttered to herself. She went into the kitchen and started organizing the silverware drawer. The spoons already nestled in a perfect stack, so she straightened the knife handles and lined up all the fork tines. With a green scrubbie, she set to work on the spotless white grout around the faucet base. An idea that had been tickling inside her head for a while was screaming to get out. When Clark finally walked into the room, Cyndi blurted out, "I need to ask you something."

"Shoot," Clark said.

"Do you need a drink?" Cyndi went to the cupboard for a cup before Clark had a chance to answer her. She got ice and water from the door of the fridge and set it on the table in front of Clark.

Clark laughed. "That's what you wanted to ask me?"

"Yeah . . . no. I was thinking, do you want to live here? We have a spare bedroom. It's a little juvenile for you, but we could change the décor. We could fix things up. That way, you'd have your own room and you could enroll in school and be settled and we could be like a family and . . ." She let her voice trail off when she saw Clark look away. "I was just thinking."

Clark's gaze fixed on her fingernails. She bit her lip.

"If you don't want to . . ." Cyndi tried to keep her voice bright, despite her disappointment in Clark's reaction.

"I can't," Clark said. "It sounds great, but I can't. Thanks, though."

Cyndi had hoped she'd say yes. Or, in the case of a no, had expected an explanation. "But, why—?"

Clark stood. "I like you, Cyndi. And I get it, but I can't. Just drop it, okay?"

Cyndi didn't understand, but she knew not to push. "Okay. Um, we should probably get back." She grabbed her coat and fumbled at putting it on. She floated the idea one more time. "If you ever need a place—"

The corner of Clark's mouth twitched. "Sure."

At least she wasn't angry. After a long pause Cyndi said, "Let's get on back now. I still want to get you those outfits, if you don't mind."

Clark agreed to the shopping trip, which yielded a couple of clean, modest outfits. Now she had something to wear when she was washing her other clothes.

That afternoon, Zach and Clark worked together wrapping silverware in napkins. Fork, knife, spoon, napkin. Fork, knife, spoon, napkin. The pile grew taller. One hundred and fifty sets of silverware made quite a stack. Those two warmed parts of her heart she'd thought long dead. Clark might not want to live with her, but Cyndi could still love her.

"Why can't we just use plastic?" Zach asked while

sliding pieces of stainless into each napkin. "It'd be so much easier."

"It's worth the extra effort," Cyndi said. She picked up one of the napkins and smoothed its crumpled corner. "It makes people feel more special to eat off real plates with real silverware."

Zach rolled his eyes, but Clark agreed. "She's right. All the other hot meal programs used plastic spoons and paper plates. Home Fires is cool."

"Besides," Cyndi said, trying to think of a line that would sway Zach's thinking, "it's saving trees."

"Oooh, face," said Clark, grinning at Zach.

"Whatever," he said and gave her a shove on the shoulder. She stumbled sideways a little, her feet tripping over each other.

Zach grabbed her elbow and pulled her upright. Cyndi expected an awkward pause, but he went straight back to sorting. Fork, knife, spoon, napkin. Clark worked beside him again. Her fumbling fingers told Cyndi more than Clark would want her to know.

Cyndi pretended to be absorbed in straightening a tablecloth.

Zach cleared his throat. "You okay?"

"I'm eighteen. I can take care of myself." She moved to shove her hands in her pockets, but the new pants had no pockets.

Cyndi made a mental note to get pants with pockets next time, to give Clark a place to hide her hands.

Clark crossed her arms across her baggy black T-shirt.

"There's no way you're eighteen," Zach said. "I bet you're younger than me. What are you? Fourteen?"

"No!" she protested. "I'm *almost* sixteen!"

"You're only fifteen?"

Just a baby. The same age as Madi after all. Cyndi swallowed a quick sob and covered her emotion by busying her hands.

"Wow. I thought you were at least sixteen, maybe seventeen," Zach said.

"Wh—? Bu—! Why did you say I was fourteen, then?"

"So you'd get mad and tell me the truth."

"I hate you," Clark said and turned her back on him. When he couldn't see her face anymore, she allowed a grin to spread across her face. She winked at Cyndi, making her a coconspirator and allowing her into the conversation. But she still kept her arms crossed and her back hunched toward Zach.

Only fifteen. Cyndi should look into the laws about how to get her off the street.

Across the room, the door opened and a grizzled old man stepped into the hall. He had the hungry look of someone who hadn't eaten all day. Cyndi recognized the same look on so many of their diners.

She started toward him to tell him the kitchen wasn't open yet and to invite him to come back in an hour. About halfway across the room, she realized who he was.

She had never seen him without his dog.

Joe felt alone without Wolf. He hated leaving the dog behind, but in order to sneak on the light rail, he had to be inconspicuous. And Wolf was anything but. So the dog had stayed behind to fend for himself.

Finding the soup kitchen was easy. It wasn't far from the light rail stop. Clean, crisply lettered sandwich boards pointed the way.

Standing in the doorway, Joe wished he hadn't come.

The room was bright and welcoming. Yellow curtains on the windows and a friendly fire in the fireplace reminded him of home. When was the last time he'd been in a room with curtains? He shuffled from foot to foot. Maybe he should just go. But that smell—was it curry?—beckoned him in.

Apparently he was early. There were a few people standing around, most of them working, most with their backs to him. One girl stood, arms crossed like she was angry, but with a smile on her face. He thought he'd seen her on the streets, but he didn't recognize anyone else.

Except for the woman who was hurtling toward him.

"Hi, I'm Cyndi. This is my place." Cyndi grabbed his hand and shook it with gusto. On second thought, she stepped in for a quick hug. Then she put a hand on Joe's elbow and led him into the room. She was awfully eager to meet him, a little too eager. "It's you, isn't it?" she asked.

"It might be." Joe knew her face, but they'd never been introduced. Not really.

"Aren't you the guy with the dog?" Cyndi's eyes pleaded, *Please say yes.*

"Uh, yes." Joe shifted his gaze from side to side and squirmed a little to escape her grasp, but she was not letting him go.

"I can't believe it's you. Mike! Come here! There's someone you've got to meet."

A balding man walked over from the serving area, wiping his hands on a dish towel.

"Mike, honey, this is the guy. The one who got me thinking about what we could do to help the homeless. This is him!" Cyndi patted Joe on the arm again, as if they were best buddies.

"Does *him* have a name?" Mike asked, reaching out to shake Joe's hand.

"Um . . ." Cyndi croaked.

"Joe," Joe said, planting his palm in Mike's. "Pleased to meet you."

"I'm Mike," he said. "Cyndi's better half."

"I gathered." Joe smiled back, like they shared a private joke. He took a step into the room, then another. Such a warm place. Such an inviting welcome. He could see why people felt at home here. Though the enthusiasm was a bit much.

"So, this is fantastic!" Cyndi said, following beside him. "I can't believe you're actually here. I've probably been downtown a dozen times looking for you. I thought you must have left town. I just can't believe you're actually here." She was over the top, this gal. Not really Joe's style, but he could see how people were stirred up by her enthusiasm.

Cyndi introduced Joe to each server down the line. "Nance, this is Joe. He's the one. Jeri, meet Joe. Joe, Jeri."

And so on.

Joe nodded to each. They all grinned back and gushed over him. He wasn't used to this much attention. At first it felt a little strange, but by the time he'd met all the workers, he was starting to feel the swelling of confidence in his chest that he used to crave. Kind of a rush.

"Oh, you have to meet Zach and Clark," Cyndi said, leading Joe to a long table where a boy handed him a napkin. Spiked hair, nice clothes.

The girl, the one who stood with arms crossed, leered at him. "Where's your dog?" she asked. So, she *was* the one he'd seen at other meals. Funny, she looked different—softer, cleaner, younger.

"He stayed home." The corner of Joe's mouth twitched up. She knew what he meant.

"Let's sit down," Cyndi said. "We've got a lot of catching up to do." As if they already knew each other. She pulled out a chair at a nearby table, but Joe walked past her to sit in one of the chairs closer to the windows.

Cyndi jumped up and scurried behind like Wolf used to do as a puppy.

Even though the meal service obviously wasn't open yet, the bald man—Mike, was it?—brought over a heaping plate of food and set it down under Joe's nose. No one else had food, but he didn't care.

Joe shoved his fork—a real metal fork—into the

pile of food and crammed it in his mouth. The warmth hit first, filling his mouth and sliding down to his stomach. Nothing like a warm meal to thaw you from the inside out. So many turned to alcohol for the same reason, but Joe was more interested in food.

Sometime between the second bite and the third, the taste of the meal—rice and curry, basil and coconut—hit his brain. Heavenly. He'd never smelled ambrosia, but it must smell something like this.

Between bites, Joe listened to Cyndi prattle on about how her life had changed, what an impact Joe had made on her at their first meeting, how her life hung in the balance because of a lawsuit.

His plate was nearly empty when she pushed back from the table. "I'd better get to work," Cyndi said. "It's time to throw open the doors to the public. "You sit and have a comfortable meal. Get more if you want. And don't leave afterward. There's something I want to talk to you about."

Joe said he'd stick around, but he didn't plan to. He went back to the serving line and asked for seconds. The server, Jeri, offered him a double helping.

"And take an extra brownie," she said, sliding two onto his plate. "Cyndi makes them every week." She scooped some rice and chicken onto a clean plate. She looked behind him to make sure he was last in line. "Mind if I join you?"

"Be my guest," Joe returned. He and Jeri made their way back across the room to the table he'd claimed. The room was full now, crammed with noise and food and the great unwashed. Body odor combined with the smells of booze and curry, brownies, and scented candles.

When they got to Joe's seat, it was occupied by a young guy with a knit hat, the kind with little braids flopping down past either ear. *He could have a home if he wanted*, Joe thought. Then again, this guy probably had his own story, his own set of circumstances that landed him here.

"Let's sit in the softer chairs away from the noise," Jeri suggested. She plopped down in one of several easy chairs and balanced her plate on her knees.

Joe took a seat facing her.

"Chess?" she asked.

"Pardon?"

"You want to play chess?" she repeated. Before Joe had a chance to agree, Jeri was already setting pieces up on a round end table inlaid with a chessboard.

Joe didn't need to concentrate to keep control of the game. He ate, more slowly this time, while his opponent agonized over every move. He took early command of the board and kept it, stringing out the game to give his opponent hope, then moving in for the kill.

"Who's winning?" Mike twisted a folding chair around so it was facing the game board.

"Joe is. Big-time. Here, you take over. I've got to get back to work." Jeri stood and Mike took her place. He gave the board a once-over. It looked pretty hopeless.

"Tell you what," Joe said. He placed a hand on each side of the table and turned it around. "Your turn."

Mike moved a pawn forward one space. "I saw you on TV," he said.

"Oh yeah?" Joe slid his bishop in line with Mike's rook. He tried to sound disinterested, but he wanted to know what Mike thought of the interview.

"You surprised me," Mike said. "Well, I was surprised to see you, first off. And what you said was kind of shocking, too. Of course, I didn't know it was you at the time, the one who drove my wife to start this crazy business. Not the kind of words I expected to hear . . ."

"From a bum?" Joe finished his sentence. "Don't judge a book by its cover."

Mike moved his rook behind a row of pawns. "Do you want to go to the trial?" he asked. "I could fix you up with a suit and you could sit in with us."

"What, and put a homeless face on your cause? Don't you think it would be better to keep me all grungy?" To think of wearing a suit again. And sitting in a courtroom. As an observer, though, not a participant.

"Not a homeless face. Your face. You're the one who got all this rolling. You're the one who changed Cyndi's outlook on life, who gave her something to believe in. You should be there."

So, this was personal.

Joe liked that. Not enough things were personal these days, at least not in a good way.

"So, what do you say?"

Joe didn't think he was quite as important as this guy thought. But it felt good to be wanted. And not just as a poster child for homelessness.

"Okay, but I'm gonna need that suit."

Sunday afternoon, Zach slouched in the passenger's seat of Cyndi's car and nibbled on a hangnail.

Cyndi leaned into the steering wheel and squinted at road signs. A year ago, she never would have ventured downtown on her own. Not in a car. These one-way streets were impossible.

"Help me look for Franklin Street," she said. "I think that's where we're supposed to turn." She watched the green signs approach and then pass behind her. Elder. Jackson. Aspen. Franklin.

"It's right there," Zach said without pointing. She made the turn and scanned the sidewalk for Clark. So many people bustling about on a Sunday, especially for a cold afternoon like this one.

"There she is!" Zach waved through the window. Clark saw the car and lifted an arm over her head like she was hailing a taxi. Cyndi pulled the car to the curb, and Clark climbed into the backseat.

"Where to, ma'am?" Cyndi asked, playing the chauffeur.

Clark played along.

"Drive south, James, and make it snappy. I have people to go, places to see." She spoke with a snotty British accent.

Zach swallowed a giggle and it came out as a snort. Bless his heart. He tried to be so cool and most of the time he succeeded, but around Clark he couldn't quite hold himself together.

"Thanks for taking me," Clark said from behind. "I think they'll take me more seriously with a grown-up along."

"No problem," Cyndi replied. "I've been curious about tent cities ever since they've been in the news." Curious? Yes. Eager to research them? Not so much. But today was a great day for a distraction.

"Well, anyway, I know you're really busy this week with the trial and all, and I appreciate you thinking of me."

"Let's not talk about the trial today," said Cyndi. "There's nothing I can do to change the outcome by worrying about it. Maybe today will help take my mind off it." Fat chance.

"So, what is a tent city?" Zach asked. He turned slightly backward to address the question to Clark.

"It's a city made of tents."

Cyndi laughed. "You asked for that one."

"Ha. Ha. No, really. What is it, and why are you so interested in visiting?"

Clark leaned forward and stuck her head between the driver's and passenger's seats, her arms draped around their headrests. "I think it's like a temporary place for people to live while they try to get back on their feet. I've heard it's safer than living on the streets and more stable than looking for a different shelter every night."

"So, is it really tents?" Zach asked.

"Yeah, I think so."

When Madi was in third grade, Cyndi had acted as

chaperone on a field trip to a Civil War reenactment. Rows of white canvas army tents covered the hillsides. Actors and war enthusiasts stayed in the tents for the weekend event. The kids had loved it, but Cyndi couldn't imagine anyone living like that these days. Not on purpose.

"From what I've heard," Clark said, "the tents are pretty nice. There's lots of rules, but that's what makes it work. But we'll just have to see."

Cyndi glanced in her mirrors, took a quick look behind her, and merged into traffic on the southbound freeway.

"How far is this place?" Zach asked.

"About twenty miles," Cyndi said.

Twenty miles. She had thought about the distance a lot. Twenty miles was forever away as far as Clark's situation was concerned. The light rail didn't go that far, so if Clark ended up at the tent city, she wouldn't be making it to Home Fires anymore.

I hope she hates it. Cyndi tried to erase the thought as soon as it formed, but it was etched in her brain.

"Next exit," Cyndi muttered. "Is anyone coming up behind me?" She reached up to adjust her rearview mirror. Zach looked backward out his window.

"All clear," he said. Cyndi put on her turn indicator and let it click twice, then eased into the right lane. Clark passed forward a crumpled piece of paper with directions scrawled on it.

"Classy," Zach said, smoothing the wrinkles out on his knee. "Turn left here!"

Cyndi jerked the car into the turn lane and ground

to a stop at a red light.

"I see it!" Clark clapped her hands like a child on Christmas morning.

Cyndi craned her neck to see where she was looking. Behind a peeling billboard, she caught a glimpse of blue nylon. When the light changed to a green arrow, Cyndi took the corner and parked along the curb. Zach and Clark tumbled out onto the sidewalk and waited for Cyndi to join them.

Old plastic bags tangled among the grassy weeds at the base of a chain-link fence near the sidewalk. Behind the fence, the billboard towered over a vacant lot. Cigarette boxes, scraps of newspaper, and a few beer cans surrounded a couple of rusted-out car bodies whose tires and doors were long since stolen. Their windows lay in slivers on the ground, sacrificed in the name of batting practice. Or, from the look of things, in the name of a gang marking its territory. Red graffiti on the bottom of the plywood sign panel marked the lot.

"Check your clothes for red," Clark advised. "The gangs don't like people wearing red around here."

Cyndi checked her clothes for anything that might make it seem like she was from a rival gang. No red, no blue, no comb sticking out of her pocket—she should be safe. Not like anyone would ever mistake her for a gang member.

"I got busted for tagging once," Zach said. "But not gang stuff. I was protesting."

Protesting with graffiti? Cyndi was glad he hadn't joined the protesters outside Home Fires. At least they hadn't destroyed any property.

"In fact," Zach said, "that's how I got kicked out of my old school. If I hadn't tagged that oil company office, I never would have met either of you."

"Tagging's lame," Clark said.

"Yeah," Zach said, as if he'd just reversed his stance on the virtues of graffiti.

Clark started up the sidewalk toward the next lot. Her step was so light, she was practically skipping. Zach doubled his steps to catch up.

Cyndi followed at her own pace. They reached a brick building, an old storefront church. Unintelligible words blotted its facade—the paint remained. A metal bar blocked the way through wooden double doors. A hand-scrawled sign posted on the door pointed to the other end of the building.

"This way, guys," Cyndi called, pointing to a gate in the chain-link fence. "It looks like we go through here."

The three made their way past the back corner of the dilapidated church building. Behind it, the rest of the block was a sea of blue, with scattered spots of red, orange, and green. Tent after tent after tent stood in rows and groups and clusters.

"Whoa," Clark said under her breath. Cyndi agreed. So many tents in such a small space. So many people crammed onto a lot where no one should have to live.

Cyndi took control. "Let's look for someone who knows what's going on around here. That one looks promising, don't you think?" She made her way to the corner of the lot, where a dark green tent stood taller than the rest. Two men played checkers under its nylon overhang.

"Excuse me, can anyone tell me who's in charge?"

"That'd be me," the older of the men said. "Hold on just a sec." He jumped two black checkers with his red one. "King me," he said to the other player. Then, to Cyndi, "How can I help you?"

The man's cheeks were round and brown, covered in constellations of freckles. Frizzy tufts of white hair poked out from under his Mariners baseball cap, and another tuft took up residence in his ear.

"I'm Cyndi, this is Zach, and this"—Cyndi made a sweeping arm motion toward Clark—"is Clark. We're from the Home Fires hot meal service. Clark is looking for a place to stay until she gets on her feet."

"Sweet," said the other man, who still hadn't kinged his opponent.

Cyndi didn't like the way he was looking Clark over.

"Shut up, Raevon. These are our guests. At least pretend to be polite." The older man waved at the three of them but didn't stand or offer to shake hands. "I'm Tamal Wilson, and I travel with Tent City Two, kind of a go-between for hosts and residents, ya know? You'll have to excuse Raevon. He hasn't been here long enough to learn any manners yet. Raevon, apologize."

"Sorry," the younger man muttered as he kinged Tamal's game piece.

"So, how does this work?" Cyndi asked. "Would Clark need to sign anything to move in?"

"Well, you can probably tell we're a little crowded. I don't think another tent could possibly fit in here. Why don't you take a look around and see if Clark—is that your real name, hon?—if she even wants to stay here. If she does . . . well, then. She and I will have a little talk and see what we can work out."

Cyndi wished she could bundle the kids back in the car and go back home. But she'd told Clark she'd take an honest look at Tent City Two. Even though she'd already formed a solid opinion about the place, she owed Clark the time. She looked to Clark for confirmation.

Clark gave a nod.

"All right, then. Anything we need to know?"

"Jes' watch your step and give people enough space. Most folks here are pretty nice, but a couple of 'em can be a bit skittish, if you know what I mean."

Cyndi wasn't sure she wanted to know what Tamal meant.

Clark took the lead on the tour, walking up and down the rows. She didn't talk to anyone, just looked around. Zach made side comments about how cold and cramped and dirty everything was. Not so subtle in his approach, but at least Clark knew his opinion.

Cyndi let her go at her own pace and didn't push her own questions or a decision until they got back in the car.

Clark didn't give any clues as to what she was thinking.

At a stoplight, Cyndi glanced over at Clark.

Clark sat in the passenger's seat, twisted backward so she could chat with Zach.

Cyndi's instinct was to tell Clark to turn around, but she didn't. The fastest way to turn off this girl was to mother her. She'd been making her own decisions for a long time.

"So?" Zach said, apparently just as eager as Cyndi to hear what Clark thought. "What are you gonna do?"

"Wasn't it great?" Clark said. "Did you see the space heaters?"

"So, are you gonna to live there?"

Cyndi hoped Clark would say no, but wouldn't blame her if she said yes. After all, the tent city did offer most of the services Clark didn't have access to.

"The tutoring center was so great. Homeless kids going to school. It's cool."

"Stink," Zach said. "You're going to move in there, aren't you?"

Cyndi braced herself for the answer.

"No. I'm not."

If Cyndi wasn't driving, she would have wrapped both arms around Clark. Zach did it for her, from behind.

"Are you serious? You're not? How come?"

"I dunno. I guess I'd miss you guys."

"Good, 'cuz that place stank."

"Quit," Clark shot at him. "I said I'm not staying there, so give it up or I might change my mind."

Cyndi kept her eyes on the road. She didn't want to do anything to make Clark change her decision.

"I dunno. It just felt too far away from home . . . Home Fires, I mean. And besides, I was thinking . . ." Cyndi waited for Clark to finish her thought, but she fell silent.

Cyndi had to supply the prompt. "Thinking what?"

she asked, sensing as she spoke that she was taking the bait for a trap, but unsure of how to avoid being caught in it.

"Just, um . . . your mall has a lot of empty land around it. Way more space than at the tent city . . ." Her voice trailed off.

"Uh-uh," Cyndi said, catching the gist of Clark's remark. "No way. In case you hadn't noticed, we're already in the middle of a huge fight over the soup kitchen." She laughed, as if to say, *You've completely lost your mind.* "Ain't gonna happen," she added, as if that sealed the argument.

Zach leaned forward in his seat again. "It's perfect," he said. "We should have thought of it earlier. Excellent!"

Cyndi pulled the car to the side of the road, threw it into park, and turned so she could see both teens.

"Listen," she said. "You can't push this. Stop now before you start. If we push any harder, we'll lose Home Fires. I'm serious, guys. I think tent cities are great, but it's impossible. We cannot host one. No."

It was ludicrous.

End. Of. Discussion.

Chapter 28

AT HOME THAT NIGHT, Cyndi and Mike stood doing dishes together like they had almost every night for twenty-seven years.

"Did you find a suit for Joe?" she asked.

"Yeah. A little short in the sleeves, but he'll look fine. What about you? How was the tent city?"

The thought of it balled her stomach up. "It was okay. Kind of disorganized."

"Is Clark going to move there?"

She sighed. "Get this. She thinks we should open one on the empty lot by the mall." The idea had been swimming in her head all day. It was crazy. It was impossible.

"That could work," Mike said.

"Are you kidding?"

"We've got the land. Why not?"

"Are you serious?" Cyndi said. "Have you lost your mind?"

"It's complicated, sure," Mike said. "I can just see it. A whole village of needy people right at our doorstep. The food is great, but if we could build a community, think of the services we could offer. I wonder . . ." He reached over Cyndi's head to place a bowl in the cupboard.

"We're already in the middle of a lawsuit. We don't need another one."

"Mm-mm," he mumbled. He dried his hands and left the room.

She followed him. "What are you doing?"

He pulled out his laptop and booted it up. It took an impossibly long fifteen seconds for it to come out of hibernation and another five seconds to connect to the Internet. She stood behind him to see what he was looking for. He tapped in "tent city" and came up with a bunch of possible sources, then clicked on the words "Are Tent Cities Legal?"

She leaned over his shoulder.

"Look at this," he said. "It says here that while not exactly legal, tent cities are also not *illegal*. Looks like some local governments are willing to bend the rules. Riverton is trying to help solve the homeless crisis. What better way than to give them places to live?"

"Mike, I just don't—"

"Look here," Mike said. "Here's the tent city you went to today. Looks like it's got a permanent location. But this one here . . ." He put his finger on the screen and scanned the paragraph for the information he needed. "Yup, here it is." Mike kept his finger on the sentence while Cyndi read it.

"This one says they move every six weeks or so. That time will be up in about two weeks. And they're looking for a new place to go. Let's do it! It's just for six weeks. We could use the vacant land behind the mall. It's away from the main road and it's plenty big."

"Mike, I don't know." Cyndi tucked some loose

hairs behind her ear. "I don't think we ought to push so hard. Besides, that lot is zoned commercial."

"And where would you ever find land zoned for the homeless? It could be perfect. Maybe God gave us that land just for this. If this is about helping people and obeying God, why would we stop at just a couple of meals a week? We're already in this up to our eyeballs; I don't see where a little deeper could hurt us more. Sure, it might make waves, especially with Spencer what's his name—"

"Ridley," Cyndi supplied.

"—yeah, Spencer Ridley." Mike paused and scratched his head. "That's funny," he said. "I've heard that name somewhere."

"On the lawsuit?"

He shook his head. "That's not it. Anyway, it would give Clark a place to stay."

A place for Clark. For that reason alone, it was tempting.

Tempting, but impossible.

"It's too crazy, Mike. We've got enough to do as it is. I can't do this, too. I'll have to come up with another plan for Clark."

"Maybe we should invite her to live with us again."

"She won't do it. I don't know why not, but she won't even talk about it. Home Fires has been great and we've helped a lot of people. But all I really want to do is give that girl a chance at life."

"Maybe the way to do that is with the tent city."

Cyndi shook her head. "I can't do that. It will have to be something else."

Chapter 29

Joe hesitated at the base of the courthouse steps. He'd sworn he'd never go through those doors again. Time, he hoped, had healed his wounds.

"Wish me luck, boy," he said to Wolf.

The shaggy beast cocked its head.

"Now go lie down." Joe shooed him away.

Wolf ambled off to find shelter in some bushes along the solid stone walls.

Joe fumbled with his borrowed tie. He smoothed his hair with his palms, but the disobedient clumps sprang back up in the wake of his hands' movement. He felt naked without the beard he'd worn for twenty years. He'd shaved it off in honor of his return to court, but after seeing himself in the mirror, he regretted it.

"You look fine," Mike said, laying a hand on Joe's shoulder. "You'll be fine. No reason to be nervous. You're not on trial here; we are." Mike let out a little chuckle, but neither his words nor his lighthearted charade quieted the thudding nervousness in Joe's chest.

Joe had missed the first day of the trial, the prosecution's arguments, but was eager to hear how the defense would argue. Would he go into free speech? Property rights?

"Cyndi should already be here. We don't want to

keep her waiting."

Joe mounted the steps behind Mike, taking them one by one. He concentrated on each creak and pop in his knees to take his mind off the looming mouth of the courthouse.

Mike held the door for him.

Joe stepped into his former life. His eyes automatically drifted to the ceiling, to the words of famous lawmakers throughout the centuries. He could have quoted them all with his eyes closed—Moses, Aristotle, Thomas Jefferson. The next thing he noticed was a new addition since his last visit, a security screening area.

The security officer said, "Empty your pockets into a plastic bin, and remove all cell phones, pagers, and other electronic devices. Then step through the metal detector one at a time."

Joe stepped through the archway, then waited as Mike dug coins, keys, and wallet out of his pocket. His new acquaintance unclipped his cell phone from his waist and tossed it in the bin. His briefcase and laptop computer went on the conveyor belt. It took a few minutes for Mike to make it to Joe's side of the metal detector, and a few more to put everything back in his pockets, on his belt, and in his hands. While he waited, Joe looked around. The lobby hadn't changed in the twenty years or so since he'd been in here last. The smell of cold marble and decades-old dust was the same. One thing was different, though: the way people looked at him. No one stared. No one avoided eye contact. It was as if he was a real person again.

"This way." Mike, now fully assembled, started toward the staircase on the opposite end of the lobby.

"If it's all the same to you," Joe said. "I'll take the elevator. I've done all the stairs I plan to do today."

"Okay, I'll meet you at courtroom G. Go to the third floor and—"

"I'll find my way," Joe said.

Mike bounded up the steps.

Joe breathed easier now that he didn't feel like a sidekick. In the elevator, everyone found a place and faced the door. No one shied away from him like they often did in the new library elevators. Joe felt the old Otis cables strain as the small room pulled itself up to the third floor.

When the doors opened, Mike was waiting. He wiped his chin with his sleeve. He must have had time to get a drink of water before the elevator arrived.

Mike pushed on courtroom G's swinging door.

Joe stepped inside. Last time he was here, the blue-and-black linoleum squares were cracking at the corners. The tables along the front had been standard-issue World War II gray, the walls the color of Crest toothpaste. Now, the room gleamed with mahogany. The rich red-brown of walls, bench, table, and chairs proclaimed that this was a place where justice would be taken seriously. "Wow," he whispered under his breath. "Nice."

"Yeah, it's really something, isn't it?" Mike said. "We're defendants, which means we get to sit up front over there." Mike pointed to the left. "You can sit in the front row, but you can't come past the partition. I'll be right in front of you. I just talked to Cyndi. She should be here any minute. She got hung up at the county clerk's."

Joe took his place thankfully behind the bar. He didn't plan to be on the other side again in this lifetime.

Mike sat in front of him in a more comfortable chair. He turned around and whispered to Joe, "It'll fill up soon."

In fact, no one was there except that reporter lady, Rebecca Whitt. She sat by the aisle near the back, jotting something in her notebook.

"You don't really have to entertain me," Joe said. "How'd it go yesterday?"

Mike grimaced. "It felt brutal, but our attorney said that's normal since their side got to do all the presenting."

It could be normal or it could be incompetence. "Tell me about it."

"Well"—Mike leaned against the rail—"our attorney didn't object as much as I was hoping. And the judge didn't side with him much when he did. But today is our turn to tell the other side. That'll even things out."

He was probably hoping his attorney would produce a surprise witness or a clever twist of the law like you always saw on court TV. Real life didn't work that way. This was going to be a tricky one to win.

"Sure," Joe said.

The doors at the back of the room swung open and shut, and the seats started filling with observers. Joe didn't turn to see them, but he could guess what kind of people they were by the sound of their footfalls. High heels tapped, men's shoes clicked and squeaked, sneakers barely whispered. The plaintiffs, Spencer and Allie Ridley, entered with their lawyer. They took their places at the table opposite Mike and immediately leaned in to consult with each other.

Joe didn't hear Cyndi's rubber-soled footsteps approaching, so he was startled when she leaned over to greet him.

"I'm glad you made it," she whispered. "You look good. Do you feel okay?"

"Like this tie might just choke me to death."

"You can take it off if you want. There's a bathroom down the hall. I have to go sit up by Mike, okay?"

Joe watched her settle into her place next to Mike. They leaned together and whispered something to each other. Cyndi looked over at the plaintiffs with a glare Joe never imagined from such a sweet lady.

Every time the door opened, Mike turned back to look for his lawyer. He glanced at his watch every ten seconds or so. As the start time for the trial approached, he turned sideways in his chair and gave himself a clear view of the aisle and door. His face registered a mounting panic. He dialed a number on his cell phone, then, apparently remembering the no-cell-phones-in-the-courtroom rule, strode down the aisle and out the back door.

Joe felt sorry for him.

A few minutes later Mike returned and whispered to Cyndi, but loud enough for Joe to hear, "No sign of him in the hall, and he's not answering his phone. I don't know what to do."

"Do you have time to wait for him out front?" Cyndi asked.

"I don't think so. And it wouldn't get him here any faster anyhow."

"I think you'd better take your seat," Joe said. "Looks like things are about to start."

The bailiff announced Judge Ferndale's arrival.

Mike winced. He took his place next to his wife at the defense table, facing the bench.

The seat to his right remained empty. Unless his attorney showed up in the next second and a half, this was going to be a short and ugly morning.

Joe's stomach knotted as the judge entered the room and called the court to order. He hated to see a judge start the day with reason to hate your side. Not that he was taking sides.

Judge Ferndale took the bench and recapped where they had left off on Friday. "Does the prosecution have anything to add?"

The plaintiff's lawyer half rose and stated, "No, Your Honor. The prosecution rests." He sat again and smirked in Mike and Cyndi's direction.

"Then we'll get going on the defense today. Does the defense plan to call any witnesses?" She looked directly at Mike. "Are we missing someone today, Mr. Finch?"

"Um, yes, Your Honor—" Mike stumbled to push back his chair and stand. "Yes, Your Honor. Um, my lawyer . . . I mean, our attorney isn't here yet. Uh . . .

can we start in a few minutes?"

Judge Ferndale squinted down over her reading glasses at Mike. "And you have chosen a very bad way to start off my Monday morning. You've got thirty minutes to come up with an attorney, any attorney. If I return and find that you are still without representation, I will render my decision. I'll be in my chambers." To the room, she announced, "This court stands in recess for thirty minutes."

Mike turned his chair around to face Joe.

"What am I gonna do? I can't find him anywhere. Schuster? They should have named him Shyster. I can't believe he's doing this to me."

"To us," Cyndi said.

"Why don't you go try to call him again?" Joe suggested.

Mike practically sprinted from the courtroom.

Joe saw panic strike Cyndi's face. She tried to follow Mike, but Joe put a steadying hand on her arm.

"Give him a minute," he said.

"We only have twenty-four minutes left. We've got to do something."

"You believe in prayer. Why not try that now?" He couldn't believe those words had come out of his mouth. Pray?

"No, I don't—praying is more Mike's thing." Cyndi looked to the doors one more time, as if salvation would appear to her there, but none did. "You can pray if you want."

"Me? Nah. That's not—I don't—"

Their awkward exchange was interrupted by the

sound of an argument in the corridor outside.

"Oh, boy," Cyndi said. "That's Mike."

Joe raced her to the door.

A crowd had gathered in the hallway around two men, Mike and the lawyer, Ernie Schuster. Once glance at Schuster told Joe he was either drunk or hungover. At nine o'clock on a Monday morning. He looked about like Joe usually did—unshaven, disheveled, and mean.

"How dare you!" Mike said, not quite shouting. "You don't even call? What do you think this is? A joke?"

"No, I—" The lawyer slurred his speech. Definitely still drunk.

"It's not a joke. It's my life!"

"Let's fight for your life," Schuster said. "Time to play ball." He took a couple of staggering steps toward where Joe stood by the courtroom door.

Joe put his arm out and stopped him easily. "You're not playing ball in there," he said.

"Says who? Move outta my way."

Joe stood firm. "Go on home now. They don't need you. You're fired."

"You can't fire me." The lawyer leaned his head back and squinted at Joe. "Who are you anyway?"

"Joseph Talbot, attorney-at-law," he said, amazed at his words—words he had sworn never to speak again.

Mike and Cyndi stared at him, mouths agape.

He took a deep breath. He was all in. "I am the Finches' new defense counsel. Your services are no longer required."

Chapter 30

CYNDI SAT BY JOE AT THE defendants' table in the courtroom. She was still in shock.

"You're really a lawyer? How——? An honest-to-goodness attorney?" She couldn't wrap her brain around it.

Joe looked a little like he'd been hit by a truck.

Mike was grinning ear to ear. He looked like it was Christmas morning.

What were the chances? They had asked and immediately received. But what do they call it when you are the answer to your own prayer?

Joe looked like he was about to be sick. "Me and my fat mouth," he mumbled.

"You're really a lawyer?" Cyndi said again.

"Yeah."

"A homeless lawyer?"

"Yeah."

She shook her head. "In good standing?"

"Yeah. Listen." He stood next to her, pulling at the sleeves to his suit. "I need to go talk to the judge and get her up to speed. Can we save the storytelling for later?"

"Go, go," Cyndi said. She shook her head again. What in the world?

Joe straightened his tie and smoothed his hair. The shock looked to be wearing off. Now he just looked alive.

"*Now*," he whispered to Mike, "it's time to play ball."

Judge Ferndale entered and took her elevated chair behind the imposing mahogany desk. She looked over at the defense. Joe could swear she did a double take. She lowered her half glasses to the end of her nose so she could peer over them.

"Well, Mr. Finch, it looks liked you scared up another attorney. Very impressive. Counsel, approach the bench?"

Joe's feet felt like they were embedded in cement as he took the several long steps to face the judge. His cheeks and hands burned with agitation and excitement he hoped was hidden by two days' stubble. He wished he had his beard back to hide behind.

"Are you the new counsel for the defense?" Judge Ferndale asked.

"I am, Your Honor," Joe croaked. "Joseph Talbot."

"Joe Talbot. Well, I'll be. It's been years. Where have you been?" The judge kept her voice professional, but a certain level of interest came through in her tone.

"I've been . . . on the road a lot." In the strictest sense, it was the truth.

"Welcome back." She leaned forward a little. "Please tell me you plan to redeem this case."

"Yes, Your Honor, I do. Since I've just been retained, though, I'd like to request a continuance to allow me to get up to speed."

"How much time would you need?"

Joe quickly calculated in his head what would be involved in reading up on case law related to this case. He didn't want to ask for too much.

"Three weeks, Your Honor."

"Granted," the judge said to Joe. Then, in a louder voice, "I'm ordering a continuance of one month to give the defense time to prepare. We will reconvene on the nineteenth of December."

"Thank you, Your Honor," Joe said. He turned back to the defense table in time to see Mike mouth *Yes!* and pull a fist down to his side.

Across the room, Mr. Ridley shuffled papers brusquely into his briefcase. He stomped down the aisle, his attorneys and wife clipping along behind him.

Joe walked back to the defense table. Cyndi practically tackled him with a bear hug before he was halfway there.

Time stopped when her soft, scented hair brushed against his cheek. He drew in a deep breath and held it. When was he last hugged? You could count the time in years, if not decades.

Mike laid a hand on his shoulder.

Joe snapped a mental picture at that instant. Needed and wanted by two people—he would cherish the moment and tuck it away to pull out on cold, lonely nights. His other happy memories had worn so thin.

Cyndi loosened her embrace. Mike removed his

hand from Joe's back to grab his overcoat.

And just like that, the moment was a memory.

"Let's get some coffee," Mike suggested. He took Cyndi's hand and escorted her into the corridor.

Joe walked behind them, watching Mike match his steps to Cyndi's. It said a lot, this give and take. They shared their small victory.

Joe, even though he'd delivered a miracle, was outside their circle. Had he ever loved anyone like that? It was hard to remember.

Outside, the frigid air slapped Joe's bare face.

Wolf met him halfway on the courthouse steps. Joe patted the old dog's head.

Cyndi knelt to Wolf's level and scratched him below both ears with gloved hands. "I remember you, yes, I do," she said in a *good boy* voice. Still petting the dog, she spoke to Joe. "He's thinner than he looks. Is he a husky?"

"Part husky, I think, or malamute. But I'm pretty sure there's some wolf in there, too. That's what I call him—Wolf."

"Where did you get him?"

"We just found each other. He's not really *my* dog. We just run together. He fends for himself."

Wolf tried to make a liar out of Joe by trotting behind him to a nearby coffee shop. No commitment on Joe's part, maybe, but the dog was devoted. Wolf parked himself under a wrought-iron table outside the restaurant. Joe let him stay there. No one was eating outside on a cold day like today anyway.

Joe yanked the door open.

Cyndi and Mike walked through ahead of him.

"Order anything you like," Mike said. "My treat."

Joe looked at the menu overhead. All the words were in foreign languages. His head reeled with the number of choices. Unable to focus or decide, he turned his attention instead to the glass-encased pastry selection. Everything looked so inviting, bathed in a warm yellow light. How could he possibly choose?

Cyndi recognized his bewilderment. "I'll order for everyone if you two want to find a table," she said.

Joe settled into a cushioned wicker chair. A few minutes later, Cyndi brought over the drinks.

"One grande caramel macchiato, extra hot, extra cream," she said, placing a drink in front of Mike.

"One grande mochaccino, whipped." This cup went in front of Joe.

"And one decaf grande chai latte, no fat for me," she said, placing her cup at an empty spot. "I'll be right back." She returned with three monstrous marionberry muffins, one for each, and some kind of egg-and-meat-filled pastry, which she slid in front of Joe.

"Wow," he said. He glanced down at the receipt: $29.06. Wow again. Just for a snack?

Mike snatched the receipt and stuffed it in his pocket. "Let's pray before we eat," he said.

Joe bowed his head and listened to Mike's conversation with God. He seemed sincere enough in his belief. He'd noticed that about Mike in the short time he'd known him, that he believed what he believed, whether right or wrong. Anyway, Joe admired the fact that Mike wasn't embarrassed by his faith like so many were . . . like his wife seemed to be.

As soon as Mike said "Amen," Joe pounced on his pastry. The muffin looked good, too, but the protein of the eggs and meat would carry him further. He crammed a third of the savory treat in his mouth and tried to chew it down into manageable mush that would fit down his throat.

Cyndi and Mike both stared at him.

Embarrassed, he put the pastry down and dabbed at the corners of his mouth with a napkin.

Mike waited until he'd polished off the pastry and the muffin before launching questions at him.

"How are you a lawyer? Why do you live on the street? How is your license still good?"

Too many questions, too fast. Joe didn't know where to start or how much he wanted to say.

Cyndi placed her hand on Mike's arm. "Slow down, dear. Let him breathe." She cocked her head to the side a little and looked at Joe. "When you're ready, Joe, why don't you tell us your story?"

Where to begin? How much did they really need to know?

"Start wherever you want to. We're all ears." She gave him a little smile, the kind you would use to comfort a frightened child on the first day of preschool.

Joe sucked marionberry seeds out of his teeth while he thought about what to say. "Okay," he said. "My name is Joseph Talbot. You heard that already. Joseph Alexander Talbot III, to be exact. I graduated from law school a long time ago, like a thousand years ago."

"Did you ever practice law?" Mike asked.

"Oh, yeah. For years. I was good, too. I worked for a pretty big firm here in town, the one down on Broad and Fifth. Worked my way up to junior partner and then full partner in record time. I earned millions of dollars a year for my firm. Crazy hours . . . I used to work eighty, ninety billable hours a week."

"So you never had a family?" Cyndi wanted to know.

"Oh, no. I had a family. Don't know where I managed to find the time to get married. They'd be grown and gone by now. I don't know where they are. I think about them all the time, wonder if they're happy . . wonder if they still remember me, if they've told their kids about me."

"What happened?" Mike asked. He didn't ask the question that begged to be asked—*What did you do to fall so far?*

"I wasn't around enough for my wife's tastes. But I think it was a trade-off for her. I mean, I kept her in a nice house, with nice clothes, a great car, a country club membership . . . anything she wanted."

Cyndi asked, "Did she leave you because you worked too much?"

"Nah." Joe pursed his lips and tried to find a way to soften the truth. But there was no good way. "She left me because I lost my job. I started double billing hours. Sometimes triple billing. It padded the firm's pocketbooks and it didn't hurt mine either. They never came right out and said to do it, but they sure never discouraged me. Anyway, those numbers came out in an audit. Lots of guys in the firm were double billing, but I was the only one they pinpointed. The firm needed a scapegoat and I was it. Big red target on my back, they gave me a choice—an ultimatum, really. I could either step down or they would turn me over for prosecution."

"So what did you do?" Mike leaned toward Joe, elbows on the table. "Did you go to jail?"

"Nah. I was too chicken. I took the deal. I stepped down from the firm and decided to lie low for a while until the whole thing blew over. Only it didn't blow over. At least, not at home. As soon as she heard I was jobless, my wife was out the door. Packed the kids along with her and moved in with some rich boyfriend she'd been seeing on the side. She had more than a few choice words to say before the door slammed shut, too. Words I'd best not say in mixed company, if you know what I mean." Joe winked at Cyndi. He tried telling the story as if it didn't matter, as if it were all water under the bridge, but the pain of the memory seared his heart.

"She served me with divorce papers before I even had a chance to think. She threatened to turn me in if I challenged her demands in the divorce. I just gave in. She got it all—the house, the kids, the cars, the money in the bank. Wiped me clean. She didn't leave me anything, especially not any dignity."

"So, is that how you ended up homeless?" Mike asked.

"Yes and no. I found a cheap apartment and looked for a job, but my name was worse than worthless around here. I couldn't find a job anywhere on the West Coast. Probably not anywhere else, either, but I never tried. I just lost heart."

"Why didn't you look elsewhere?" Cyndi asked.

Joe felt a tear well up in the corner of his eye and then escape, rolling over hills and through the crags of his cheek. He brushed it away with the back of his hand.

"It was your children, wasn't it?" Cyndi answered her own question. She fished for a tissue in her purse, but gave up and handed Joe a napkin.

"Yeah," Joe said with some difficulty. "I wanted to be close by so they could visit me, but they never did."

"Never?" Mike sounded as incredulous as Joe felt.

"Not once. Sometimes I wonder if they live in the city. I wonder if either of them has ever dropped a coin in my can. If they walked by, I'm sure I wouldn't recognize them. They're old enough to have careers, to have kids of their own."

"You could be a grandpa," Cyndi said.

"Yeah, I could. Actually, I am." He pulled the printed birth announcement from his pocket. "That's my grandson."

Cyndi squinted at the paper. "Hard to see," she said. "I'm sure he's a cutie."

"So, I've got a question," Mike said, "not to change the subject."

"Shoot."

"Are you legal? I mean, are you allowed to practice law?"

"Am I disbarred? Is that what you mean?"

"I guess so."

"Nah, I'm legal. Like I said, it never went through channels."

"But, don't you need a license or something?"

"Yeah—I've got one. It's all up to date, too. That's been a pain, but I've managed to pay the fee every year. It was important. Helped me hang on to a little dignity, I guess. Made me feel like I was still somebody."

"How did you pay—?" Mike started, but Joe stopped him.

"Don't ask. You really don't want to know."

Joe had shared as much as he could. He drew the line at admitting that he'd paid for his lawyer's license with coins fished from public fountains.

Chapter 31

CYNDI HAD A LOT TO THINK about. She really wanted to talk to Clark, but she couldn't burden the girl with her legal woes. And she certainly wasn't ready to share her spiritual ones. Nance was out for the day, and Mike was too close to the situation.

She needed a break from Home Fires anyway and decided to take a stroll around the block to clear her head. She walked the main road down the entrance of her neighborhood. Cars sped by, too close for her to feel safe. As soon as she could, she turned onto a smaller road, away from aggressive drivers and people in a hurry to get to places they probably didn't even want to go.

The fresh air did wonders in clearing her head. With a little quiet time to revive her, she felt more ready to face the day. She didn't want to ruin her mood by going back out on that crazy main drag, though, so she decided to see if there was a way to cut through the greenbelt between the neighborhood and the mall.

From a distance, she looked for a place to cut through the trees. There wasn't an obvious path, so she walked closer. In a couple of places, the underbrush had been trampled down, forming paths into the trees.

Cyndi had a bad feeling about this. She should

probably walk around. But she'd come this far. She was probably spooking herself for no reason.

"Hello?" she called. "Anyone there?"

No one answered.

She tromped down one of the makeshift paths. A blanket of leaves crinkled under her leather boots. She ducked under a low limb and came into a small cleared area under a canopy of branches. A tattered tarp and two filthy, crumpled blankets told the story of the people who had slept here. So did the legless plastic lounge chair, three mismatched shoes, and a molded black purse, probably stolen from someone's car.

Cyndi felt the sudden urge to scrub her hands. She couldn't believe there were homeless people living right here, not one hundred yards from the mall. Had they been here before, or did they move in because of Home Fires?

As she went back toward the office, she wondered how many other homeless people made themselves at home in the bushes. She was willing to bet those weren't the only ones.

She didn't want to talk to Mike about it. Not yet. On a whim, she went to the craft store. She stopped outside the front door, hesitant to enter. Bins of silk flowers and discount fall items overflowed with sunflower yellow and tulip pink. The automatic door opened. She felt like a fool, standing here on the sidewalk.

In or out.

In, she decided, making her feet follow her resolve.

A gum-chewing teen ran the front cash register.

Cyndi pretended to browse down the scrapbooking aisle and through yarns to the fabric department, watching for Amanda on every aisle. She found the older woman in the sewing center at a pristine white sewing machine.

"What are you working on?" Cyndi asked. She pulled a stool over to see the project.

Amanda lifted her foot off the pedal long enough to say, "Hi, sweetie. I'm making a sampler quilt for a class I'll be teaching in January." The machine whirred quietly under her sure guidance. "Can I help you with anything?"

"I was wondering if you have a few minutes. Can I treat you to a sandwich over at the sub shop? Or to leftovers at Home Fires?"

Amanda stopped sewing again and turned her head toward Cyndi. "I think that's a grand idea," she said. "Let me go tell Chip so he can hold down the fort for a little while."

Chip was in models. "You girls have fun," he said. "Take your time. I'll be fine."

Cyndi pulled some leftover spaghetti from the industrial fridge in the Home Fires kitchen and heated it in the microwave on paper plates.

"It's not fancy, but it's what we've got," she said.

"What you've got is fine."

Cyndi poured two cups of coffee from the pot and zapped them in the microwave. Sitting across the table from Amanda, she wrapped her hands around her mug.

"What's going on?" Amanda asked. "Did you get news on the case?"

"Not yet. We've got a month before we have to go

back to court. I'm nervous about it, but I don't have the energy to worry all the time, not with everything else that's happening."

"What everything?"

"Keeping Home Fires going. Loving the people who come through the door. Taking care of Clark. And Mike. Did you know they're conspiring to build a tent city on our vacant lot?"

Amanda whistled. "That's going to go over well, isn't it?"

"It's not happening," Cyndi said, although the scene in the bushes pushed into her consciousness. People were living in the greenbelt right behind them.

"Mm-hmm. I believe you." She didn't even try hiding her smirk. "The place looks great. Real homey."

Cyndi grabbed at the change of subject. "It does. Thanks to you."

"But that's not why you asked me to come over, is it?"

No, it wasn't. But she didn't know how to broach the question. Or even what the question was. She took a swig of her coffee. Bleh—sludge.

"This must be yesterday's. Sorry." She grabbed Amanda's drink, too, and tossed it down the sink, watching it sploosh up against the stainless steel walls and then gurgle down through the drain.

Amanda got up and turned on the teakettle. "It's not about any of this, is it?"

Cyndi wanted to tell her about the prayer, about Joe. Wanted to talk about how God hadn't listened to her prayers since Madi died. Maybe even before that.

Why would he listen now? Or was it just a coincidence? She didn't know why she expected Amanda would have the answer, didn't even know if she was a believer.

"It's not about anything, really. I guess I'm just tired."

Amanda didn't press her. "So what happens next?" she asked.

"We wait. Joe has a little less than a month to pull together some compelling arguments."

"That's really something that Joe's an attorney, isn't it? Kind of hard to believe."

"Very hard," Cyndi said.

"Must be a God thing."

So she was a believer. "You think so?"

"I can't think of any other explanation myself."

"No, me neither, I guess." Much as she wished she could.

Chapter 32

"NO, NO, NO, NO, AND NO!" Joe ignored the law about being quiet in the library.

Mike motioned for him to shush, but Joe had already taken about as much of Mike as he could stand.

He turned the page in one of the law books open on the table in front of him and tried to ignore Mike's insistent whisper.

"It won't take long, I promise. It would really help to see it through your eyes."

"I need to get this research done on zoning ordinances, or did you forget?" Joe pretended to read, though he couldn't concentrate.

"I'm not saying we're going to start a tent city," Mike said. He leaned into Joe's personal space, close enough that Joe could smell the designer coffee on his breath. "No commitment. I just want to visit. Have you ever been to a tent city?"

"Have I been to one? Are you kidding? I've been to every shelter, tent city, soup kitchen, freeway rest stop, and campground in this state and a bunch of others. I'm busy here. Go away." Joe fiddled with a stack of books at his elbow.

"I'll buy you lunch."

Now that wasn't fair.

"And I'll teach you how to do research on the Internet so you don't have to pore through these huge tomes."

He'd never give up, would he? "I'll pass on the Internet lecture," Joe said. "I like real books just fine. But if you buy lunch, and throw in a pair of reading glasses, and promise you'll leave me alone after we eat, you've got yourself a deal."

Mike grinned. "They're printing those words smaller than they used to, aren't they? I've noticed that too." He placed both palms on the table and stood up. He started stuffing scraps of paper to hold Joe's place in the various books.

Joe stashed the books on a cart. He pulled on his jacket and his fingerless gloves. He still felt strange in the new clothes Cyndi had picked out for him.

On the sidewalk, Joe whistled for Wolf. "Come on. We're going for a ride."

Mike pushed a button to unlock the doors on his car. He opened the back door first and spread a towel on the bench seat, then patted his knee until Wolf jumped onto the towel.

Joe got in the passenger's door. He ran his hands over the velvety seat. It felt like the Christmas dresses his daughters used to wear when they were little.

"Buckle up," Mike said. "It's the law."

Joe had heard about that. Safety First campaigns were hard to miss, though it puzzled him why so much effort was put into getting people to take personal responsibility and not so much into getting them into affordable housing. Joe reached for the seat belt, but fumbled with buckling it.

Mike reached over and snapped the belt into place. He turned the key and the vehicle hummed to life. "How long since you've been in a car?"

"I don't know—years." The whole dashboard was computerized, flashing bluish-green lights to indicate speed, miles per gallon, even the outside temperature. Joe pointed to a slot above the radio. "Is that a CD player?" he asked.

"Yep. And there's a DVD player, too, if you want to watch a movie. Look under the seat—there are some discs, though I'm afraid they're mostly chick flicks. Here—" Mike reached across and grabbed a rectangular screen from the glove compartment. "You'll have to use the remote screen. The fixed screen is for backseat passengers."

He slid a disc into the player, and within seconds, Joe was watching a miniature version of *Sleepless in Seattle* on his lap. Incredible.

Joe started getting into the story. The main character had lost his wife. His son had set him up to talk to a radio show host when the screen went black. Joe shook the screen.

"We're here," Mike said.

Joe pushed the big red button on his seat belt to release himself. He felt around the door for something that might be a handle. He was still searching when Mike came around to his side of the car and opened the door for him.

"Thanks." Joe had been to this tent city before. It was the permanent one on the vacant city lot. They kept talking about fixing it up to be more like Dignity Village in Portland, but nothing had been done to take it beyond the hodgepodge array of tents.

Joe followed Mike around a brick building to the entrance of Tent City Two through the village, looking for people to talk to, but the city seemed to be deserted.

"Where is everybody?" Mike wondered aloud. He poked his head inside a couple of tents. "Nobody home."

"Okay, good. Let's go," Joe said. He didn't like this place. All the rules of suburban life without any of the amenities.

A large black man approached.

"Can I help you?" He addressed his question to Joe. Joe looked down at his clothes, amazed that this guy would assume he was in charge.

"I'm just tagging along," he said, inwardly disappointed that his quick escape had been interrupted. "My friend's the one with the questions."

"Can I help *you*?" the huge man asked. This time he directed his inquiry at Mike.

"Yeah, I'm Mike Finch. My wife and I run Home Fires. It's a hot meal service out in Riverton. I'm just doing a little research on tent cities, wondering what it takes to run one."

"Tamal Wilson's the name. You might say I'm in charge around here." Tamal held out a hand in greeting.

"My wife told me about you," Mike said. "Cyndi? She was down here the other day with a couple of teens. They're all gung ho about starting a tent city on our property. I'd like to know what that would involve."

"I remember her. She was with Clark? I'll be happy to give you any pointers I can. Anything to get people off the streets, give them a chance at a better life. Know what I mean?"

Joe knew exactly what he meant. But putting them up in tents was like putting a Band-Aid on an amputated leg.

"Come on over to my place. I'll get you some coffee."

Once they were seated under Tamal's awning, the tent city director started to talk. "The most important thing is to lay down the rules and enforce them," he said.

Joe cringed at the us-versus-them vocabulary.

Mike pulled out a notebook and some paper, ready to take detailed notes. "What kind of rules?"

"No drugs, no alcohol, no violence, things like that. Treat each other with respect. Pick up your own garbage. No noise after ten p.m. And everyone looks for a job. In the daytime, I expect all my residents to be either out working or looking for work. No loitering around here all day. If you want to live on the streets, that's your choice. But if you want to make something of yourself, you've got to put in the effort."

Joe wasn't surprised. Most of the shelters had the same type of policy.

"Of course, if you host a tent city on your site, it would be different. Temporary tent cities only stay in one place for six weeks or so. That comes with a whole other set of rules. But one of the most important goals is to keep the neighbors happy."

"Too late for that," Mike said.

That was an understatement.

"We were just curious," Joe said. "We're not hosting a tent city. Come on, Mike. Let's go. We've got hungry people to feed tonight." He tried to speak with authority. He stood up and, without saying good-bye, stalked to the car.

It was locked.

Joe crossed his arms and leaned against the back door. Wolf whimpered inside.

When Mike came out a few minutes later, he didn't hide his disgust. "That was rude," he said as he unlocked the car.

"I'm not in the mood." Joe buckled his seat belt without help.

Mike started to say something, but didn't. He pursed his lips, gripped the steering wheel, and drove. After a few minutes of tense silence, he spoke. "I wasn't—"

Joe held his hands up in surrender. "Do I look stupid to you? It's written all over your face. Count me out." Joe pulled the seat belt away from his neck. "Just get me a drive-through lunch and drop me and Wolf off at the library."

"What about the glasses?" Mike asked.

"Bring them later."

Mike sulked all the way to the library, which was fine with Joe. He didn't need Mike's approval or his friendship. And he sure didn't need to get sucked into his ideas.

When Joe got out of the car, Mike asked, "Will I

see you at Home Fires tonight?"

He knew he'd be there, but Mike needed to sweat a little. After all, Joe didn't belong to him. Didn't belong to anyone.

"Don't count on it," he said.

Chapter 33

TUESDAY NIGHT AFTER THE crowds left, Cyndi, Mike, Nance, and some others stayed behind to set Home Fires up for the Thanksgiving meal. Mike unloaded the industrial dishwasher and put away the dishes. Just like home, except here they were dealing with dishes for dozens, not just for the two of them.

"Why *couldn't* we host the tent city?" he asked the room.

Cyndi cringed.

He kept asking the same question, in different ways and to different people. "We've got the property, the county is turning the other cheek, so I don't think we'd have legal issues . . ."

"Um, earth to Mike," Nance said. "If you haven't noticed, we've got legal issues."

Cyndi cheered inwardly.

"Yeah, but those are going to work out. I'm talking about a temporary thing that could really change people's futures. I mean, Home Fires is good and it's building community, but it's more of a crutch than anything. This would be something for people who are really trying to better themselves."

Cyndi bit her tongue. She scrubbed the pots and pans with more vigor than usual, grinding the aluminum surfaces to a shine. Every time Mike opened his mouth, she wanted to scream. The very idea—inviting homeless people to live on their property. It was incomprehensible.

"So, I was thinking," Mike was saying. "We put the tent city on the extra five acres. It's off the main road. I think all we'd need is some porta potties. And I'd need to make a phone call to the police to increase their rounds. If the police are on board, the neighbors couldn't cause more trouble than they already are. Right?"

A choked-back guffaw burst from Cyndi's mouth. "Excuse me," she said and left the kitchen. Was he kidding? Did he really think the neighbors would just lie down and take it?

She'd put her foot down. They were already doing more than enough.

On Sunday, at church, Cyndi took her regular seat at the front of the auditorium. She didn't sit alone now, even though Mike was ushering. A lot had changed this year. New friends sandwiched her, Clark and Zach on one side, Joe—who hadn't darkened a church's door in forty years—on the other. Clark and Zach probably came to have a warm, dry place to hang out together. Still, her heart warmed to have them by her. She was starting to love them for who they were, not for how they reminded her of what should have been.

Mike looked jittery this morning.

Cyndi feared he would use his assigned time to

pray from the pulpit to pitch his idea for the tent city.

Cyndi tried concentrating on the songs, but she was distracted by Zach and Clark, and especially by Mike.

His turn was after this song.

He didn't wait for the song to end before taking his place behind the podium.

"'Give thanks in all circumstances; for this is God's will for you in Christ Jesus,'" Mike began. "When Paul wrote those words to the Thessalonians, he wasn't just offering a suggestion. And he wasn't talking about being thankful one Thursday in November between the turkey and the football game, either. Give thanks in all circumstances."

Cyndi relaxed a little at the traditional opening to the time of prayer.

"What do we have to be thankful for?" Mike asked the congregation. Most people didn't answer, but he encouraged their participation and a few tossed out answers.

"Family." This from off to the right.

"Jobs."

"Our health."

"Sure, yeah. Good answers. Easy ones for us," Mike said. "Anything else?"

"Limitless wealth?" a voice from the back offered. A light chuckle rippled from back to front.

"Nice try, Scott," Mike returned.

More people threw out suggestions.

"Shelter."

"Cars."

"Food."

"Freedom."

Apparently Mike had enough examples to run with now. He cut off the sharing by shifting from a conversational tone to his lecture voice.

"You mention all those things—family, house, car, freedom—as if those are givens. We think of people in other parts of the world who are starving or who can't afford to see a doctor. But we often fail to see those who are right in front of our faces. We've got hungry, lonely people all around us."

Cyndi bit her lip and steeled herself for what she knew was coming.

"Would everyone who has helped out at Home Fires in the past year, either with setup or legal work or food prep or anything else, please stand up?" Mike lifted both arms to encourage the workers to stand. Cyndi heard rustling behind her. Zach and Clark stood beside her. Clark tugged at her sleeve to get her to join them. She turned her head to see if anyone else was standing, then turned all the way around. Astounding—more than half the audience was on its feet. She hadn't realized how many different people had volunteered.

And those left seated squirmed in their seats.

"Great!" Mike said. "I think all these workers deserve a hand, don't you?" The audience obediently clapped for the workers, for themselves. Clark let out a whoop, and Zach actually wolf whistled right in church.

"Besides the workers, we've also got some Home Fires guests here today."

Cyndi felt Joe tense beside her.

"Don't worry, guys, I won't make you stand. I just

wanted everyone to know that we're not just helping the people *out there*, we're bringing the people *in here*, too. I think we're off to a good start. But I don't think we're doing everything we can yet.

"It has recently come to my attention that there are not enough shelters in the metro area to host all the homeless people that reside here. I've also come to realize that not every homeless person is a down-and-out bum. Clark? Would you come up here, please?"

Clark shrank down beside Cyndi. Zach gave her a little push, and Cyndi leaned over to whisper, "You might as well go up. He's relentless."

Clark whispered, "Jerk," but she stood and made her way to the podium beside Mike. Poor thing. She didn't want to be singled out.

Cyndi writhed inside for her.

"This is Clark. She's been coming to Home Fires for months. She helps out every time we open our doors. Comes all the way from downtown. And she's homeless." He put a hand on Clark's shoulder as if to comfort her in her pitiful state. "Clark's not a bum. She really wants to do something with her life. What is it you want to be, Clark?" Mike thrust the microphone in Clark's face. She jerked back from the sudden movement, then leaned a little too close to the microphone to say her two words.

"Social work." The words came out scratchy through the sound system. She could have said "Circus act."

"You want to be a social worker?" Mike asked. "That's a very noble goal. Thank you, Clark. You can sit down."

The girl returned to her seat, her face red with embarrassment.

"So, that's Clark," Mike said. "She has dreams. But her life consists of searching for a place to sleep and something to fill her empty stomach. She's got to worry about things no young woman should need to worry about."

Cyndi bristled.

"I'd like to suggest that we make a short-term commitment that could help people like Clark get the start they need. Cyndi and I would like to host a tent city on the vacant lot behind Riverton Plaza. But we're going to need help—lots of help."

Cyndi could almost feel the wind in her hair as the congregation took a collective gasp. If she had more courage, she'd get up and walk out.

"Tent City Three is looking for a temporary home. I've been to Tent City Two and seen how it's run. I really think we could do this. It will take a lot of work for a short amount of time. The city usually moves on after six weeks. So, what that would mean for us is that we'd have to mow the field, arrange for some porta potties, form a committee to set some rules and guidelines. It would mean ramping up the food service at Home Fires to serve dinner every night for the six weeks. Usually tent cities don't serve meals because of health department regulations, but we're in a unique situation where we can offer both if we've got the manpower. The kicker is, it would mean making this commitment during Christmas season. They need a new spot to set up in less than two weeks."

"Question."

Cyndi turned to see who was talking. A man on the opposite side of the building, about halfway back, stood. Was his name Jim something?

"Yeah?" Mike acknowledged him.

"I thought you guys were already in hot water with the neighborhood over Home Fires. What makes you think they'll let you—us— just bring in a whole city full of homeless people?"

"Well, we've got a crackerjack new attorney here, Joe Talbot. Joe, would you stand?"

Joe stayed seated, arms folded across his chest. Mike didn't force it.

"Joe is on track to get us off the hook in the Home Fires lawsuit. That should be wrapping up pretty soon. We shouldn't run into any legal problems with the tent city, but if we do, it's on my family, not on you. I'm willing to take the risk. What about you?"

Now Joe stood, with some effort.

"Excuse me; let me clarify something," he said, speaking directly to Mike. "I'll help with the trial, that's fine. But that's as far as my commitment goes. I don't like tent cities, don't even like the concept of tent cities, and I refuse to fight for one. I think they're a bad solution to a problem that can be fixed other ways. Sure, the shelter system is flawed, but we should fix the system we've got instead of coming up with different ideas to mess things up. It spreads the limited resources too thin, and it steals our dignity. This battle's all yours."

Mike blinked, clearly at a loss. He cleared his throat. "I still say we give it a shot. It's only for six weeks, one time. And it could really make a difference to a lot of people. I can't see any better way to help out at Christmastime. Who's in with me?"

Clark and Zach shot their arms up in the air right away. Cyndi turned again to take in the response from the rest of the crowd. A few hands went up, then a few more, and still more. Cyndi even saw some people who used to oppose Home Fires step up. She looked back to her husband. He beamed with excitement.

Cyndi raised her right hand, slowly, and only as high as her ear.

Mike made eye contact with her and grinned.

Chapter 34

NANCE STUCK HER HEAD INTO Cyndi's little office at the back of Home Fires. "The reporter is here."

"Thanks." Cyndi wiped her sweaty palms on her pant legs. It might be silly to be nervous at this point in the game, but this would be her first television interview. At least the first one on purpose. "How's my hair?"

"You look radiant."

"I know better than that. I mean, is my makeup all right? How's my hair? I wish I had a mirror."

"She's interviewing outside, isn't she? Have you noticed it's drizzling? I don't think your hair or makeup is going to matter."

"I know. You're right."

The shadow of a woman passed behind Nance.

Rebecca Whitt stepped into the doorway as Nance stepped out of the way.

Cyndi smiled and waved her in. "Come in, come in. I'm Cyndi. Come in, welcome. Have a seat."

"If you don't mind, I'd rather just get on with the interview. Is that okay?"

"Yes, of course. I just . . . I'm a little nervous."

"No problem. Why don't you give me a tour of the place, we'll get some roaming shots, and then we can set up the camera for the interview. That way we can get to know each other a little before I put you on the spot." Cyndi suspected Rebecca's practiced smile was meant to put her at ease, but it wasn't working.

"Okay, um, would you like to look around Home Fires first?"

"Actually, if you don't mind, I'd like to go straight outside. The soup kitchen is good, but that's yesterday's story. Today's news is the tent city."

"Tent City Three it is, then. I'll just grab my coat."

"Great, I can't wait to see it. Say, will Joe be here?"

Cyndi reached for her jacket. "You know Joe?"

"From the special I did on homelessness last summer. So, is he here? I'd love to talk to him."

"I haven't seen him tonight. But my husband is outside. He's kind of running things."

If Rebecca was disappointed, she didn't say. She followed Cyndi outside.

A crew worked at setting up tents in the adjacent field. The cold drizzle worked its way through the layers of Cyndi's clothing. For now, the only way to get to the tents was to slog through the grass. They were planning to lay some paths, but it was down the list a ways. By the time she'd taken two steps off the pavement, cold water was already seeping into her tennis shoes. Her corduroy pants wicked up the wet until her cuffs hung heavy.

Rebecca was two steps ahead of her in the field and in foresight. She'd been smart enough to wear waterproof hiking boots and a Gore-Tex shell. Even the cameraman had wrapped his device in a rain jacket of sorts.

Cyndi trudged behind the reporter through the overgrown sedge. Tiny grain heads popped as she brushed past them, the seeds clinging to her pants like Velcro. She wiped wet bangs off her forehead.

Before she reached the tents, she started scanning for Mike's red jacket. At least a half-dozen workers wore red, but only one was bald. "There he is."

He started walking toward a truck parked on the gravel drive on the far side of the field.

She adjusted her path to intercept him. "Mike," she called. He didn't hear her, so she called a little louder. "Hey, Mike!" she yelled, but he kept walking away. She jogged toward him.

"Mr. Finch!" she yelled, waving an arm over her head.

He stopped and looked around for whoever called his name.

Rebecca stepped forward to greet him. "Rebecca Whitt. I'm here to get some footage and pick up a couple of interviews for the evening report."

"Help yourself. I've got to get some folks to unload this truck."

"What's on the truck?"

Cyndi expected her to pull out a little notepad or something, but she just asked.

"We've got to cover the whole ground with waterproof tarps before the tents can go down. That group over there is pitching tents. And we've got tables and chairs and stuff to unload. Cyndi, why don't you and the news crew take a look around?"

"Well, if you're sure you're fine—I'll just wander around and give Rebecca a chance to talk to some people."

Finding someone to interview wasn't hard. Lots of people had plenty to say about the new tent city. Thankfully, most of it was good. No one complained about the weather or about the fact that they were about to have a couple hundred squatters living in their neighborhood. Some of the new residents pitched in to help, too, though Rebecca wasn't too good at picking out who was an affluent volunteer and who was a tent dweller.

"Let's go talk to him," she said, pointing out an older man who seemed to be struggling with putting tent stakes in the ground. Cyndi stood back a few feet while Rebecca approached him.

"I'm with News Channel 7. Do you mind taking a break for a minute and answering a few questions?"

The elderly man pushed himself up to a standing position.

"You must be an angel of mercy," he said. "I just can't work on the ground like I used to. Who did you say you were?" He wiped his right hand on some faded Carhartt jeans before extending it.

Rebecca put her business card in the grimy hand.

"Rebecca Whitt, News Channel 7. I'd like to talk with you about the tent city, if you don't mind."

"Not at all. But let's find a place to sit, if *you* don't mind. Looks like they're pulling folding chairs off the truck now. Maybe we can snag a couple."

Cyndi hurried over to ask for three chairs from the

teens who were unloading the truck. She set them on a bare spot in the grass and indicated that the man and reporter should take a seat. She felt like a hostess of a tea party or something, only without the tea, the fancy clothes, and the roof.

She sat down on her own chair, but as her weight settled into the curve of the seat, she pitched forward. The chair's right leg had sunk into the saturated ground.

"Guess I could stand to lose a few pounds," she quipped, trying to extricate herself from the embarrassing position.

A quick hand and easy rescue were offered by the elderly man. "Let's move up onto the gravel, shall we?"

They moved their chairs about ten feet to the shoulder next to the truck. The cameraman stood behind them and circled as they talked.

"Now," Rebecca said. "Let's start over. I didn't catch your name."

"Don't believe I threw it. My name's Stern. Chip Stern."

"And what is your affiliation with Tent City Three?"

"I don't know as I'd say that I'm affiliated, not in any official way, that is. I'm just helping out."

"So, do you live in the neighborhood?"

"You might say that. I work over there." He pointed toward the end of the mall where Home Fires had made its home.

"You work at the craft store?"

"Not if I can help it. I'm the owner."

Reporter or not, Rebecca couldn't hide the shock

on her face.

"You're the owner? But I thought the owners were protesting."

"Some of them, sure enough. And I've got to tell you, when Cyndi here first started talking about a soup kitchen, I was dead set against it. I thought it would ruin our business and bring in a bunch of riffraff, bring down the town, you know."

"But now you're helping out. What changed your mind?"

"Honestly?" Chip rubbed his chin. "My wife. Amanda and I came into Home Fires before it even opened to complain about all the damage that would happen, and Cyndi roped us into helping with the decorating. Put our skills to work. We hadn't felt so useful in a long time. I mean, work's work, but this was something else."

"What do you mean?"

"Well, how can I say this?" He rubbed his chin again. "One of the things about getting older is that the youngsters think you don't know how to do anything. Now, I was a carpenter for years and years. A good one, too. I won't climb ladders anymore, but I still know how to swing a hammer. Home Fires and now this tent city have given me the chance to get my hands dirty again. Makes me feel young . . . well, except when I have to stand up off the ground. That's getting hard to do."

Rebecca leaned toward him. "I know you've had some antagonism from the neighborhood over the soup kitchen. What about the tent city? Any problems over it?"

"Ya know, not so much as I'd expected. I haven't heard a whisper of protest over this project, which kind of makes me nervous."

"How so?"

"Well, people were so outspoken about the soup kitchen, but now it's just silence. Makes me wonder if they're planning a different attack. Now, don't quote me on that. It's just a feeling, probably just the jitters."

Rebecca rose. "Thank you for your time, Mr. Stern," she said. "I'll let you go back to your tent stakes now."

"Oh, no, ma'am. I'll not be groveling on the ground again today. Maybe I can go help serve hot cocoa. It's about time for that, I think. I'll take your chairs, though, if you like." Chip folded the chairs and carried them toward Home Fires.

Cyndi was pleased with what Chip had said. Of all the people for Rebecca to interview, he gave the situation a nice spin. "Why don't you show yourself around a little more and meet me back inside when you're ready?" Cyndi suggested.

She took Rebecca's silence as permission. Instead of walking back across the field, she opted to minimize the damage to wardrobe and pride by skirting around to the street and walking back on dry ground. The gravel drive wasn't bad to walk on. She just had to watch for puddles.

As tarps went down, tents were going up in organized rows. Unlike Tent City Two, here they had room to spread out with space left for walking and gathering. Near the road, Cyndi noticed Clark and Zach working together to set up a tent.

Clark was pulling on one edge of a rain fly while Zach staked down the cords on the opposite side. When he finished, he brought the mallet around.

Cyndi walked over to them and was going to greet them, but was stopped short by the intimacy of their conversation.

Clark handed Zach the cord. He took it, along with her hand. He leaned down and spoke in a low voice. "I like your hair like that."

She reached up and felt her hair. The drizzling rain wasn't enough to soak it, just enough to mat it down. Her latest color was pink, but she hadn't dyed her hair in weeks, which meant almost an inch of black roots gave her a backward skunk stripe.

He grinned his silly grin at her, and she pushed him away.

"Be nice."

"You want nice? I'll show you something nice." He closed his eyes and moved his face toward hers.

Cyndi wasn't sure whether to interrupt or back away. They were standing out in an open field in the rain. What did they expect? Privacy? She cleared her throat.

The teens jerked away from each other. Zach ran his hand around his mouth to wipe away either the moisture of Clark's kiss or his embarrassment at being caught.

"Hey, Cyndi. What's up?" Clark acted all cool, like nothing had happened.

"Nothing, I was just headed back to the kitchen.

We're trying to gear up for dinners every night, and there's still so much to do. I saw you two over here and thought I'd say hi before I go back in. How's the tent?"

"It's like the most beautiful thing I've ever seen. Look, come over here." Clark led her around to where the front door still drooped near the ground. "The zipper's open. Stick your head inside."

Cyndi had to lean down to get her head in the door. Wet nylon brushed her cheek. Once she had her head in, she looked around. "It's empty in here."

"No, no, it's not," Clark said from outside. "Take a deep breath."

She inhaled the acrid plastic-y smell of a sporting goods store. "I don't know what I'm smelling for here." She pulled her head back out.

"It's *new*. Like, brand new. I bet this is what heaven smells like."

Between the mud and the tarps, this place was far from heaven. But the fact that Clark and others like her saw it that way confirmed to Cyndi that they were doing the right thing. The risk was worth it.

Though so far, there had been no reaction from the Ridleys and their crew about the tents.

Strange. And unsettling.

A woman's voice interrupted, the reporter calling from the other side of the tent. "Hello? Is anyone back here?"

"Yo!" Zach answered. "Who's there?" He waved a hand in the air.

"Rebecca Whitt, from the TV station," she called. "Where are you?"

Cyndi was ready to answer her, but Clark put a finger to her lips to silence her. The girl turned her head, looking for something, then reached for the tent flap. She dove into the small blue room and zipped the flap behind her. From outside, you couldn't tell she was in there.

Rebecca walked around to meet Cyndi and Zach on their side of the tent.

"Oh, hi," she said when she saw Cyndi. She was looking for new people to interview, so Cyndi just nodded and let her talk to Zach.

"I'm trying to find people willing to do interviews on camera or give me a quote or two about the tent city. Would you like to do that?"

"Um, sure," Zach said. "I guess so."

"I just need to go get my cameraman. He's taking some footage over by the truck. I'll meet you back here in a few minutes, okay?"

Clark gave Rebecca plenty of time to get out of earshot before clamoring out through the tent's floppy door. Zach gave her a hand and pulled her up to his level.

Clark pushed against his chest and tromped away.

"Hey!" Zach called, running after her. "What happened? What did I do?" He reached her side and matched his pace to hers. Cyndi struggled to keep up. The damp corduroy around her calves chafed against her skin with each step.

"Hey, guys, wait up!" she called. Zach tried catching up, but Clark kept moving away from him.

"I gotta go," she said.

He grabbed at her elbow, but she pulled herself free and continued a beeline path toward the street. Zach picked up his pace to get directly in front of her.

Clark tried to sidestep him, but he grabbed her shoulders. By the time Cyndi caught up, Clark's eyes were clouded with tears. Her shoulders sagged, and she wore the weary look of the woman Cyndi had seen under the bridge so long ago, the look of one grown old before her time.

"Hey, sweetie, what is it?" Cyndi asked in the gentlest voice she could muster. She wanted to reach up and brush the tear off Clark's cheek, but didn't want to spook her.

"I just . . . I can't . . ." Clark's chin trembled.

Cyndi felt tears welling. If only her tears could fix Clark's trouble, she'd gladly let them fall. But she knew Clark needed her to be strong. She tightened her jaw against the impulse and swallowed down saliva so salty it made her tonsils ache.

Clark clenched and unclenched her jaw. "I can't be on camera. No one can know I'm here."

When she started to walk away, Zach reached out to stop her, but Cyndi motioned him to let her pass. Instead, he walked beside her, picking up her hand in his own.

Cyndi fell into step behind them, proud of Zach for his sensitivity. He didn't pry for her story.

But Clark offered it anyway.

"I'm not supposed to be on my own," she said. "I'm only fifteen. But I can't go back home. I won't. Ever."

Zach still didn't say anything, just squeezed her hand a little tighter and stayed with her. Cyndi laid a hand on her shoulder in what she hoped would be a gesture of comfort and support.

At the street, the three of them turned right and headed toward the light rail station.

"I saw my picture once on a mailer card. My picture, my name and birthday and description on one side and a carpet-cleaning coupon on the other."

"Was it really that bad at home?" Zach asked. "Worse than on the streets?"

Cyndi couldn't imagine a life so hard that it drove Clark to make the choices she had.

"Mom was okay. I miss her sometimes. But her choices of husbands . . . She's been married five—no, six times. My latest stepdad, he"—Clark sniffed and wiped her nose with the back of her arm—"he was a jerk. Yelling, screaming, calling me names. He hit my mom a couple of times. That was in the daytime. At night, he'd come into my room to apologize. He'd act all sorry and then . . . I couldn't take it anymore. I thought he was gonna kill me. If he didn't, I thought I'd kill myself."

Holding back tears was useless. Cyndi released them and felt their warm sting as they sprang, one after another, from her heart. "Oh, honey," she whispered, pulling Clark into an embrace. This girl, this child she held so dear, had seen the worst life had to offer. Cyndi prayed for wisdom. "Clark, you don't have to go through this alone. We could call someone who can make sure he'd never hurt you again."

"No!" Her emphatic answer faded to a whimper. "No, I've got things figured out for now. No cameras. No interviews. No pictures. I've done it for a year. I can keep it up for a few more months until I'm old enough to file for emancipation."

Thoughts and wishes raced through Cyndi's head. She searched for an answer among them but found nothing. When they reached the station, just a bench under a plexiglass shelter, Zach held Clark in a comforting hug, nothing asked, nothing demanded, until the train sighed to a stop. He gave her a soft kiss on the cheek and whispered, "Everything'll be okay."

He walked her, hand in hand, to the open train door. At the edge, Clark stepped away, still holding Zach's hand as she passed through the sliding doors. Their fingers were the last things touching. And then, nothing. Just a palpable space and longing between. The doors hissed shut. Clark's face and palms, pressed against the window, grew smaller as the train rushed away.

Zach burrowed his hands in his deep pockets and walked away, shoulders sagging, back to the tent city.

Cyndi, still on the platform, could fight the tears no longer. She slumped to the bench and gave in to heaving sobs.

Chapter 35

MIKE INSISTED CYNDI GO out for a nice dinner with him. It had been so long. Months, maybe. And after tomorrow they would be tied down with the tent city for six solid weeks. It was their last chance to spend time alone together until the six weeks of hosting Tent City Three were over.

"It's an illusion, you know," Mike said.

"What is?"

"The idea that you have everything under control."

"Are you reading my mind?"

He smiled at her, the lines around his eyes accentuated in the shadows cast by candlelight. "I don't have to read your mind. I know you too well. You're worried that things will fall apart without you. We're only gone for a couple of hours, and the crew is going to be fine. You deserve a night off, and I've got to admit, I need one too."

"You're right. But I just can't help it—it must be the mother in me." She chose a piece of French bread from the basket between them and slathered it with butter. She let her mind drift as she observed the scene outside the restaurant's plate-glass window.

Well-dressed couples strolled by, their eyes twinkling in the warmth of street lamps and Christmas lights, and entered the symphony hall across the street.

Cyndi pushed her water glass away from to make room for the scorching bowl of soup a waiter slid in front of her. Its Gruyère crust glowed golden yellow. The robust scent of country French cuisine drifted into her sinuses.

"Lovely. I haven't had soup like this in ages. Do you think we could make it at Home Fires?"

Mike rolled his eyes.

"I know, we're supposed to be taking a break, but I can't help myself. I've got Home Fires on the brain. I was just thinking the onions and bread and broth are cheap, but the cheese might be too much. I'm sure the food bank wouldn't supply us with Swiss cheese."

"Why don't you just enjoy your soup?"

While she was waiting for it to cool, she looked out the window again. A middle-aged man walked alone. His pants hems hung below the bottom of an oversize trench coat but only reached to midcalf, revealing mismatched socks. She let her gaze drift up to his face. Six-day shadow and wrinkles so deep they could be called crevasses told his story. He passed, oblivious to his observer on the other side of the glass. A year ago she wouldn't have seen him. Now she wanted to run out and invite him to Home Fires.

The broiled Gruyère crackled when she pushed her spoon through its crust. Strings of melted cheese hung like cables between spoon and bowl. She bit through the strings with her front teeth, slurping to suck the loose ends in. She lifted a second spoonful to her mouth, leaning over to avoid dripping on her silk camisole and wool jacket. As she did, she saw another homeless man, this one with a dog, out the window. The dog looked just like—it couldn't be—

"That's Joe!" she exclaimed, pointing out the window. Why was he dressed like a bum again? Where was the well-dressed lawyer she'd made over?

Mike looked out at Joe. He waved to try to grab their new friend's attention, but Joe either didn't see him or didn't care to acknowledge him.

"Excuse me." Mike pushed back from the table and left the restaurant. Cyndi followed him out to the street. Mike approached Joe, but Cyndi held back.

"What's going on?" Mike demanded.

"What do you mean?"

"You said you're with us."

Joe pulled on his beard. "I'm not trying to pull you down. I just think you're going about things the wrong way. Getting the neighbors riled up against us doesn't help the homeless at all!"

"What do you know about what helps and what doesn't?"

"I'm living it!"

"You look for quick fixes, but you don't want to really get out of your situation. If you did, you'd do something about it!"

Cyndi couldn't believe Mike had just said that. If there was a line to cross, it was somewhere behind them.

"Like what? Go live in your tent city? You honestly think it would make a difference?" Joe was right up in Mike's face now. He was making Cyndi nervous.

Mike leaned closer to Joe's face. "It's getting people off the streets."

"Being on the street doesn't make you a bad person, you know."

Cyndi couldn't keep quiet any longer. "We know," she said. "We've come to appreciate you all so much."

"Us all? What are we, a breed? You think you're so different, so much better, than everyone else? Well, you're just the same. Just wait and see. When things go wrong for you, you'll show everyone who you really are." Joe stepped closer to her, and Mike stepped in between them.

"That's not—" She was thinking of specific people, people who had changed her life this year.

"Go inside, Cyndi," Mike said.

Joe waved his hands above his head. "What, are you afraid of me? The scary homeless man?"

Mike held a hand out to stop Joe from getting any closer. "Cyndi, go inside."

She didn't want to leave the two alone, afraid of what Joe would do to Mike. Or what Mike would do to Joe. But when Mike took on that tone of voice, she knew better than to cross him.

"I'm just going to get our coats," she said.

Before she walked away, though, she had one more thing to say. "Joe, I just want you to know that I love you no matter what."

Joe stared back at her. He said, "We'll see about that."

His words and his tone rang in Cyndi's ears all the way home. She lay awake that night. What did he mean?

Was he going to do something to test her love for him? Was it a threat? Or just his way of talking? If he knew her, he'd know her commitment to him was real.

"Hey, everyone! Let's gather up for a prayer." No one in the soup kitchen paid any attention to Mike, so he resorted to clapping his hands. Eventually the others quieted down to listen.

"If everyone could make a circle, we'll have a prayer before the guests arrive." He glanced out the narrow windows that framed the front doors. The "guests" stood with faces pressed against the glass, waiting for the doors to the banquet table to swing open. Running a tent city and a soup kitchen at the same time was nuts. The workload had at least quadrupled.

It's only for six weeks. Cyndi repeated the mantra over and over.

The Home Fires workers held hands and bowed their heads for Mike's prayer. They wore weary expressions.

"Holy God," he prayed. "We ask you to fill this room with love and renewed energy. Give us what we need to get through the next few weeks. And, Lord, please help us treat our guests with dignity and respect."

Everyone scattered to the workstations, and Mike went to open the door. He greeted each guest with the instruction to eat quickly to make room for the extra diners.

Cyndi stood by him. "How's it going?"

"Crazy busy," he said. "You know. It's worth it, though."

"I sure hope so," she said. "I'm proud of you. I think we're fighting for a good thing. I'm just tired." She gave him a side hug. He turned his head and bent down to kiss her. With a quick squeeze, he gave her a word of encouragement.

"I'm sorry about last night. I was being stupid," he said. "You're my rock. What would I do without you?"

"I love you, too," she replied, patting his cheek with one hand before letting go. "I'll see you after dinner."

She started to walk away, relieved to have the latest fight behind them, but Mike grasped her hand and held her at his side. Together, they greeted people as they came in. Some they knew by name, some by face, others not at all. So many people coming through the doors. So many lives to touch and change. Some made eye contact, most did not, but Cyndi made an effort to look each individual in the face and acknowledge each soul as important, even the ones she knew were just there to use her. And she kept a special eye out for Joe.

A scuffle at the back of the crowd pressing at the door drew her attention. She rose up on tiptoe to try to look over the tumult of bodies to see who was causing those in the middle to complain, "Stop pushing. Hey! Wait your turn!"

Clark squeezed out from between two obese women into the front of the mob, her recently styled hair now in disarray. Her eyes shone with anger; her cheeks flushed with rage. "Who did it?" Clark screamed.

Mike reached his arm in front of her to keep her from lunging after someone. "Whoa, whoa, whoa! Slow down." He struggled to stop her. She had enough momentum that his arm alone couldn't hold her back. He blocked her with his body.

She kept screaming. "Who did it? I'll kill him!" She wrestled to get out of Mike's grip, to swing out at something, at someone.

Mike closed his arms around her in a wrestling hold.

Cyndi closed in behind Clark and laid a calming hand on her shoulder. Both Mike and Cyndi spoke in soothing tones, which Clark couldn't hear above her tirade.

"Shh, honey, shh," Cyndi said over and over as she rubbed Clark's back. "What's wrong? What happened?"

Mike took a more direct approach. He held Clark's struggling body against his chest and tried to reason with her.

"Clark, dear, you've got to calm down. Clark, stop screaming. Clark, if you don't settle down, we'll never know what's wrong. What's the matter?"

When she finally stopped yelling, the anger and tension in her muscles melted away so suddenly that she might have sunk to the ground if not for Mike catching her by the armpits. She leaned into him and began to sob. That didn't make communication any better, since she was still unable to form an intelligible sentence.

The crowd streamed around the three of them, as if in fast-forward while Mike, Clark, and Cyndi were on pause. After the tail end of the line passed by, Clark stood on her own feet. She wiped at her red, puffy, tear-stained face with her overlong sleeves.

"Clark," Mike said, "you've got to tell us what happened."

She sniffed and swallowed. "They slashed the tents."

Cyndi's didn't even think to put on a jacket or ask any questions. She sprinted toward the tent city across the empty field. Who slashed the tents?

Frosted blades of grass cracked and snapped under each pounding step. She sucked in icy air. The cold shot through her lungs and into her sides. Not even halfway there, she slowed to a loping jog and, finally, to a complete stop. She stood, bent over with hands on knees, and waited for the oxygen she gulped in to reach her muscles.

Two sets of footsteps crunched through the grass behind her. Clark and Mike caught up to her, each took one of her hands, and together they made their way across the dark field to the temporary lights of Tent City Three.

The damage was worse than she feared. A dozen tents lay slashed open and upended, their contents spilled out onto the makeshift walkways. Electric cords had been severed, draping the northern corner of the campsite in complete darkness. Large orange insulated jugs of water and coffee had been shoved off their tables. Their contents spilled out over the upended tents, and already fingers of frost laced the newly formed puddles.

Mike pulled out his cell phone and punched in 9-1-

1. "Yes, I have some vandalism to report," he said. He raked across his head as if he still had hair and answered the dispatcher's questions with short responses.

Mike Finch.

Riverton Plaza.

Vandalism.

"Okay. Thank you." He punched the end button on the phone and looked at Clark and Cyndi, who both stared at him as if waiting for him to set things right.

"The police are on their way," Mike said. "I'll stay here to meet them. You two go secure the doors at Home Fires and make sure any potential witnesses stay put."

Numbness blanketed Cyndi, not just her fingers and toes but her mind as well, as she trudged back across the field. By the time she got the soup kitchen secured and trusted workers posted at the exits, the edges of Cyndi's numbness had frayed away. Hot anger rose to the surface, but she pushed it down. She'd need to be calm to speak with police and to face all the work to be done tonight.

Tromping back toward the tent city and the flashing lights of three police cars, Cyndi started ticking through her list of who had a grudge against her and Tent City Three.

Tent City residents? She quickly discounted this possibility. Why would anyone who benefited from the temporary housing want to destroy it?

Spencer Ridley? It wouldn't surprise her. He'd been so hostile toward the soup kitchen yet strangely silent about the tent city.

Zach? He had confessed to some acts of vandalism. Wasn't it arson? But he loved the kitchen and the tent project. He wouldn't do anything to hurt it.

Joe? The name came unbidden to her mind. Joe was a friend. Or was he? How much did they really know about each other, anyway? One thing for sure, Joe was not happy with the tent city. His hostility ran deep. And last night—maybe that really was a threat.

Clark wouldn't have done it. That show of emotion was too real.

Honestly, it could be anyone. How much did Cyndi really know the people living on her grounds? She wanted to trust them, but honestly, of all the homeless people she'd been in contact with, she knew Clark the best. And she couldn't even predict what color hair she would show up with, much less what angst and passion drove her.

It took more than an hour for the police to gather the evidence they needed. One officer took notes while another measured and photographed the scene. Two of the officers headed over to the soup kitchen to interview witnesses and another questioned Mike, Clark, and Cyndi.

When the tent city residents were released, Cyndi eyed each one with suspicion. The residents without tents milled around, unsure of how to go about replacing or repairing their downed homes.

Cyndi stood and stared at the mess.

"Hon, why don't you just go home? We'll take care of things here," Mike offered.

Even if she'd wanted to leave, she didn't think she

could get her feet to move. Everything—hands and feet, but especially her brain—was numb. Her heart ached. "I—I don't know where to start."

"We could start with a prayer."

She hated the idea. What good had prayer ever done? What good would it do now, when it was too late? She found herself, once again and against her will, holding hands with Mike, who held hands with Nance, who held hands with Amanda and on around the circle.

They had so many words that seemed to gather on the ground in the middle of the circle, a pile of prayers that would rot in place.

Somewhere in the middle of the prayer, the dulling shock started wearing off. A knot burned in her gut, a small hot kernel that grew and caught and blazed up into anger—at whoever did this, at Mike for being so calm, even at God. When Mike finally said amen, she jerked her hand out of his and stomped off to the farthest tent.

It lay smashed and deflated.

She didn't need to undo the zipper to grab the never-used sleeping bag and foam pad through the jagged cut in its side. She yanked on them. The sleeping bag snagged on the hole. She pulled harder. The bag ripped and bled feathers into the air.

"Aaarrh!" Cyndi threw the bag on the ground. She stomped her feet. She was done.

Done!

"Hey, hey!" Mike came up behind her. "Calm down, hon."

"Calm down? Calm down!" She couldn't control

the rise of her voice, didn't want to, really. "It's ruined!"

"Shh." Mike pulled her into a hug.

She pulled against him, but he didn't let up. She pulled again, then realized he wasn't letting her go until she relaxed into him.

He stroked the back of her head. "Shh. It'll be okay."

She buried her face in his shoulder. "I don't see how."

He tilted her head back so he could see her eyes. "I know you don't, but it will. A good night's sleep will do us all a lot of good."

"Speaking of sleep," Nance said.

Cyndi hadn't seen her standing there.

Nance fiddled with a tent rod. "Speaking of sleep, where are we going to put everyone tonight? We can't exactly send them out to find other shelter this late at night."

They couldn't, but what else could they do?

"Maybe . . ." Mike said. He let go of Cyndi. "Maybe we should open up the dining room for the night. Everyone can sleep inside."

Cyndi shook her head. "I don't think that's a good idea." There was the fire code. And the fact that one of them might be the vandal. And—

Mike laid his hand on her shoulder. "It might be our only choice. We invited them here to get them off the street. I don't think we should send them straight back out the first time something goes wrong. We've got forty people inside who are counting on us to provide a warm dry place for the night. I think we should take care of them."

Nance dropped the tent pole as if she was ready to run inside and start setting up beds.

"Wait," Cyndi said. "What if one of them is the vandal? We can't afford to have the kitchen trashed too."

"Hon, it's God's kitchen. He can take care of it."

"Like he took care of the tents?" She felt hysteria rising in her again.

"In this world, you will have trouble," Mike said. "He doesn't promise everything's gonna be easy. But he does promise he's bigger than all the mess. Trust me, Cyn. If you can't trust him, trust me. We need to get everything moved inside so people can get some sleep."

She did trust Mike. Mostly.

Nance was already hauling stuff out of the nearest tent. There was no stopping people with big hearts and good intentions.

Cyndi walked over to Nance and picked up a foam mat.

"Just for tonight," she said. "To get everyone out of the cold."

Chapter 36

IN THE MORNING, CYNDI walked through the field surveying the damage. In filtered, foggy light, things looked worse than the night before. A cold December drizzle lent a wilted look even to the tents that still stood.

Clark found her own tent, picked up a corner, and dragged it toward the huge Dumpster they'd had brought in to clean up the site. The nylon rain fly dragged behind her in the mud like a dead snake.

Cyndi wanted to cry for her. She knew Clark had already cried plenty last night. She'd heard her quiet sobs in the Home Fires dining hall long after the other guests had gone to sleep.

Clark stopped near her. Around her eyes was puffy and dark. She shook her head. "I can't believe it."

"Me neither, sweetie." Cyndi wished she had something else, something more powerful to say.

"It was stupid of me to think a tent and a sleeping bag would really make a difference."

"Not stupid, just optimistic."

Zach walked up beside Clark. He slipped his arm around her waist. "I'm so sorry."

She buried her face in his sweatshirt and wrapped her arms around him. "It's not your fault."

Cyndi had never seen Clark like this. Her defensive facade was broken down, and she was actually letting her real emotions show through. Problem was, her spunk was gone as well. It was just a small bump in the grand view of Clark's hard and complicated life. For the moment, though, the girl must feel like she couldn't catch a break.

A blinding light shone in Cyndi's eyes. She put a hand up to shield her eyes and see where the light came from. By the time she realized a TV camera was trained on her and the two kids, Zach was already hurtling toward it.

He thrust his hands out to cover the camera lens. "What do you think you're doing?" he demanded.

Clark pulled her jacket up to block her face. She took off at a sprint across the field.

Cyndi knew she couldn't catch her on foot, so she ran for her car. She slammed the door shut and turned the key.

Immediately, the windows fogged. She flicked the defroster on high. "Come on, come on," she whispered, as if her words would make the fog dissipate. She leaned forward and wiped the opaque windows with her bare hand.

Which way did she go? At the street, Cyndi randomly chose to go right. She turned right again into the Riverton Heights neighborhood, her eyes peeled for movement.

Where was she? Every second stretched.

Cyndi tore up and down the streets. She didn't see her. She sped back to the main road and went into the next neighborhood. On the third street, she caught a glimpse of Clark dashing into the park.

Cyndi careened into the curb and threw the car into park. She jumped out of the car and ran after her. "Clark! Stop, honey! It's me!"

Clark kept going.

Cyndi jogged to catch up. When she was close enough, she reached out to Clark's shoulder. "You don't need to run."

Clark gasped for breath. She halfheartedly tried to pull away.

Cyndi lowered her hand to Clark's and led her to a park bench. "It's okay. Just breathe."

Clark's cheeks burned red.

Cyndi's heart ached for her. She clutched her hand tighter. "I wish I could make everything better for you." She wished for adequate words of comfort. She knew Clark well enough now to give her silence to work out her own thoughts.

They sat without talking for several minutes.

Clark sniffed and leaned forward on her elbows. Cyndi rested a hand on the middle of Clark's back.

Cyndi started feeling cold. She thought about going back to her car for the old army blanket she kept inside, but she didn't want to break the moment with Clark. Her patience paid off.

"I used to play in a park like this one," Clark said. "I'd swing as high as I could. I thought if I went high enough I could fly away. See that house?" She pointed across the street to a beautiful Tudor whose brick facade and manicured hedges hinted at the type of people who lived there. "I used to live in a place like that. Bigger, though. We had beautiful flower gardens. I had blue frilly curtains on my bedroom windows. But all the fancy stuff on the outside was hiding ugly stuff you couldn't see."

Cyndi looked more closely at the house and wondered if it hid dark secrets.

"He said not to tell anyone. He said people wouldn't understand, that what we had was special. But it didn't feel special—it felt wrong . . ."

Cyndi took in what Clark was saying, though she didn't want to understand.

"He said he'd hurt me if I told anyone." Clark scoffed. "Like he hadn't already. I was more afraid he'd hurt Mom. Or maybe kill her. I thought I could keep her safe by doing what he wanted. It was stupid. I couldn't protect her."

Cyndi couldn't begin to understand the amount of suffering this child had lived through in her short life. "Your father?" she asked.

"Stepdad. The last one. Did you know my mom died? Two years ago. In a car accident."

"I didn't know."

"I couldn't protect her."

Cyndi thought of Madi. She gasped out a quiet sob. "Sometimes things happen." She dropped her hand to squeeze Clark's. "You know it wasn't your fault, don't you?"

"In my head . . . but my heart—I couldn't stay. I can't go back there."

"We won't let that happen. Hey—" She checked

the words before she said them, made sure they weren't on a whim. "What if you live with me and Mike until we can work out something permanent for you?" It wasn't the first time she'd thrown the idea out there, but she thought this time Clark might grasp on to it. She knew the girl wouldn't fling herself on the ground in gratitude, but when Clark shrank down even more, she didn't know what to do. "What is it? What's wrong?"

Clark looked away. She mumbled, "I just, I know the streets."

Of course. Cyndi didn't have to know how to read minds to understand what Clark meant. She was afraid to be in a house, with a man, behind closed doors. Mike would never hurt her. He loved her almost like he'd loved their own daughter. But if Clark wasn't comfortable, Cyndi wouldn't force her.

They sat awhile longer, not talking. Far down the street, Cyndi saw Zach jogging toward them. When he reached the edge of the park, he slowed to a walk. He plopped down on the bench on the other side of Clark.

"Hey," he said. His breath hung in the air.

"Hey," Cyndi said.

Clark just crossed her arms.

"I caught up with that reporter." Zach wiped his mouth. "I explained your situation. She was shooting live before, but she promised she won't run that clip again. There's no way he was watching local news on a Friday morning . . . is there?"

Clark shrugged.

Zach put his hand on her arm. "It's gonna be fine. He didn't see it."

Clark stared down the road as if the answer she needed lay at the other end. "I don't know."

Zach laced his fingers through Clark's. He stood and tugged at her. "Come on."

She dragged one foot after his, then the next.

Cyndi followed them to her car. She drove them back to Home Fires and let Clark hang out in her office.

She took a seat facing her.

Clark ran her thumbnail along the edge of the desk, back and forth. She dug into the surface of the wood.

"Don't—" Cyndi started. She stopped herself. Don't squash her, she told herself. Don't smother her. Give her space. After a few minutes, she caught herself picking at the worn spots on the knees of her jeans. She was just as fidgety as Clark. They couldn't just sit here forever, but where else could they go?

"Tea?" Mike stood in the doorway, holding an insulated mug.

Cyndi nodded. "Clark?"

The girl shook her head.

"Then I'll take it. Thanks." She wrapped her fingers around the cup as if its heat would soak through. She walked out into the hallway with Mike, thankful for the distraction.

"Come outside," Mike said, tipping his head toward the front door. "You need to see the progress we're making."

What difference did it make what kind of progress they were making? They hadn't caught the vandals yet. What would keep them from striking again?

The scene in the field surprised Cyndi. Half a

dozen Home Fires workers were setting up brand-new tents.

"Wha—how?"

Mike grinned. "All donated. People who saw the news last night have been dropping off tents and other supplies all morning." He leaned over to pick up the torn packaging from one of the new tents. He walked over and tossed it into a nearby Dumpster.

A patrol car turned up the road. Its tires crunched through the loose gravel. It pulled over along the curb near where Mike and Cyndi stood. An officer climbed out and approached them. "Morning, folks."

Cyndi's stomach knotted.

"Good morning," Mike said. "Any news?"

The officer held out his hand to shake Mike's and Cyndi's. "Sergeant Stanislaus," he said.

"Mike Finch."

"Mike, you're the one I'm looking for. I have questions about a couple of people."

Cyndi offered, "We could go inside. Home Fires is warmer."

They walked across the field together. Inside, Mike dragged three chairs into a corner where they could speak in private. "Coffee? Doughnut?" he offered.

Sergeant Stanislaus laughed. "Coffee, black. Hold the doughnut."

Cyndi poured the coffee. She took the third chair. "What did you find?"

The officer referred to a small notebook. "We've eliminated nearly everyone we interviewed who was inside last night."

"What about neighbors?" Mike said. "Did you talk to Spencer Ridley? He's been antagonistic."

"We did. He's got a solid alibi. It wasn't him."

"What about his wife?" Cyndi asked.

The officer shook his head. "We'll look into it. I wanted to talk to you about someone else. Joseph Talbot?"

"Joe?" His name caught in Cyndi's throat.

"We know him," Mike said. "But he wouldn't—"

Sergeant Stanislaus stopped him. "He's just a person of interest at this point. But I do have some questions."

"Shoot," Mike said.

"Is it true he threatened the tent city?"

"Yes, but—"

"And your wife?"

"Yes, but—"

The only time Joe had threatened them was when they ran into him on the street last week. Cyndi tried to think who might have seen the argument.

"It was just words," Mike said. "In the heat of the moment."

"What exactly did he say to you?"

"I don't remember the exact words."

Cyndi did. They were burned in her mind. *When things go wrong for you, you'll show people who you really are.* When he'd said it, she'd taken it as a threat. Maybe that's not what he meant, though.

"Joe didn't do it," she said. "He couldn't have." With the idea planted in her head, she couldn't shake it. Of course he could have. He was that mad.

Stanislaus closed his notebook and rose to leave. "Thanks for your help. We'll keep you apprised if there are further developments."

Mike showed him to the door.

As soon as they were out of earshot, swells of emotions burbled up in Cyndi. Joe was her friend.

Wasn't he?

In her gut, she knew. But she wouldn't believe it until she'd talked to him face-to-face.

Cyndi bundled up in hat and coat. She threw her purse over her shoulder.

"Where are you going?" Mike asked.

"Downtown. I'm going to look for Joe." She didn't want to confront him, but she had to know if he was the one. Now that the officer had suggested it, she couldn't shake it loose. She'd start at all his regular haunts. Maybe someone at one of the shelters would know where to find him.

She was almost to her car when she heard the barking.

Wolf bounded across the parking lot toward her, ears flapping, tongue lolling out the side of his happy mouth. He stopped at her feet and leaned against her leg.

She scratched his head. "Hello, boy. Where's your person?" Wolf wouldn't be here without Joe.

As it turned out, Cyndi didn't have far to look. She walked across the field to check on the progress at the tent city before heading downtown to look for Joe.

The sun had burned through the fog, but the grass was still damp. The ground would take days to dry even if it didn't rain.

Wolf led Cyndi straight to Joe. She found him on his hands and knees, wiping ground tarps with a ragged towel. She stopped short of the tarp edge and folded her arms across her chest. "What brings you down here?" she demanded. What she really wanted to ask was "How dare you?"

"I heard you had some trouble here last night," Joe said, twisting his neck to look at Cyndi.

"Yeah." She watched his face for signs of guilt. This was a man who knew how to keep secrets. How was she to know what he had done or not done? She couldn't know anything for sure unless he said it. And even then—

"Thought I'd come on down and help out. Now that I'm down on the ground, though, I don't know if I'll ever be able to get up. I might have to move in after all. Just pitch a tent over me right here."

Joe chuckled in his wheezy kind of way.

It was too much. He'd been so against the tent city, so adamant. And now here he was, joking about moving in.

He leaned over again to keep wiping down the tarp.

The end of a folded switchblade stuck up out of his back pocket, a scrap of blue string snagged on it. The string was the same color as the tents they'd lost.

He must have done it.

Who else?

She turned away. No longer angry, she was awash

in sadness.

When she was far enough he couldn't hear her betray him back, she dialed 9-1-1.

Chapter 37

THE PHONE BURNED in Cyndi's hand.

The police would come soon, sirens blaring. They would find him in the field, pretending to help, with evidence in his back pocket.

Motive and opportunity.

She sighed. When he was just some homeless guy, he'd had a certain charm. But now that she was getting to know him and his story, she was disappointed by the pattern of destruction he lived without remorse or care.

She went to the kitchen to pour herself a cup of tea. There she found Clark, slouched down against the industrial-sized refrigerator.

"Where's Zach?" Cyndi asked.

Clark just shrugged.

"You okay?" Cyndi slid down beside her.

"Yeah. I guess." She brushed a stray clump of hair off her face, revealing her blotched, swollen cheeks.

Cyndi helped her to her feet. "You hungry? Can I get you a shake or something down at the sandwich shop?"

She shrugged again, but when Cyndi stood and reached for her hand, she got up. She shuffled behind her out onto the sidewalk.

They were halfway to the sandwich shop when

some shouting out near the field stopped them. Cyndi looked across the parking lot. Someone was getting into it with Mike.

She ran across the lot to see what was going on. It was that awful Spencer Ridley and his horrid wife.

Spencer's anger rose as a trumpet sound, but the words were lost before they reached her ears.

She kept running, Clark right behind her.

"—or I'll call the police!" Spencer was right in Mike's face. If he didn't have an alibi, they'd already have him locked up. She couldn't believe he wasn't the vandal.

"Please step back." Mike's voice was firm but calm. By the look on his face, he was close to losing it. He stepped closer to Spencer.

"Hey, man!" Spencer threw his hands in the air, palms away from Mike as if inviting a fight. "Back off or I'll have a restraining order slapped on you so fast, you won't know what hit you."

Just then, strobing red-and-blue police lights flashed atop an approaching patrol car. The sirens blipped a couple of times, and the car pulled to a stop next to Tent City Three. A blue sedan pulled in behind the squad car, and a man and a woman in business attire got out.

Cyndi's stomach churned.

When Mike walked toward the officer, he had to pass Spencer.

"Back off, man!" He took a fighting stance.

"Settle down," Mike replied, thrusting his open hands still higher in surrender. "I'm not going to touch you. I've got to see what this officer wants."

Cyndi wished she could grab Mike by one hand and Clark by the other and drag them home—home to a life of peace and normalcy. It would be so easy just to step away, one step at a time, and never look back, so wonderful to click her heels together and be whisked by magic to a happy place. But all she could do was stand and watch helplessly as the inevitable chain of events unfolded in slow motion.

Mike tried to sidestep Spencer to get to Sergeant Stanislaus, but Spencer wouldn't let him by.

A second police officer stood behind the sergeant, the two from the sedan behind him.

The two police officers ignored Spencer's posturing. Their eyes were trained on someone else.

Cyndi turned to see who the officers were targeting.

Just beyond her, still wiping down tarps, knelt Joe. His back was turned to the commotion as if he hadn't heard anything.

So they'd come for him.

Whatever she'd hoped to feel, this wasn't it. It was like she still held the handle of the blade she'd stabbed into his back.

What had she done?

The sergeant stood, feet spread to shoulders' width, arms crossed with an air of authority. "Joseph Talbot?"

Joe turned his head to see the officer. "Yes?"

"You're under arrest."

Joe looked to Cyndi for help.

She turned away. She couldn't look him in the eye.

"You have the right to remain silent. Anything you say can be used against you in a court of law. You have the right to an attorney . . ."

Cyndi walked away, as if removing herself from the scene would ease the pain in her heart. She didn't know what hurt worse: Joe's betrayal of her trust, or her betrayal of their friendship.

She walked past Stanislaus, not sure where to go. She just wanted to get away.

The plainclothes police officers walked toward her. She sidestepped to let them by.

They walked past her. She turned to see where they were going.

Clark was right behind her.

All the togs of the puzzle clicked into place. Cyndi wanted to tell her to run.

Clark's fearful glance darted between the police, a known threat, and these two and their undisclosed intentions.

"Clarisse Ranier?"

Clark's only motion was the expansion of her chest as she tried to draw breath.

"Are you Clarisse Ranier?"

Still she didn't answer. The air crackled with tension.

Something had to give.

It was Zach. "Leave her alone," he said.

"Shut up, Zach," Clark spat.

"So you are Clarisse?"

"Clark," she said. Despite the firm set of her chin, she looked like she was going to cry.

Cyndi knew exactly how she felt.

The woman from the sedan placed a hand on Clark's elbow. "We're here to take you home."

The woman steered Clark to their car.

Cyndi's heart dragged behind her, stretching the bond between them but not breaking it. She couldn't let them take her. "Stop!" she yelled. "Let her go."

The woman let go of Clark's arm. She pulled out her wallet and flipped it open to her ID. "Child Protective Services. JoLynn Arnold," she said. "We've been looking for Clarisse here for some time."

"You can't take her—" Cyndi started.

JoLynn stopped her. "It's my job to make sure she gets home safely."

"Please don't make me," Clark pleaded. "I'd rather die."

Cyndi didn't know the law, but she knew Clark belonged with her. "Can I just talk to her for a minute?"

The man with JoLynn piped in. "Clarisse's father is very anxious to see her."

"Stepfather," Cyndi said. "He's not her father."

From the corner of her eye, Cyndi could see Joe being put in a squad car. Sergeant Stanislaus pushed the old man's head down to keep him from knocking it on the doorframe, gave a gentle shove to put Joe's head all the way into the car, and closed the door. Joe rested his head on the window.

Cyndi's heart tore in two.

The sergeant walked over with Mike. "Everything's under control now, ma'am. We've got your vandal. You might want to contact a lawyer to discuss where to go from here."

The absurdity of his statement made Cyndi want to cry. But if she started, she'd never be able to stop.

"Where are they taking Clark?" Mike asked.

Cyndi turned back to see the CPS workers putting Clark in the car, not unlike the police had just done with Joe. "They're taking her. We've got to stop them."

Mike turned to Stanislaus. "Can you help?"

The sergeant walked over to the CPS workers. He took JoLynn's badge, scrutinized it, and handed it back.

Cyndi took Mike's hand and squeezed it hard. "Can they just take her away?"

"I don't know, hon."

Cyndi went to the car window. The look of panic on Clark's face fed her own panic. She wanted to shout that everything would be all right, but Clark deserved more than empty promises.

JoLynn was showing Stanislaus a piece of paper. He skimmed its contents and handed it back. He came around to Cyndi's side of the car.

"It looks like everything is in order," he said. "She's a runaway. Her family is worried about her."

"Family?" Cyndi spit out the word. You couldn't call a monster like that family.

"Isn't she old enough to be independent?" Mike asked.

"She's fifteen," JoLynn said, a touch of frustration creeping into her tone. "She's been on the run for over a year. Her father has been worried sick. And now we're going to place her back with him."

"Wait!" Zach blurted. "You can't take her back there. He'll hurt her. He's dangerous."

"I hope that's not true," JoLynn said. "We've got no evidence or reports to say he is. We'll assign her a new caseworker who will check in with her regularly. If anything is amiss, we'll pull her from the home. But for now . . ."

The tall man—Cyndi didn't catch his name—folded himself into the front seat of the car. JoLynn walked around to the driver's side.

"Wait," Cyndi said, desperately searching for any words that would keep Clark away from danger. Knowing her words had failed before. "When can I see her?"

"Ma'am, we are not prison guards. We're not even the police. Once she's home, she's home. If she wants to see you, I'm sure you can arrange something."

Through the closed window, Clark shouted her address and phone number. Mike scrawled them on a scrap of paper.

Cyndi put her hands against the window. "Don't worry. We'll come for you. I love you."

Zach stood, hands crammed deep into his sweatshirt pocket, shoulders hunched forward, jaws clenched, face white.

Cyndi shared his pain, a physical ache that came from deep in the soul. It felt a lot like losing Madi, only more sudden, like a Band-Aid being ripped off instead of being pulled off slowly.

The love stretched even tighter as the sedan pulled away.

Cyndi stood on tiptoe and shouted, "I will come for you!"

Chapter 38

JOE COULDN'T HEAR WHAT was happening with Mike, Cyndi, Zach, and Clark from his seat in the back of the squad car. But body language spoke.

Despair . . . written in their stance, in the way they hung their heads. He almost forgot his own predicament while he watched the drama outside his window unfold. When the man slammed the car door, Zach and Cyndi stood together in shared grief. From behind, they could be mother and son. And when the sedan rolled out of sight, the two gave in and wept on each other's shoulders.

Love hurts.

He hadn't realized it when he was young. But when he learned, he learned it good. Since then he'd carefully shielded himself from the unnecessary pain of it.

Wolf wandered over to Joe's window and pressed his wet nose against the glass.

Joe listened to the faint whine through the window. He felt the dog's anguish in his own heart.

"Hey, old boy," he whispered. "I've got to go away for a while. I'll be back, though. You take care of yourself. I'll be back soon." Joe's voice cracked. He swallowed the salty knot forming in the back of his throat. "Tell Cyndi and Mike I didn't do it. They'll believe you. And, Wolf?"

The dog cocked its head.

Joe tapped on the glass. "Wait for me, will ya?"

The officers got into the car and slammed their doors.

Mike and Zach looked up when the engine started. Cyndi actually looked away. She didn't run to his rescue like she had for Clark. No one ran to save him.

They thought he was guilty.

Chapter 39

Cyndi sank to the ground, her heart crushed within her.

Mike knelt down beside her. "It'll be all right."

"How can it?" She buried her face in her hands. Hot tears pressed into her palms. "I promised I would take care of her. I let her down."

"She'll make it. She's a tough kid."

She shook her head. "That's just her mask. She's not tough. She's just a baby." Clark's toughness was convincing, but not to Cyndi. She closed her eyes.

"She's not Madi, you know. She's strong. And she's going to make it."

"He's going to hurt her."

Mike cleared his throat. "Just because she ran away doesn't mean he's abusive."

Why did everyone assume this jerk was the one who was being maligned? "He is," she said. "Clark told me." Briefly she related what little information Clark had shared.

"Then we'll get her back." He stood and paced. He got on the phone to the police. He was talking to CPS. All this before Cyndi even found legs to stand on. Every time the door was closed by a negative answer, Cyndi's spirit sank.

She couldn't just sit here. She had to *do* something. She needed to find Clark.

Mike drove and Cyndi checked the map on her phone. The address Clark gave them was closer to downtown. It wouldn't take them long to get there, but it seemed like forever. Why were they hitting every red light?

Cyndi watched the dot on the map move closer to their destination. "Take the next right. No, that one where the car is coming out."

Mike followed her directions into a high-end neighborhood. "Are you sure this is right?"

"Yeah, I'm sure. Hard to imagine her living here, though, isn't it?"

"Hard to imagine living on the streets after this."

Not if home life was as bad as she described it. Cyndi looked at the map again. "134th is up ahead."

Mike drove up the street, watching the house numbers increase.

"It should be in the next block. There it is." Cyndi's stomach fluttered.

He parked by the curb, even though it looked like this was one of those communities where street parking was forbidden. "Is that a For Sale sign?"

That couldn't be right. They must have the wrong address.

She double-checked what she had scribbled on her hand. This was it, all right. Cyndi got out and grabbed a flyer from the For Sale sign and brought it back.

"It's for sale." She said the obvious but couldn't grasp what it meant. Were they in the wrong place? Did Clark's stepdad even have the right to move her?

They walked up to the front door together. Cyndi's stomach did flips in her throat. Oh, how she wanted to hold Clark close.

Mike rang the doorbell.

No one answered.

He rang it again.

Cyndi listened, hoping to hear something. Maybe someone was inside, just not answering. She peered in the vertical window beside the door. A sheer curtain blocked most of the view. She moved around to peek through another window.

"What are you doing?" Mike hissed. "Stop spying on them."

"I'm not spying," she said aloud. "There's no one here. It's completely empty." No furniture, no rugs, no decorations. Only freshly washed Italian tile floors and an end table with real estate cards scattered on it. Mike joined her at the window. He cupped his hands against the glass to cut down on the glare.

"Oh, Cynthia, I have a really bad feeling about this."

Not as bad as Cyndi's feeling. If Clark wasn't here, they had no way to find her.

She wasn't just lost to them. She was lost and in danger.

The next morning, Cyndi sat at the kitchen table

with the newspaper and a cup of tea. She wore her robe and slippers. She tried to read the front-page stories, but the words blurred together.

Mike padded into the kitchen in a ragged old sweatshirt and some sweatpants that didn't match and poured himself a cup of coffee. His face looked bruised. "Did you get any sleep last night?" he asked.

"No."

"Me neither."

"I can't stop thinking about Clark. I'm so scared. I don't know what to do."

"We're doing all we can. Pray and wait."

Cyndi lowered her head to the table. She was waiting—what else could she do? "It's not enough."

"I know, but it's out of our hands. You know what we can do, though?"

"What?"

"Get Joe out of prison."

Yesterday it had seemed so important to get justice for the tent city damage. Important enough for her to turn in a friend. What difference did justice make in the long run? But to get him out? He deserved to be in jail. He was guilty. To bail him out was to condone his crime.

She pressed on her temples. "I don't know—"

"We need to help him," Mike said. "Who else does he have?"

Who else? Who in the first place. She felt terrible about turning him in, but not that terrible. "I'm tired, babe. I think I'll lay down for a little while."

Cyndi curled up on her bed and tried to rest. The

ache of loneliness and helplessness gnawed at her. Loneliness, but not aloneness. So many faces, many without names, people she had served and tried to love swam in her mind. A year ago, they'd been just faces, toothless, ugly people who smelled bad and needed food. Now she saw them as souls, and sometimes she even got a glimpse of how beautiful they could be if given a chance.

Mike poked his head in the door, and Cyndi's thoughts scattered like marbles on tile. He went to the closet and took out a clean shirt.

Cyndi patted the mattress beside her.

Mike sat next to her and laid a hand over hers. "Feeling any better?"

"It's so much all at once."

"You really love that girl, don't you?" He squeezed her hand.

"More than my own life. I thought I could protect her, but I was helpless. I *am* helpless."

"I think we always have been. Control is just an illusion."

"But that doesn't mean we have to surrender every time something bad happens. I lost years mourning for Madi. I don't want to lose that much time again."

"We won't. We'll find her."

They sat quiet together.

"Hon?" Mike squeezed her hand.

"Hmm?"

"We need to take care of Joe, too."

She sighed.

"He needs us as much as she does."

He didn't. He couldn't.

He'd stabbed them in the back. But then, hadn't she turned around and done the same thing? She hadn't asked, hadn't given him the chance to tell his side. She'd just assumed his guilt and acted on that assumption.

"You go if you want. I think I'll stay home."

He pulled on her hand. "I don't want to leave you here like this. Come outside. It'll do you good."

He could make her get in the car, but he couldn't make her go inside the jail.

Chapter 40

ON THE INTERSTATE, CYNDI alternated between biting her lip and worrying her fingernails. She'd never been to the jail before and didn't care to go now.

They parked in a visitor's spot.

Mike got out, but Cyndi stayed in her seat.

He came around to her side of the car and opened the door. "Come on, hon."

She crossed her arms. "I don't want to go in."

"Well, then, we'll wait until you do."

He went around to his side again and got back in the car.

That was easy.

Only he didn't start the engine. He sat on his side, she on hers

"Aren't we going home?"

"Nuh-uh. We'll go inside in a minute, when you're ready."

She sighed. His quiet stubbornness was so infuriating. And effective. She knew he'd never give up. She sighed again. "All right. Let's get this over with."

Mike held her door open and escorted her to the entrance.

She wanted to die.

"May I help you?" The police academy flunky

behind the desk couldn't have been more than twenty.

Mike read the young man's name tag. "Um, yes, Officer Angelo. We're here to see Joseph Talbot. He's being held here."

The officer punched Joe's name into his computer.

"May I see your ID." It wasn't a question.

Mike and Cyndi both handed over their driver's licenses.

Cyndi crossed her arms and looked around the room while they waited for Officer Angelo to verify their identities. The cinder block walls were painted a dark gray that sucked light out of the room. The fluorescent lights flickered.

He handed back their IDs. A gray metal door to his right buzzed. "Sir, ma'am."

Mike pulled at the door handle. It swung open with a *chunk*. He waved Cyndi through in front of him and stepped behind her into another waiting area, painted the same industrial gray as the first.

Through a small rectangular window in the door, Cyndi stared back at the facility's entrance. An identical door across the room led, presumably, to the cell blocks. Was that what they were called, or was that just the term they used in the movies?

"Nice place, huh?" Cyndi said. She chose a black plastic chair, one in an attached row of four. She sat bolt upright, her hands resting on her knees. Despite the strong odor of bleach, dust balls and hair collected in corners and along the black rubber baseboards.

After a few minutes, the second door buzzed open and two officers entered the room. A female guard instructed Cyndi to follow, and Mike went with the male guard.

After a thorough, but not too thorough, search of her belongings and person, Cyndi met Mike in the visiting room. She'd expected to talk with Joe via telephone through safety glass, but it looked like they'd be sitting at a table with him. She'd rather not get that close. He'd be able to read her eyes.

"Choose a table. We'll bring the prisoner here to speak with you." The female guard stood in the doorway in a masculine stance. The other left and returned a few minutes later with Joe.

Joe actually looked better than normal. He wore a clean orange jumpsuit, his hair was combed, and he appeared well rested.

Mike shook his hand.

Cyndi sat across from him with arms crossed.

Mike led the conversation. "How are you?" His concern came through in his voice.

"I'm okay," Joe said. He scratched his beard. "The food's not half bad in here, but the company stinks." He let his words hang in silence for a moment before muttering, "It was a joke."

Ha. Ha.

"And, by the way, I'm innocent. But I know what you're thinking. Nobody in jail is guilty, right?"

Nobody but you, Cyndi thought. She wondered if the police had sent the blue thread and the knife to the crime lab for forensics.

"They must have found some incriminating evidence against you," Mike said.

"I don't know. They don't tell you anything in here. I guess I'll find out at my arraignment hearing. It's not until Monday."

Mike slid a Bible across the table. "I thought you might like something to read."

"No offense, but there's a hundred of those lying around and they don't really seem to be doing anyone any good. So, thanks, but no thanks." Joe pushed the book back to Mike. "Now, if you've got a newspaper, I'd take it."

"Do you have a lawyer?"

"Nah. I figure I can defend myself. No point in turning my life over to a stranger at this late date."

"We could find someone for you—"

"Like you found someone for your defense? No thanks. We'll have to settle for the same attorney."

"Oh, drat," Mike said. "I forgot. We're supposed to be back in court on Monday morning with my new attorney all ready to present his case. I guess you won't be able to make it."

"Sorry. I'm booked." Aside to Cyndi he whispered behind a cupped hand, "Pun intended."

She fought the little smile that tickled at the corner of her mouth. Jokes aside, Joe had put them in a bad position. Without his defense at the trial, the suit was up in the air, along with the fate of the mall and Home Fires. And with the vandalism at the tent city . . .

The hardest part was that she'd befriended him and been inspired by him—inspired to fill the hole in her life with meaning. Founded or not, she'd trusted him. Friendship betrayed, trust shattered. "Mike, I think it's time for us to go." When Cyndi stood to leave, a guard moved toward the table to escort her and Mike.

"Just a minute," Mike said. He faced Joe. "Is there anyone we need to contact about you being in here? Any family or friends?"

"No, no one." There was no loneliness or regret in Joe's expression. "There is one thing, though. Well, two things, really. First, I didn't do it."

Cyndi rolled her eyes.

"Honest," Joe said, a hint of angst in his tone. "I hope you'll believe me. I might not have liked your tent city, but I didn't wreck it."

"Thanks for saying that," Mike said. "What's the second thing?"

Joe scratched his neck, tipping his head to the side and wincing a little in embarrassment.

"Could you, um . . . would you take care of Wolf until I can be there for him again?"

A corner of Cyndi's heart melted at the old man's love for his dog. And his admitting it. Not all of it, mind you. Just a corner. The rest of her was still hurt and angry.

"Done," Mike said. "Don't you worry about Wolf. He'll stay with us for as long as it takes."

She might be disappointed and angry over Joe, but she'd take in Wolf. Starting with giving him a bath.

"That wasn't so bad, was it?" Mike asked once they were back in the car.

"It's not the jail that bothers me," she said. "It's Joe. In my gut, I know he did it."

"Innocent until proven guilty, remember?"

It was a nice sentiment when it wasn't personal. But Cyndi knew he was guilty. She also knew it was her fault the police had figured it out.

She didn't know which was worse.

The third night after Clark was taken, Cyndi still didn't get much sleep. She tossed and fumed in bed, worrying over the girl and what horrible things were happening to her. Whenever she started to drift off in sheer exhaustion, she would jerk awake. She couldn't go on like this. She needed sleep. But more than that, she needed Clark.

Sometime in the darkness, it occurred to her that she hadn't heard from Zach since that afternoon. If anyone was likely to know where Clark was, it was Zach.

How late did teenage boys sleep on weekends? Probably late, but she didn't care. As soon as the clock turned seven, she dialed the number she had for him, the one he'd used on his volunteer paperwork for Home Fires. She hoped it was a good number.

On the third ring, he answered. "Hello?"

Thank goodness. "Zach? This is Cyndi."

"Hi."

"How are you holding up?"

"I've been better. They haven't told us if he's going to come out of the coma or not. It's pretty tough seeing him like this, and Mom's exhausted."

Coma? "Wh-what are you talking about? Who's in a coma? What's going on?"

"I thought you knew. Dad had a terrible stomachache. He passed out. He hasn't woken up yet. That was . . ." He paused. "I think it was three days ago. I've kind of lost track of time."

"Are you okay?"

On the other end of the call, Zach choked up. "I'm pretty scared."

"Which hospital are you at? I'm coming over."

"Riverton Memorial."

Cyndi let out the breath she'd been holding. "I'll be there in a little while. You hold tight, okay?"

"I will."

She was about to hang up when he asked, "What were you calling about?"

"Sorry?"

"If you didn't know about my dad, why did you call? You've never called me before."

Cyndi didn't know whether to mention Clark or not.

He already had a full plate. But he also had the right to know what was happening with the girl he loved.

"I—we—went by Clark's place, the address she gave me, and she's not there. The house is empty. I was hoping you had heard from her."

"No," he said. And then an aching silence.

"Zach? I'm sorry. I just, maybe I shouldn't have said anything."

"It's okay," Zach said in a flat voice. "I, um . . . I've gotta go."

The connection broken, Cyndi slammed her phone

down on the table.

Why now? Why was God putting so many burdens on them at once?

"Mike?" she called up the stairs. "I'm going to the hospital. You're on your own for breakfast!"

She didn't hear an answer, but she didn't exactly wait for one either before she closed the door behind her.

Cyndi found Zach curled up on the waiting room couch in the critical care wing.

She sat near his head and smoothed his mussy hair. "Are you awake?"

He rubbed his eyes and sat up. He looked worse than she felt. Neither one of them had slept in days. "Kinda."

"You don't look so good. Let's go get you something to eat."

In the hospital cafeteria, Zach chose a bagel and cream cheese, but when they sat at the table, he pushed it away.

Cyndi took a knife and spread the cream cheese on his bread. "You've got to eat," she said, thrusting the food at him. "What happened?"

"Like I told you, he got a really bad stomachache. He turned kinda green; then he passed out."

"Do they know what it is? Appendicitis, maybe?"

"Pan-something-itis."

"Pancreatitis?" She didn't know much about the disease, but knew it could be very, very bad.

"Yeah. The doctor said it can come from drinking too much or doing drugs, but my dad didn't do any of that kind of stuff. He said it's—hold on." Zach opened his hand and showed her his palm. Written on it in ballpoint pen were the words *hypertriglyceridemia* and *necrotizing pancreatitis*. "He said it could be hereditary. That means I might have it, too, right?"

Cyndi placed her hand over his to cover the words. "No, Zach. Not necessarily."

"He might die. They didn't say it in front of me, but I overheard them. They said he has a 30 percent chance of full recovery. That's not very high."

"No, it's not. But it's not nothing." They weren't promising odds.

"They've got him lying on his back. He hates sleeping on his back. If we folded his arms across his chest, he'd look like a corpse." Zach pulled the bagel toward him and took a bite, then another and another. It didn't take him long to down the whole thing and chase it with a full glass of cola. "I need to get back up there," he said. "I don't like leaving Mom alone for too long."

Chapter 41

ZACH LED CYNDI DOWN the hall to his father's room.

Cyndi paused outside the door, unsure whether or how to intrude on his parents.

He motioned her in, holding a finger to his mouth to tell her to be quiet.

His father lay in the bed.

From the doorway, Cyndi could see the bumps his feet made in the pink woven blanket.

Zach's mother sat next to his bed, her back to the door. She held her husband's hand, caressed it with both her thumbs.

The heart monitor beeped out a steady rhythm, its green line spiking with each beat. A respirator sucked and sighed, and its accordion pump danced up and down like a morbid jack-in-the-box.

Cyndi wanted to clamp her hands over her ears. Hospital disinfectant stung her nostrils with its nursing home scent.

"Spence?" Zach's mom whispered. She took a sip of water from a paper cup on the dining cart. "Can you hear me?"

Cyndi shrank back in the doorway, not wanting to intrude but not wanting to abandon Zach.

Even Zach didn't go all the way into the room. He stood, frozen, letting his mom have her moment with his dad.

"You wouldn't believe the huge words the doctors have thrown at me today. *Thrombophle*—I can't even pronounce them. No one will even tell me if you're going to get better or not. I don't know what to do."

Zach's mom rested her forehead on the back of her husband's hand.

"Mom?" Zach said.

She startled.

He walked around to talk to her.

"What time is it?" she mumbled through a fog of exhaustion.

"I don't know. Morning. How's Dad?"

"He's okay," she said, based on nothing but wishful thinking. "We'll know more later today. You should go home and get some rest."

"I'm not leaving, Mom." Zach waved Cyndi into the room. "We've got a visitor."

Cyndi took a step or two closer to the bed.

"Mom, this is Cyndi. Cyndi, this is my mom."

Zach's mom turned around. Her eyes, hollowed with exhaustion, met Cyndi's.

No. It couldn't be.

Zach's mom was Allie Ridley. And there in the bed lay Spencer Ridley, the leader of all the protests against Home Fires.

Could it be?

Zach's parents were the ones suing her.

Fight or flight.

Cyndi's legs chose flight. She ran down the hospital corridor, her scarf streaming behind her.

Why, oh why? Why did his parents have to be the Ridleys?

She burst through the doors of the chapel. She hadn't meant to come here, didn't mean to end up here. How many hours had she spent in this very room, begging for the life of her daughter? How many times had God answered no?

Diffused light streamed in through a giant blue skylight in the ceiling. A round stained-glass window in the front of the room drew her to the first row of chairs. The chapel, large enough for thirty or more, had only ever held her.

Her alone.

She spoke aloud.

"Do you think this is funny? Well, it's not."

Her words echoed back to her.

"You're not clever or funny . . . or nice. You're . . ." She searched for the right words. "You're a bully."

He wasn't. She knew it. But it sure felt like it. She wanted to hit something. They should put a punching bag in front near the altar. She would have worn it out long ago. Her and a lot of other people.

She went to the wall and pressed her face up against the cool paneling. "Why?" It was a question to which there was no answer.

The room filled with all her memories, all her disappointments, all her failures.

And the faintest of whispers, not even loud enough to be heard.

"Love."

"I can't," she said. "It's too much."

She thought of those she'd loved and lost, like Madi and Clark.

She thought of those she'd loved in spite of . . . like Zach and Joe. Now she found herself struggling over her feelings for Zach. When he was an edgy skater kid with a big heart, he was easy to love. But as the child of those people?

And Joe. Homeless Joe. How could she not love him? Until she didn't. Helpless Joe she could love. Independent Joe? Not so much.

And now Allie and Spencer.

"I can't do it, God," she said. "I can't. They've done nothing but tear us down, humiliate us, *sue* us."

She shook her head. "I can't."

And in the depth of her heart, she felt the word *love*.

She put her head in her hands and prayed. "You have to show me how."

How long she sat in silence, letting his love wash over her, she didn't know. When she was finally ready to leave the chapel, she did the thing she least wanted to do in the world.

She walked down the hallway to Spencer Ridley's room and tapped on the door. "Allie?" she whispered. "Sorry to bother you. Do you want me to sit with your husband so you can go home and get some rest?"

Chapter 42

MONDAY MORNING CYNDI and Mike arrived at the courthouse early, hoping to catch Judge Ferndale before court reconvened.

In the judge's reception area, Cyndi found herself sitting on a Naugahyde seat worn shiny and thin by years and posteriors.

"Do you think she'll grant us another delay?" she asked Mike, who sat across from her, his knees almost touching hers.

He looked up from his phone. He'd been staring through it. "I don't know. We can only hope."

And pray. The thought came unbidden. "What if she won't talk to us? What if she'll only talk to our attorney?"

"Well, we don't exactly have one, so . . . I don't know what else we can do."

The second hand on the wall clock ticked off the seconds. Cyndi cleaned under her fingernails. Time stood still.

Ten minutes before the trial was to start, Judge Ferndale's secretary said, "Mr. and Mrs. Finch?"

Cyndi and Mike both looked up. "Yes?"

"The judge will not be able to see you before going into the courtroom."

"We'll make it quick—"

"I'm sorry. You can go on in and find your places."

Cyndi leaned over to pick up her purse and followed Mike into the hall. "Do you think she's angry with us?" she asked.

"I hope not." Mike grabbed her hand, smearing it with the cold sweat of his own. "I guess we'll find out soon."

In the courtroom, they walked the long, lonely path down the aisle to their table on the defense side of the room. The plaintiff's table was also at half strength. Mr. Ridley's two attorneys sat upright, their unopened briefcases squared off on the table in front of them. Cyndi thought Allie Ridley might have come without her husband, but she wasn't here. Cyndi hadn't seen her since she left the hospital the other night. Allie had refused her offer to sit with Spencer, but just making the offer had shaken the shackles from Cindy's soul.

At the "All rise," everyone stood until Judge Ferndale took the bench. The imposing mahogany desk dwarfed the judge.

Cyndi wiped her hands on her skirt. She looked over at the plaintiffs' table, at the empty seats. She should be thrilled that the Ridleys failed to appear. But after seeing Allie's face in that hospital room, after seeing the fear in Zach's eyes, she found her own heart thawing toward them. No matter what the outcome of today's hearing, Cyndi determined to show grace to the Ridleys, if not for their own sake, then for the sake of their son.

The judge leaned in toward her microphone and

spoke. "This court has come to order. I understand the defense has a question?" She looked at the empty chair next to Mike. "Where is your attorney?"

Mike half stood up and stammered, "He's, um, indisposed, Your Honor. Permission to approach the bench?"

Cyndi wanted to sink through the floor.

"You may approach."

Mike stepped forward alone.

Cyndi wasn't sure if she was supposed to go up there or not. She could only catch a few of Mike's words, though she knew what he'd been planning to say.

". . . unable to be present today . . ."

The judge's reaction was inaudible, covered by a shuffling sound from the prosecuting attorney. Cyndi peeked over at him. He pulled out his cell phone and looked at the screen.

". . . arrested. He's in jail . . ."

Judge Ferndale released Mike to return to his seat and spoke to the room as a whole.

"Due to some extraordinary circumstances, I am granting, once again, a short recess. This court will reconvene in twenty minutes." When she stood and left the room, so did the other attorney.

Mike trembled. "I don't ever want to do that again. I've never felt so hung out to dry as this morning. Joe's left us in a pretty bad spot."

Though she knew banter and worry were not helpful, she joined Mike in a verbal dance. She whispered one possibility of what might happen, and he countered with another. Back and forth, they went over all the contingencies they could imagine, none of them very good.

A few more people filtered into the courtroom, including Rebecca Whitt, that nosy reporter who had exposed Clark. A whole new level of emotion welled up in Cyndi as the girl returned to her thoughts. She lifted a quick prayer that if one of them had to lose, it would be herself, not Clark.

The prosecuting attorney returned to his side of the room just before the judge entered again. "It has come to my attention that, due to unforeseen circumstances, the defense is once again without an attorney," Judge Ferndale said. "I am considering granting another brief stay to the defense. Would the prosecution have any objection?"

The prosecution evidently did, since he asked to approach the bench. Minutes dragged by before he was allowed to sit down again.

Judge Ferndale pinched the bridge of her nose between her eyes. She put on her glasses and riffled through some papers in front of her. "The court would like to recognize the prosecution at this time."

Cyndi turned and watched the lawyer rise.

He got permission to approach and stood in conference with the judge for long enough to make Cyndi uncomfortable.

When he backed away, the judge looked out at the room. "Well, this morning is starting off full of surprises. The plaintiff is asking to drop the lawsuit against the defendant."

Cyndi's stomach climbed her throat. Even the chance that the case would be dismissed . . . She held her breath and waited for the judge's ruling.

The judge removed her glasses and spoke to both sides. "Case dismissed."

Cyndi and Mike exhaled as one.

Before the news had time to sink in, the judge rose and left the room. The great wooden door closed behind her, and the courtroom was doused in silence.

Cyndi swiveled in her chair and faced Mike, who wore the same stunned look that she felt.

A second later, a grin broke out on his face, followed by whoops and hollers from the defendant's side of the courtroom. Cyndi stood, still in shock, and reached for him. She squeezed her arms around his neck. Was it truly over?

Mike picked her up off the ground and spun her around. "It's over!" he said into her ear. "We're free!"

"You're choking me," she whispered back.

He set her back on her feet.

The Ridleys' attorney swung wide on his way out. He placed an envelope on the table by Cyndi and kept walking.

Cyndi picked it up. She tore it open and pulled out the index card inside. In perfect handwriting, three words.

"Thank you. —Allie."

Cyndi pressed the note to her chest. She hadn't done much, but it was enough.

Instead of heading out the front doors of the courthouse, Mike led Cyndi down the hall on the ground floor to one of the smaller courtrooms.

She didn't have to ask where he was leading her. Joe's arraignment was set to start any minute. She expected a reluctance to rise inside her, but as they approached the room, she felt none of the anger, hurt, or betrayal she'd harbored against Joe over the past several days. It could just be the relief of the suit being dismissed. She didn't have to worry about losing their house or Home Fires. Or was it, perhaps, more than that?

Joe, even guilty Joe, needed them to be there for him.

They entered the criminal court. The room was smaller and more run down. The judge's bench was raised only six inches or so above the rest of the floor. Instead of heavy wooden pews, spectators sat in molded plastic chairs with shiny metal legs.

The front row was filled with men in orange.

Cyndi scanned the row until she found Joe's gray hair. Fifth in line if they were going in order.

Mike nudged her to the right. Cyndi wondered if it was like at a wedding where you had to pick sides. She made herself as comfortable as she could on the slippery plastic chair.

The assistant to the district attorney brought one man after another before the judge. Most of the accused sat with shoulders hunched forward. From the back, Cyndi imagined them with eye patches and missing teeth, ball and chain around their ankles.

Court-appointed attorneys droned through lists of reasons why their clients were innocent, were not flight risks, could not be expected to meet a high bail. The judge released two under their own recognizance and sent the other two back to jail to await trial.

When Joe's name was called, he shuffled to the podium on the defense side. She couldn't see them, but Cyndi could tell from the way Joe walked that his wrists were cuffed in front.

"Where is your attorney?" the judge asked.

"I'm representing myself," Joe answered.

"I strongly advise against that. You do know that an attorney will be appointed to you at no charge?"

"Yes, Your Honor, I understand. And I waive my right to an attorney. I choose to stand in my own defense."

The judge spoke to the room for the stenographer's benefit. "Let it be noted that Mr. Talbot has refused his right to an attorney. Proceed."

"Your Honor?" Joe said.

"Yes?"

"May I request permission to have these cuffs removed during the arraignment?"

The judge indicated that the accompanying officer should remove the restraints.

"Your Honor," the prosecuting attorney said, "Mr. Talbot is accused of acts of vandalism against a tent city. A witness places Mr. Talbot at the scene of the crime on that day. He had motive and opportunity. And he's homeless; therefore he's a flight risk. We request that Mr. Talbot be held at the county jail until a trial date."

"Mr. Talbot?"

"Yes, Your Honor." Joe did not hang his head as the other accused men did.

"How do you plead?"

"Not guilty."

"And what do you have to say for yourself?"

"First of all, Your Honor, just because I'm homeless does not mean I'm a criminal. If you check my record, you will find that it is clean. Also, I am not a flight risk. I have lived in this city for over thirty years, and I don't intend to go anywhere. And third, and definitely not least, I am innocent. I request that you release me without bail."

"Mr. Talbot, you know I can't do that. I am setting bail at ten thousand dollars. If you do meet bail, you will be expected to provide the court with a permanent address."

The judge brought his gavel down on its pedestal. "Next case?"

Cyndi sat, stunned, as they clicked the handcuffs back around Joe's wrists and led him, shuffling, out the side door. She'd been so sure in her moment of happiness, she never considered . . . But of course they weren't going to just let him go.

She elbowed Mike. "Let's go," she said. "We need to spring a friend from jail."

The Finches were just walking through the door after their Christmas Eve service when the phone rang. Cyndi picked it up with a prayer it might be Clark.

It was Zach.

"Hi, Zach. What's going on? Is everything okay?"

"Yes . . . no, actually. My mom's going to stay at the hospital with Dad. Our house is just so big and empty and I—"

"Oh, sweetie, it's Christmas Eve. You can't stay alone. Come stay at our place."

She made up the guest bed for Zach. It would be good to have someone stay in that room again.

In the morning, Cyndi stood outside the guest room door, her fist poised to knock. On second thought, she'd let him sleep. She tiptoed downstairs to start breakfast. Her traditional cinnamon rolls were already done, but she still needed to fry the bacon and cut up some fruit for a salad.

She sliced strips of skin off a pineapple, letting her mind wander as her hands took on the familiar task. Two weeks and not a word from Clark. Her number didn't work, the house was empty, and CPS was no help at all. She spent every afternoon on the streets, looking for Clark, talking to people who might know where she was. This afternoon she'd go out again.

How could God let an innocent person suffer at the hands of an evil one? For she knew in her heart that Clark was suffering.

"I just don't get it," Zach had said late last night. "She was trying to make a better life. Why did he have to find her? I knew she didn't want to be on camera, and I just wasn't paying attention. If I'd had my eyes open, I could have—"

"Don't even consider the mighta, coulda,

shouldas," Cyndi said. "We can't change what happened. The past is past. All we can do is pray for a better future."

"Can we?"

Cyndi looked at him. "Can we what? Pray?"

Zach nodded.

"Right now?"

He nodded again.

She was new back to it. Since her prayer that night in the hospital, she'd talked to God several times, just not in front of anyone. "Do you want to pray, or do you want me to?"

"Um, you." He fidgeted a little, but he leaned forward in prayer posture when Cyndi reached for his hand. In the instant between when Cyndi said, "Father God," and when she started to word her prayer, she relaxed into the arms of her Lord. She knew from experience that it was safe to say anything she wanted and that he would listen. Mike was relaxed too, snoring softly in his easy chair, but Zach was completely present. She could feel his agreement as she poured out her heart, carrying Clark before the throne.

After several minutes of talking to God, Cyndi felt Zach squirm again. She peeked up at him. He chewed on his bottom lip.

"Did you want to say something?" she asked.

"I don't know how."

"You just talk. Say whatever is on your mind, and God will hear you. Okay?"

"I'll try," he said. He bowed his head again and coughed, then cleared his throat. "Um, God? This is

Zach. I was wondering, while you're listening, could you help my dad get better too? I know we haven't got along too well the past year or so, and he's kind of been a jerk to a lot of people, but he's still my dad and it's pretty bad what's happening to him. And to Mom. She's a mess. Can you make things a little easier on her?"

He stopped talking and just waited. Cyndi waited with him for a moment before concluding the prayer with an "Amen."

"Thanks," Zach said with a small, crooked smile.

"You know prayer is not a magic formula, don't you?" Cyndi didn't want to discourage him, but she hoped he didn't get the impression he could force God into doing something just by praying. "God's will is a complex thing."

"I don't expect any miracles, I guess. I never talked to God before. And he really hears when you talk to him that way?"

Cyndi beamed inside when she answered that question. "You know, I think he really does."

"And he'll make sure Clark is okay?"

She shook her head. "I hope so, Zach. I really do."

Cyndi thought back on the prayer as she made Christmas breakfast.

"Smells good." Mike stood in the kitchen door and rubbed sleep out of his eyes. He shuffled across the kitchen to the coffeepot and poured himself a cup. "How late were you two up last night?"

Cyndi ran a hand through her not-yet-combed hair. "I think it must have been three or three thirty. We had a good talk, though."

"Yeah, we did."

Oh good, Zach was awake.

Mike offered him a cup of coffee. "How'd you sleep?"

"Okay, I guess," Zach said.

"Breakfast is almost ready," Cyndi said. "We've got regular Sunday worship this morning, a van load of presents to deliver to the tent city, and a whole team of people lined up to serve lunch at Home Fires. And I want to check all the regular places this afternoon for Clark. It's going to be a busy day."

"Could we make time to swing by and see my folks?" Zach asked.

"Of course we can," Cyndi said. She checked her voice, hoping the strain of seeing the Ridleys for the first time since finding out they were Zach's parents wasn't showing through. At least with the lawsuit off the table, that huge elephant was taken care of.

Chapter 43

A YEAR AGO, JOE NEVER COULD have predicted that he would spend this Christmas serving hot meals in a soup kitchen. Of course, he couldn't have predicted that he would use his law license again, either, or that he would be arrested. It had been a big year.

"Merry Christmas, old man!" Cyndi greeted him. She was the last in line. The other couple hundred or so were already seated at their tables. Most had already eaten. "Grab some food and we'll sit together," she said.

Joe plopped turkey, mashed potatoes, and gravy on his plate and slipped a roll in his pocket for Wolf. He peeled off his latex gloves and joined Cyndi at a table.

"Quite a year, huh?" she asked as Joe crammed food in his mouth. Years of hunger bred horrid table manners, he knew, but he didn't care.

"Yep, quite a year," she repeated. "And it's not over yet. We promised Zach we'd go down and see his parents at the hospital this afternoon. I can't believe it. First that they could have such a great kid. I hope he's not too disappointed if we can't just waltz in and patch everything up with his folks after all they've done to try to hurt us. I know God doesn't really punish people for their sins, but in this case—"

Joe almost gagged on his turkey. How could Cyndi

drone through tragedies in other people's lives and then suggest that they were fair punishments? "Really?"

She paused, fork halfway to her mouth. "What?"

"I can't believe you said that. You talk like you want to help people. Sounds like you want to choose who you're nice to. He's in a coma."

Cyndi held her voice at a low level, but her face screwed up in frustration. Her clenched fists pressed against the tabletop. "How dare you? If it weren't for me, you'd still be on the street eating tossed-out food from Dumpsters. If it weren't for me, you'd still be in jail. Who bailed you out?" She half stood and leaned toward Joe.

Joe wiped the corners of his mouth with a napkin and tossed the soiled cloth on the table. "You did," he admitted. "You did. But you also called the cops on me."

"I—I—" She stammered out some nonsense syllables.

"A right doesn't erase a wrong." He stood with a little more agility than normal. "And, for the record, I. Didn't. Do. It."

Chapter 44

"COME ON, MIKE. LET'S get out of here." Cyndi interrupted him as he was about to sink his fork into a piece of pumpkin pie. "I want to get this hospital visit over with so we can go look for Clark."

"I haven't even had my pie yet," he said. He turned back to the group of guys he was with, most of them homeless, most of them regulars.

"I'll be in the car," Cyndi said. "Bring Zach when you're ready."

She sat in the passenger's seat, the windows fogging her into an opaque capsule. How dare Joe talk to her like that after all she'd done for him? From the moment she met him, she'd been giving—first the hat and scarf, then food, shelter, a job, and now forgiveness and a get-out-of-jail-free card.

Mike pulled up on the handle of the driver's side door. "Spill it. What's going on?" he said.

"Do you think I'm a jerk?"

"Of course not."

"Joe thinks I am."

"How come?"

"I just said Spencer Ridley's illness seemed too coincidental to be a coincidence."

Mike cleared his throat. "You said that?"

She shrugged. "Kinda."

"Hon, Spencer's not in a coma because of the lawsuit or the protests. If that's the way God works, we'd better cover our heads against the next lightning strike. God doesn't mete out illnesses as punishment, no more than he gives Christmas bonuses to all the good little boys and girls."

"In my head I know it, but in my heart it feels that way."

Mike stroked her cheek. "I know it does, sweetheart, but Spencer Ridley no more caused his illness than we caused Madi's. It's not a cause-and-effect world."

"Who made you so smart?" Cyndi said. It'd be so much easier if it was, if you always knew whose fault things were. She wiped her cheeks. "Here comes Zach."

Mike flashed the headlights to signal for the boy to come over. "Let's drop this for now," he said. "Zach has enough on his mind without suggesting his dad is anyone's fault."

Zach tried the handle, then tapped on the back door window. His mouth moved and he pointed to the lock.

"Don't worry. I'll keep it to myself." Cyndi pushed the unlock button, and little black posts jumped up with a soft *cachunk*. She needed to think about all of this, anyway.

Once Zach was tucked behind his seat belt, they headed for the hospital.

Cyndi usually didn't like silence when they drove, but today she didn't feel like striking up conversation.

Life was complicated.

Cyndi felt Mike tense as they walked to the elevator. How many times had they been here over the years with Madi? She'd taken her first and her last breath in this building.

One the critical care floor, they followed Zach as far as his father's door. They hung back until Zach had a chance to let his mom know they had visitors. Zach came back to the door to invite them in.

Cyndi extended her hand as she approached the thin, bedraggled woman who barely resembled the Allie she remembered from not too many days before. "I don't know if you've officially met my husband Mike."

She did look horrible, nothing like the primped and coiffed beauty from the other side of the courtroom. "Hi, Mike. I'm Zach's mom. But you know that."

Zach. Safe territory.

"He's been a terrific help this year. I'm sure you're very proud of him." Cyndi could tell Mike was struggling for words.

Allie forced a smile.

She glanced over at Spencer, lifeless on the bed, surrounded by blipping machines.

"Do you need anything? Can we help with anything?" Mike asked.

"There is something," Allie said. She fidgeted. "Um, why don't you sit down?"

"It's okay," Cyndi said.

Allie ignored her. She dragged her chair to the end of the bed, next to the only other chair in the room. She motioned for Mike and Cyndi to sit. Once they did, she sat on the bed near Spencer's feet.

"I don't know how to say this . . ." Allie stared at the floor.

The ventilator hissed and moaned, hissed and moaned.

Allie pressed her hands between her knees, then wiped them on her jeans. Whatever favor she was about to ask would be a huge one.

"I—I appreciate how you've taken Zach in. He's a completely different kid from when we moved here."

Cyndi smiled up at Zach.

He blushed at the attention.

Mike said, "We enjoy him. He's a big help."

"Yeah." Allie put her hand to the back of her neck. "I, um . . . What I wanted to say is . . . it's my fault."

It was the same thing she'd said to Joe that he got so mad about. But now, hearing Allie say it, she heard how ridiculous it sounded. "No, no. It wasn't anyone's fault. Zach said it's something hereditary. Something in the pancreas or spleen?" Did her words ring as hollow to the others as to her?

"Pancreas," Zach said.

"No, not that," Allie said. "I know that's not my fault. I mean the tents. It was me. I mean, I slashed the tents."

Cyndi felt the blood drain from her face.

"I can't stop thinking about it. I thought it would make everything all right. I can see now it was craziness."

Complete craziness. Cyndi tried to grasp what was happening. Not Joe?

The words poured from Allie, as if the pressure of a million pent-up thoughts could no longer be contained once the first and hardest ones were out. Most of them didn't register. Surely she wasn't trying to justify this heinous act. "If only I could get Spencer to slow down and see. If I could get Zach to spend more time at home and . . . well, you know."

Cyndi looked to see Zach's reaction, but he was gone.

Mike spoke in a comforting, controlled voice. He must be outraged, too, but he hid it well. "Do you mind if we pray about this?"

"No," Allie said, a hint of excitement creeping into her voice. "I already did. I told God about everything I did, and I didn't get struck by lightning or anything, and I think maybe he wants to forgive me, and I just can't believe that's possible, but it must be possible or I wouldn't feel that way, would I?"

Cyndi didn't know what to say.

Allie pressed on. "I've cried so much lately. I know it's weird to be asking you, but you're the only people I know who say they know God. Can he forgive me?"

Cyndi thought she was going to hyperventilate.

Mike leaned toward Allie and laid a comforting hand on hers.

Cyndi staggered out into the hall. She leaned over the drinking fountain and pressed against its metal bar. A stream of tepid water brushed against her lips, but she did not drink. Every fiber told her to reject Allie's cry for mercy and to prosecute her for the damage done. For months, she had sought her downfall, and now she wanted forgiveness? She'd wrongly sent Joe to jail because of this woman.

Forgiveness? Impossible.

Cyndi straightened her back and released the water fountain bar. She paced down the hall and back again. On her way past the waiting area, she caught a glimpse of Zach, leaned over with his head between his knees. She had no comforting words to offer, no answers, only questions.

At the end of the hall, she turned around to take another lap, as if that would help. Mike stood in Spencer's doorway. She tried to step around him, tried to avoid his inevitable rationality, but he grasped her arm and kept her from walking past.

"What are you doing?" He kept his voice low.

Cyndi was not so soft spoken. "Why are you siding with her?" She twisted out of Mike's grip and stomped away.

"She said she was sorry," he yelled at her back.

She spun around. "Sorry! Sorry?" Cyndi stalked back to him. "All she has to do is say she's sorry and it all goes away. Is that it? So what if she slashed the tents? So what if she's done everything in her power to ruin my life? If she's *sorry*, that makes it all better." She let the sarcasm drip off each word. "Sorry doesn't cut it. She deserves punishment."

"Now hold on," Mike said. "We can discuss it."

Discuss? What was there to discuss? She had broken the law. "I'm pressing charges."

Allie stepped into the doorway behind Mike, her eyes full of pain. Well, good.

Cyndi walked away. At the elevator, as she waited for the doors to open, she could feel Allie's pleading eyes boring into her head. On second thought, she'd take the stairs.

Cyndi took her keys in hand before crossing the dark parking lot. She found the car key and stuck it between her fingers with the tip pointing out as a precaution against would-be attackers. It was a silly habit she'd picked up in a self-defense class years ago, and she'd always scoffed at the thought that the tip of a key could actually hurt someone bent on taking down a woman her size. Tonight, though, she had enough anger and adrenaline pumping through her to take on the biggest threat. Lucky for any lurkers, she made it safely to her car.

Once inside, she waited for the defroster to kick in. Despite the freezing cold, Cyndi's face burned hot with righteous indignation. She'd intended to go hunt for Clark, but she was on autopilot. Before she knew it, she was back at Home Fires.

Cyndi burst in through the door of the dining hall.

Joe was wiping down the tables from the Christmas dinner.

She stormed past him to her little office and slammed the door behind her.

After a few seconds, Joe tapped on the door and pushed it open a little. "You all right?" he asked.

"It's been a rough night," Cyndi admitted.

"No fooling?" Joe let himself in. "I'm not much good at comfort, but I'll give it a try. What's up?"

"People are hard to love. Or even like. I thought

we were good together, like family. Only you don't seem to want a family, and I can't seem to hang on to one."

"Love hurts, you know," Joe said. "It'll rip your heart right out if you let it. I've been scared of that kind of hurt for a long time. But I've gotten to feel a bit of it lately. This place gets under your skin; you people do too."

"I thought I was being—"

"A jerk? Yeah. You were, but that's what family does, is stick together even when not everybody is lovable."

Cyndi let a small smile sneak across her face. "Thanks, Joe. That means a lot," she said. She took a deep breath. "I owe you an apology."

"What for?"

"You were right. I turned you in. I saw the knife sticking out of your pocket with the blue thread stuck in it . . . But now I know it wasn't you."

"I coulda told you that."

"You did. Several times. But I'd figured it all out."

"They found him, huh? I'll be. Who was it?"

"So I guess I owe you an apology. Now I have someone else to be angry at."

"Who?"

"Zach's mom."

"The protest lady? Figures."

Cyndi was surprised. "You knew that was his mom?"

"He talked about her."

Cyndi put her head in her hands. "I feel like I'm

being tumbled in a dryer. Everything keeps getting mixed up. I'm angry at you, then I'm not. I'm sorry for her, and she stabs me in the back. I couldn't look at her face anymore. Even now, I feel like punching someone."

Joe laughed. "I guess that'd have to be me. Don't close the door on Zach because of what she did. He'll need you more than ever now. He's a good kid, just needs some direction. You and Mike can give it to him if you can keep your cool and keep your feelings for his folks out of the mix."

At Zach's name, Cyndi snapped. "Oh no! I left Zach and Mike at the hospital. They'll need a ride." She grabbed her keys and coat. "I've gotta go. Do you want a ride home?"

She caught herself, too late. "I'm sorry. I meant I can take you wherever you're staying tonight."

He chuckled. "If it's all the same to you, I was planning to pull a quilt off the wall and curl up on one of the couches. These nights when the chill settles, I can't stand the thought of sleeping outside."

"You can curl up here if you want to," Cyndi said. "But just for the night; then you'll need to find a more permanent solution."

"Fair enough," Joe said. "I noticed you've got a pretty nice tent city set up over there. Think they've got room for one more?"

Cyndi patted him on the back. They'd both made progress tonight.

292 | PATTY SLACK

When she got back to the hospital, Cyndi tried calling Mike to tell him to meet her in the car. His phone went straight to message, though. It must be off.

She reluctantly climbed the stairs and walked toward Spencer's room. She hoped to catch Mike's attention without having to face Allie again. But when she looked in the window, she was surprised to find only Mike sitting by Spencer's bed.

"Where's Zach and his mom?"

Mike looked up. His eyes were swollen like he'd been crying. "They went home. Allie is going to turn herself in, and they wanted a few minutes alone together before they have to face whatever comes next."

"And you trust her to actually call the police?"

He nodded. "Yeah. I do."

Cyndi took a deep breath. She pulled a second chair up beside Spencer's bed. Such a handsome man, now reduced to a pile of flesh held together with life-giving machinery. It was hard to hate someone who had fallen so far. She reached out tentatively and placed her hand on his arm. She'd almost expected it to be cold, but it still held the warmth of life.

"God help me, Mike, I can't live with all the hostility. I sustained it as long as I did because they kept egging me on. But with him like this and Allie facing her punishment, I just don't think I can keep up the fight."

Mike laid his hand on top of hers and pulled it to his lap. "I've been sitting here thinking about how we've been sidetracked from what's important. The only fight I want to keep up is to get Clark back."

"Me, too." Cyndi leaned her forehead against

Mike's. "Me, too."

Once Allie turned herself in, Cyndi's hard heart started softening. Slowly, but it was softening. That's how she could stand to sit at a table in Home Fires a couple of months later with Joe and Mike and watch a recap of the day's events play out on the news.

Rebecca Whitt stood on the courthouse steps, her hair blowing about her face. She yelled into her microphone to be heard above the wind. "A few minutes ago, in a bizarre turn of events, Allie Ridley, wife of the plaintiff in the recently dismissed lawsuit of Ridley v. Riverton Plaza, was sentenced for the crime of vandalism. She pled guilty to slashing and upending sixteen tents in Tent City Three, which, at the time of the crime, was housed on the property of the very group her husband was suing. The tent city has since moved to another temporary location. Criminal damage of this degree is a class-six felony, which carries a maximum jail term of one year.

"When the judge gave her opportunity to express her remorse to the court, Mrs. Ridley made the following statement."

Footage of Allie Ridley standing before the judge in a black business suit played behind Rebecca's voice. The words were burned in Cyndi's memory, but she listened anyway. The sound faded to the courtroom as Allie read a prepared statement.

"Your Honor, I wish to express my sincere regret and remorse for what I did. I had no excuse for destroying those people's homes. I thought, somehow, that I could scare them out of my neighborhood. But I see now that my actions were unreasonable and wrong. Even if they had produced the results I sought, they would have been wrong, and I am truly sorry for what I have done. I am ready to pay for my actions. I've changed a lot in the past three months. I've learned to look less at myself and more at the people around me. Please give me a chance to prove my change of heart."

Cyndi imagined the words might sound insincere to people watching the newscast, but she'd spent enough time with Allie lately to know the woman had truly changed.

So had Cyndi.

Rebecca resumed her report on the cameraman's cue.

"Mrs. Ridley confessed in December, two weeks after the crime was committed. The judge today sentenced her to four months in jail, but suspended this portion of the sentence. She was also sentenced to four hundred hours' community service. The owners of Home Fires, the very soup kitchen she was suing, have requested that her community service time be spent with them, serving the homeless people she tried to hurt.

"Whether she has truly turned over a new leaf, only time will tell.

"I'm Rebecca Whitt, News Channel Seven."

As soon as the story was over, Joe turned away from the news on TV and back to Cyndi and Mike, who sat across from him.

"I guess that's a wrap," he said. "I don't think they'll have anything to report about us again."

"I sure hope not." Cyndi was done in. It had been a rough few months for everyone, but she felt like the men carried their fatigue more easily. The problems with Allie were nothing compared to Cyndi's continuous worry over Clark. She stayed awake every night praying for the girl's safe return, every afternoon searching the streets for her.

"It's only a half hour until we're supposed to meet with Allie," Mike said. "You look beat, honey. Why don't you go home and rest, and we'll take care of making arrangements with her."

Cyndi didn't want to rest . . . couldn't rest. "I'm fine," she said. "I'll go with you." Not that the men couldn't show her everything, but this felt like Cyndi's mountain to climb, a last challenge in overcoming the bitterness that still fermented in corners of her heart. She knew it was her problem, not Allie's, but she was ready to get through it.

Cyndi knew her own scars were still tender. "I feel like it might be too soon."

"It's never too soon to love," Joe said.

Crotchety old Joe. Cyndi wasn't the only one who'd changed lately.

"She can learn a lot from you guys and from your guests, especially that old woman with the imaginary pet monkey."

"Can we trust her?" Cyndi asked. What she really meant was "Can I trust myself with her?"

Joe said, "You've been great at loving the people

who are different from you. Sometimes it's harder to love the person who *is* like you."

Cyndi cringed at being compared to Allie, who was everything she didn't want to be. Or maybe everything she was.

The more she thought about it, the more she realized he had a point. She'd started reaching out to Joe and Clark and all the homeless people at Home Fires in order to make Madi proud. Along the way, she'd learned a lot about loving and caring for people, but she still struggled with loving the people who lived in nice houses, drove nice cars, had steady jobs. People who couldn't admit they needed help. People like herself.

"It's an ongoing struggle, I guess," she said. "I've got a long way to go, but if I have you two to help point out my flaws . . ." There was a piece of paper in her pocket. She pulled it out and stared at it. It was a used sugar packet. She pressed the tiny paper rectangle flat and ironed it with her fingertip. "With critics like you pushing me to do things I resist, I might just end up a little like Jesus in the end after all."

"Well, we can only hope," Joe said.

"And pray," Mike added.

"But you're going to need to recruit a new critic," Joe said.

Cyndi squinted at him. "What do you mean?"

"I mean I'm moving on. I'm taking the money you paid for my attorney fees, and I'm going to get off the streets."

Mike's "That's great!" and Cyndi's "Wonderful! I'm so happy for you" mingled in the air.

"What's great?" Zach asked, coming in the door. "Mind if I squeeze in? Mom'll be here soon."

Joe scooted over to make room for the teenager.

"Joe here said he's moving off the street," Mike said. To Joe he asked, "Do you need any help finding a place? We could probably drum up a lot of good used furniture from some friends."

"Actually, I'm thinking about leaving town," Joe said.

Cyndi crumpled the little paper in her hand and rolled it into a tight, tiny ball. She dropped the small yellow sphere on the carpet under the table. "Seriously?" She furrowed her brow. "Do you think that's a good idea?"

"Yeah, I do. I've just hung around here for so long in case my kids look for me. But they're not going to."

"You don't know that," Mike said. "They might come around."

"They might, yeah, but there's this wonderful new invention called the Internet. I think if they really wanted to find me, it would be easier to locate a Joseph Talbot, attorney-at-law, almost anywhere in the country than it would be to figure out, or even admit, that Homeless Joe is their dad. I need to start over in a place where no one has any expectations about me. I've thought about it a lot, and I'm ready to go."

"Oh, Joe," Cyndi said, laying her smooth white hand over his gnarled, calloused one. He didn't flinch like he used to. "We'll miss you so much. And we'll pray for you every day. You will keep in touch, won't you?"

"Sure I will. I'm not going to let myself be alone

ever again."

"What about Wolf?" This from Zach, who stared at Joe like he'd said he was moving to Mars.

"Wolf can go with me. He's the oldest friend I ever had. Won't he be surprised to sleep in an apartment and eat dog food every day?"

"He sure will," Cyndi said. Joe moving on. Unbelievable. "When do you go?"

Joe reached in his pocket and pulled out a scrap of paper.

"What's that?" Mike asked.

"My bus schedule. I leave at eight o'clock."

"Eight o'clock on which day?" Mike pressed him.

"Tonight."

"Aren't you full of surprises?" Cyndi said. She prayed her cheerful voice would not betray the shock and dismay she felt at losing him. "Good for you. Where's your ticket for?"

"Chicago. I figured I could start in the middle and then decide from there. I'm hoping to find a nonprofit group that helps the homeless that's looking for an attorney. I'm way past the age of wanting to build a career. But building a legacy might be nice."

Allie knocked on the door.

"Come on in!" they all yelled.

She let herself in and joined their circle. She pulled a sandwich out of a paper bag. "I hope you don't mind. I'm so sick of cafeteria food."

"Go right ahead," Cyndi said. She made a mental note to take some fresh snacks up to Spencer's room.

"How's Spencer?" Joe asked.

"The same. He has his bad days and his worse days. The doctors are past promising he'll recover. I feel like they're just putting Band-Aids over holes in the dike." Allie unloaded an apple and a bottle of water from her sack. "Hey, thank you all for being in court this morning. It meant a lot to me."

"No problem," Mike said. "That's what we're here for."

Cyndi still couldn't word her support that enthusiastically, but didn't disagree. Allie needed their support.

"And, Cyndi," Allie said, "I can't tell you how much it means to me that you're going to let me work at Home Fires. We got off to such a rocky start"—that was a huge understatement—"but I won't disappoint you again. I promise."

Cyndi had to go through with it. "Come tomorrow at three, and I'll show you the ropes."

"I won't disappoint you," Allie said. "I won't."

Zach beamed at his mom. Funny what a little felony could do to bring a family together.

Chapter 45

THAT NIGHT, MIKE AND Cyndi stood hand in hand behind the Greyhound station and waved to Joe as he mounted the steps to his new life.

Wolf was tucked safely away in a Goodwill kennel in one of the bus storage bays. Joe, freshly shaven and dressed in clean, pressed clothes, waved back. He'd never looked happier.

Cyndi wiped a tear away.

The bus started with a cough and a groan. It pulled away, and all that remained of the months they had spent with Joe was a cloud of blue diesel smoke, a soup kitchen, and a new perspective on love and forgiveness.

"Let's go home," Mike said.

"Sounds good," Cyndi answered. "I'll fix us a pot of tea. But since we're downtown, can we drive around and look for Clark for a few minutes?"

"Of course."

They'd memorized these streets in the past months. They'd been up and down them so many times . . . on foot, in cars, together and alone. Cyndi knew every alley, every bridge that offered shelter from the elements. She knew the names of the regular caseworkers at every shelter. She knew the phone numbers of CPS and the rescue mission by heart.

As they wove up their regular grid through downtown, Cyndi pressed her forehead against the passenger's side window, staring into the night for a glimpse of their girl. All she wanted to do was bring her home safe.

"Come on, Clark. Where are you?"

Mike looked over at her. "We'll find her. We will. Maybe not tonight, but someday."

After they'd covered every street twice, Mike called it a night. "We'll come out in the daylight tomorrow. We won't give up."

Cyndi's heart still ached for the child. She closed her eyes for the short trip home, crying out, "How long?" in silent prayer. By the sound of tires on pavement and the number of turns, she knew they were pulling into the driveway.

"Cyndi?" Mike said. He put a hand on her knee.

She opened her eyes.

A young woman sat on their front porch.

Could it be?

It was.

Cyndi opened her door and jumped from the car while it was still rolling.

"Clark!" she cried. She ran into the arms of the waiting girl. "Is it really you? You've grown! And your hair!"

Clark had grown out all the pink. Her dark brown hair lay soft and clean around her neck. Her grin was wider than her face.

Cyndi wrapped her arms tight around Clark and let tears of relief flow. "I can't believe it's you."

Mike encircled both of them in a hug and whispered, "Thank God."

Thank God, indeed.

Cyndi pushed away from Clark so she could see her again. She'd never seen anything so beautiful. "Where have you been? Come on, come inside."

Clark picked up a backpack and followed Mike in. "I ran away the first day."

"You—you what? We were so worried. We couldn't find you."

"I wanted to come back, but I couldn't. I knew he'd find me."

"Why didn't you call? Or let us know you were okay?"

"I couldn't risk him finding me again. But now it doesn't matter. He has no right to take me again. Today's my birthday. I'm sixteen."

"Are you here to stay, then?" Mike asked.

Cyndi held her breath and held in her prayer.

"Is that okay? Could I crash here for a while?"

Cyndi's happiness overflowed. "For as long as you want," she said with a grin so wide it hurt. "For the rest of your life, if you want. Our home is yours."

To Get Help

I wish I could send you to a national organization who is solving the problems of homelessness and food insecurity, but the best resources, at least in my area, are locally run.

If you or someone you love is houseless or sleeping outside, search online for local homeless shelters or walk into any church to find out what resources are available.

If you or someone you know is a victim of intimate partner abuse or other domestic violence, please seek help. Call your local police, or the National Domestic Violence Hotline at 1-800-799-7233.

To Offer Help

- Volunteer at a Hot Meal Program
- Help staff a homeless shelter
- Donate $50 at agapecoc.org to fill a waterproof backpack with winter supplies. Click "support church" and designate "fill a pack" on the donation page.
- In Portland, OR, volunteer for Night Strike to build community with people under the Burnside Bridge at bridgetowninc.org
- Find out what is happening in your community and join in!

Acknowledgments

Thank you to the men and women who volunteer tirelessly on behalf of the houseless, the invisible, the hungry, the poor, the frightened. You make our world a better plan.

To the people at Loaves and Fishes, at Share House, at the Winter Hospitality Overflow, at Agape Church of Christ, at Marriage Team, and the many, many others who stand in the gap to see and to serve those who need it. Thank you.

To my critique group, my beta readers, my walking buddies who heard and listened to this story as it formed in my heart and mind and as it shaped me in my quest for answers.

To Ron and Lori Clark at Agape Church of Christ, who always remind me that people deserve to be treated with dignity and that every person is loved by God.

To Mara for serving in ways we never see or hear about. You are an example to me.

To Nick and Kathy whose dog Darion posed as Wolf. And to Tabi who posed with him.

And always, especially, thanks to the God and Father of our Lord Jesus Christ, who sees me in my messy life, who rescues me, and who loves me no matter what.

About the Author

Patty Slack hopes her stories transport you to places you've never been. From the hills of Pennsylvania Coal Country to the farmlands of West Africa to the Inside Passage of wild Alaska, Patty hopes to take you on a journey.

Her love of travel and fascination with all kinds of people has exposed her to varied and fascinating cultures. But Patty, like Cyndi, discovered that it can be harder to love the people in your own neighborhood than it is to love people halfway across the world. She will never perfect the art of loving well, but, with God's help, she plans to keep trying.

Patty and her family find themselves at home in the beautiful Pacific Northwest. Hikes in the Columbia River Gorge and the perfect climate for growing fruits and vegetables more than make up for the long drizzly winter.

If you enjoyed this book, please consider leaving a
review on Amazon or Goodreads.

Other books by Patty Slack

To learn more about Patty Slack's fiction or to contact
the author, visit clayinkpotpress.com

Made in the USA
Charleston, SC
20 November 2016